'A spiffing read... calculated to grip blue-rinsed Conservative ladies and make socialist eyes pop'
Matthew Coady
THE PEOPLE

'Preposterous'
Paul Johnson
DAILY TELEGRAPH

'Compulsive reading'
CITY LIMITS

'Rattling good'
Anne Sofer
LONDON REVIEW OF BOOKS

'A curious molotov cocktail'
FINANCIAL TIMES

A VERY BRITISH COUP

Chris Mullin

ARROW BOOKS

Arrow Books Limited
20 Vauxhall Bridge Road, London SW1V 2SA

An imprint of the Random Century Group

London Melbourne Sydney Auckland Johannesburg
and agencies throughout the world

First published in Great Britain by Hodder & Stoughton
Coronet edition 1983
Corgi edition 1988
Arrow edition 1991

3 5 7 9 10 8 6 4 2

Printed and bound in Great Britain by
Cox & Wyman Ltd, Reading

ISBN 0 09 986230 1

*To Joan,
who will never lose faith*

'I could easily imagine myself being tempted into a treasonable disposition under a labour Government dominated by the Marxist Left... Suppose, in these circumstances, one were approached by an official of the C.I.A. who sought to enlist one's help in a project designed to 'destabilise' this far left government. Would it necessarily be right to refuse co-operation?... Coming from the representative of any other foreign power such a request would not be entertained by me for a moment. But the United States is not just any other foreign power. I am and always have been passionately pro-American, in all sense of believing that the United States has long been the protector of all the values which I hold most dear. To that extent my attitude to the United States has long been that of a potential fellow traveller.'

When Treason Can Be Right
by Peregrine Worsthorne,
Sunday Telegraph, November 4, 1979

1

The news that Harry Perkins was to become Prime Minister went down very badly in the Athenaeum.

"Man's a Communist," exploded Sir Arthur Furnival, a retired banker.

"Might as well all emigrate," said George Fison, who owned a chain of newspapers.

"My God," ventured the Bishop of Bath and Wells, raising his eyes heavenward.

As the Press Association tape machine in the lobby began to punch out the first results of the March 1989 general election it became clear that something had gone horribly wrong with the almost unanimous prediction of the pundits that the Tory-Social Democrat Government of National Unity would be re-elected.

Kingston-on-Thames was the first to declare. The sharp young merchant banker who had represented the seat saw his majority evaporate.

"A mistake," said Furnival when he had recovered his composure.

"Bloody better be," grunted Fison. No one could remember the last time a seat in the Surrey stockbroker belt had returned a Labour Member of Parliament.

The machine was now giving details of a computer forecast to the effect that if the Kingston swing was reproduced across the country Labour would have a majority of around 200 seats.

"To hell with computers," muttered Furnival. Fison took a sip of whisky. The Bishop dabbed his forehead with a purple handkerchief.

There were those who had argued that computers had rendered elections obsolete. That very morning a professor from Imperial College had been on the radio describing how he had fed the entire electoral register into a computer which had then selected a perfect cross-section of the population. He had polled the sample and confidently predicted that his results would be accurate to within one quarter of one per cent. Harry Perkins was about to put the learned professor and his computer out of business.

"Freak result. Means nothing." The party around the tape machine had been joined by a man in a double-breasted Savile Row suit. Sir Peregrine Craddock's *Who's Who* entry said simply that he was 'attached to the Ministry of Defence', but those who know about these things said he was the Director General of DI5.

For the next few minutes Sir Peregrine's optimism seemed justified. The National Unity candidate held Oxford with a majority only slightly reduced. Braintree stayed Tory. So did Colchester and Finchley. Then at about quarter to midnight came the first results from the North. Salford, Grimsby, York and Leeds East were all held by Labour with doubled, even trebled, majorities. It was at this point that Arthur Furnival disappeared to ring his stockbroker.

At a few minutes to midnight Worcester went Labour, bringing down the first of six Cabinet ministers who would lose their seats that evening. Sir Peregrine took a sip of his orange juice. George Fison rushed back to Fleet Street to dictate an editorial for the late edition of his newspaper. He was last heard shouting that the British people had taken leave of their senses.

By 12.30 it was clear that the National Unity bubble had burst. South of the Wash the Social Democrats were being annihilated. Richmond, Putney, Hemel Hempstead and Cambridge all fell to Labour in quick succession. North of the Wash only the seaside resorts and the hunting country remained in Tory hands.

Like so much else associated with the twentieth century, television sets were banished from the Athenaeum. But in view of the impending national disaster a delegation from the crowd of elderly gentlemen now gathered around the tape machine had been despatched in search of the club secretary, Captain Giles Fairfax. The captain said he would see what he could do and within ten minutes reappeared carrying a small portable set borrowed from the caretaker's flat. It was now installed beside the tape machine on a table taken from the morning room. "All very irregular," said the captain with an apologetic glance at the portrait of Charles Darwin which overlooked the scene. Nevertheless, he stayed to watch.

There was a groan as the television screen immediately focused upon the beaming face of Harry Perkins who was awaiting the declaration of his own result in Sheffield town hall. Perkins, a former steel worker, was a stocky, robust man with a twinkle in his eye and dark, bushy brows. His greying hair was long at the sides and combed over his head to hide his balding crown. His face was deeply lined and rugged, burnished by the great heat of a Sheffield steel mill in the days when Britain had been a steel-producing nation. He was smartly dressed, but nothing flashy. A tweed sports jacket, a silk tie, and on this occasion a red carnation in his buttonhole. Harry Perkins was going to be quite different from any Prime Minister Britain had ever seen. The programme on which he was in the process of being swept to power was quite different from any ever presented to the British electorate.

On the television screen a commentator was now reciting the highlights. Withdrawal from the Common Market. Import controls. Public control of finance, including the pension and insurance funds. Abolition of the House of Lords, the honours list and the public schools.

The manifesto also called for 'consideration to be given' to withdrawal from NATO as a first step towards Britain becoming a neutral country. An end to Britain's 'so-called nuclear deterrent' and the withdrawal of all foreign bases from British soil. There was even a paragraph about 'dismantling the newspaper monopolies'.

For weeks all opinion polls and all responsible commentators had been predicting that there was no hope of the Labour Party being elected on a programme like this. Ever since Harry Perkins had been chosen to lead Labour at a tumultuous party conference two years earlier, the popular press had been saying that this proved what they had always

9

argued – namely that the Labour Party was in the grip of a Marxist conspiracy. Privately the rulers of the great corporations had been gleeful, for they had convinced themselves that the British people were basically moderate and that, however rough the going got, they would never elect a Labour government headed by the likes of Harry Perkins.

Picture, therefore, the dismay that swept the lobby of the Athenaeum as the television showed Perkins coming to the rostrum in Sheffield town hall to acknowledge not only his own re-election with a record majority, but to claim victory on behalf of his party.

"Comrades," intoned brother Perkins.

"*Comrades*, my foot." Sir Arthur Furnival was apoplectic. "Told you the man's a Communist."

"Comrades," repeated Perkins, as though he could hear the heckling coming from the Athenaeum. He then delivered himself of a dignified little speech thanking the returning officer, those who counted the ballot papers, party workers and all the other people it is customary for a victorious candidate to thank. Then he got down to business.

"Comrades, it is now clear that by tomorrow morning we shall form the government of this country."

He paused to let the cheering subside. "We should not be under any illusion about the task ahead of us. We inherit an industrial desert. We inherit a country which for ten years has been systematically pillaged and looted by every species of pirate, spiv and con man known to civilisation."

"Scandalous," muttered Furnival.

"Disgraceful carry-on," said the Bishop of Bath and Wells.

"All we have won tonight is political power," continued Perkins. "By itself that is not enough. Real power in this country resides not in Parliament, but in the boardrooms of the City of London; in the darkest recesses of the Whitehall bureaucracy and in the editorial offices of our national newspapers. To win real power we have first to break the stranglehold exerted by the ruling class on all the important institutions of our country."

"Treason," whispered Furnival, "that's what I call it, downright treason."

Perkins paused and then, speaking slowly and looking directly into a television camera, straight into the eyes of Sir Arthur Furnival, he said, "Our ruling class have never been up for re-election before, but I hereby serve notice on behalf of the people of Great Britain that their time has come."

Such language had never been heard from a British Prime Minister before. Although received with rapture in Sheffield town hall, Harry Perkins' words burst upon the Athenaeum as though the end of the world was at hand. Which, in a manner of speaking, it was.

"South of France for me, old boy," said Furnival.

"Certainly looks like the game's up, Arthur," murmured the Bishop, whose faith in divine providence had temporarily deserted him.

From nearby Trafalgar Square came a burst of firecrackers as crowds of young people celebrated the election result.

By 1.15 the scale of the disaster was apparent to everyone. The television commentators were now citing a computer prediction that Perkins would have an overall majority of around ninety seats. Gradually the cluster of eminent gentlemen around the television dwindled. Some donned overcoats and slipped miserably out into the night. One ancient member dozed on a Chesterfield in the lobby, his head resting on the marble wall, pince-nez dangling from a cord around his neck.

Not everyone went home. Some drifted upstairs to the huge drawing room and sat in urgent little groups discussing what life in Harry Perkins' Britain held in store for them.

"Early days yet." The speaker was Sir Lucas Lawrence, former permanent secretary at the Department of Industry. He was standing at the end of the drawing room overlooking Carlton House Terrace. On the mantelpiece behind him were white marble busts of Alexander Pope and Edmund Burke. Below in the grate a pinewood fire crackled.

"These Labour chappies are all the same," Sir Lucas went on. "Always shooting their mouths off in opposition, but once

11

they've got their backsides in the limousines they're as meek as lambs." After retiring from the Department of Industry Sir Lucas had joined the board of an arms company. There had been one or two raised eyebrows at the time. The odd parliamentary question drawing attention to his dealings with the same company in his capacity as a public servant, but it had all blown over and now Sir Lucas was chairman of the board, his civil service pension intact.

"Pretty damn serious if you ask me," boomed Lord Kildare, a portly landowner with a castle and 30,000 acres in Scotland and a town house in Chelsea. He was standing facing the huge mirror above the fireplace. His considerable bulk rested on the back of one of the green leather armchairs. The mirror afforded a panoramic view of the vast room behind him. In the distance he could see stewards in red jackets and black bow ties silently commuting between the bar and the little groups of elderly gentlemen scattered around the room. He shook his head sadly. A way of life was coming to an end. "Pretty damn serious," repeated Kildare gazing absently into the fire.

Sir Lucas was not convinced. He drew deeply on his Havana and exhaled vigorously. "Mark my words," he said firmly, "once the boys in the private office get to work, these Labour chappies won't know what's hit them."

Kildare side-stepped to avoid being engulfed by an oncoming cloud of cigar smoke. "All very well," he said miserably, "but I've never heard any Prime Minister talk like that fellow Perkins tonight."

Sir Lucas was unruffled. "You forget," he said. "I've seen all this at close quarters. Mind you, I am not saying it was plain sailing. One or two Labour ministers always prove difficult, but in the end we sorted them out."

"How?" asked Kildare, who already had visions of a life in exile. He pictured himself in a white suit and a straw hat sitting alone on the verandah of the Bermuda Cricket Club, a daiquiri in one hand and an out of date airmail edition of the *Daily Telegraph* spread on the table before him. No, thought Kildare, give me the grouse moors any day.

Sir Lucas adopted a confidential tone, "I'll tell you how." He lowered his voice and touched Kildare reassuringly on the forearm. "We turned the whole damn machine loose on them. More than any man can stand. Whenever my minister insisted on giving money away to co-operatives or any of his other harebrained schemes, I would give old Handley in the Cabinet Office a ring and put him in the picture. He'd get his people to produce a brief opposing ours which would be distributed to all other departments. If necessary he'd follow up with telephone calls to sympathetic ministers and when the matter came up at Cabinet my minister would find himself totally outgunned. After a while he got the message and resigned. Just as well, otherwise we'd have had him reshuffled."

"All very well, Lucas, when you've only got one or two extremists in the government, but what if you've got a whole Cabinet full of them?" Kildare ran a finger round the rim of his whisky glass.

Sir Lucas smiled wanly. "In that case something bigger's called for." He glanced over his shoulder as though afraid of eavesdroppers. "One or two runs on sterling. A whopping balance of payments crisis. Only takes a few telephone calls to lay this sort of thing on. If you'd seen, as I have, the Prime Minister's face at 2.30 in the morning when sterling's going down the drain at a million pounds a minute, you'd soon realise how right I am."

"If you ask me, we've got a job of work on our hands preserving civilised values." The newcomer to the conversation was Sir Peregrine Craddock, who had been quietly sipping his orange juice on the fringe of the gathering. Speaking as though he was dictating a top secret memorandum, Sir Peregrine continued, "Very serious situation. Whole country crawling with extremists. Everything we stand for threatened. Fight back essential."

With that he placed his glass, still half full of orange juice, on the mantelpiece, turned on his heel and strode out of the drawing room. The lobby was empty now except for the member with the pince-nez who was still dozing. It was silent too, apart from the sporadic patter of the tape machine. Sir Peregrine put on his hat and coat, paused to peer at the latest offerings from the Press Association and walked out into the night. It was exactly 2 am on Harry Perkins' first day as Prime Minister.

Broadcasting House, the headquarters of the BBC, lies just north of Oxford Circus and about a mile from the Athenaeum. On general election nights it is the custom for the Director General to give a small drinks party for the governors, their spouses and a handful of senior executives. The party takes place in a sterile suite adjacent to the Director General's office on the third floor of Broadcasting House, down the corridor from the special radio election unit.

BBC governors are a small body of impartial men and women, whose job is to uphold the commitment to fairness and balance enshrined in the Corporation's charter. Although BBC governors are supposed to reflect a wide cross-section of society, it is fair to say that the political views of Harry Perkins were not within the spectrum of opinion which they embraced. As the alcohol flowed and the scale of Perkins' election victory was becoming clear, the wafer-thin veneer of impartiality which normally shrouds BBC pronouncements began to give way to something less dignified.

"CAT-AST-ROPHIC." The Belfast brogue of Sir Harry Boyd, who twenty years earlier had been the last Unionist Prime Minister of Northern Ireland, broke the gloomy silence around a television set which was delivering a computer prediction of a Labour majority of at least 100 seats. "Catastrophic," repeated Sir Harry quietly, collapsing into an armchair.

"We could be in for civil war," said Jonathan Alford, a rather correct man in his late thirties and a senior television news executive. Civil war was something Alford knew a bit about since he was also a major in the territorial Special Air Services. He was one of a number of senior BBC personnel whose spare time was spent scrambling over assault courses in

14

Herefordshire and attending lectures in army staff colleges on strike-breaking and riot control. The outgoing government had trebled the territorial army budget and left recruits in no doubt that they would have a rôle to play in the event of large scale civil disturbance.

Major Alford was just beginning to enlarge, rather gleefully, some felt, on the prospects of civil war when he was interrupted by a shrill cry of, "Oh Christ, there goes Roddy," from over by the television set.

The scream, for that is what it was, emanated from the considerable frame of Dame Margaret Carrington, Justice of the Peace and chairperson of the Historic Homes Association. Roddy was Lieutenant-General Sir Rodney Appleton, until now Member of Parliament for Taunton, of whom it was once said, "If there was a canal in Taunton he'd send a gunboat up it." Sir Rodney was a neighbour of Dame Margaret's in Surrey.

Over by the door the Director General, Sir Roland Chance, was administering a stern warning to Jack Lansman, link-man on the breakfast-time radio news programme. It would be Lansman's job to break the news of Perkins' election victory to those members of the British public who hadn't sat glued to their television sets into the small hours. "I do hope we've got this straight, Jack," drawled the Director General. "You can't go on describing these people as 'extremists'. After all, they are now the government."

Lansman was unrepentant. "I've been calling them extremists for years, and nobody's ever complained."

The DG was sympathetic. "You really mustn't take this personally, old chap. I don't like them any more than you do. It's just that they've *won* and we shall have to take them seriously."

"If you say so," sighed Lansman, "but what about the moderates? Surely I can identify a moderate or two? Damn it all, the public have a right to know what they are in for."

"They'll find out soon enough. The public don't need any guidance from you. Just give it to them straight. No more labels. Do you understand?" Lansman nodded sulkily. The

15

DG sidled off to commiserate with Dame Margaret, leaving Lansman muttering, "I'll give it to them straight all right."

On leaving the Athenaeum, Sir Peregrine Craddock crossed Pall Mall and headed up a side street into St James's Square. He cut the corner by the London Library and turning left walked crisply up Duke of York Street, then through Church Place and into Piccadilly, emerging by the Church of St James. Although the buses had long since stopped, taxi cabs were doing brisk business and private cars still cruised towards Piccadilly Circus.

Turning left, Sir Peregrine walked quickly past Hatchards and Fortnum and Mason where he had recently purchased a pound of caviar to celebrate his daughter's birthday. Past the Royal Academy on the other side of Piccadilly, its huge metal gates locked shut, and past the Ritz Hotel. All symbols of everything he found best in the British way of life.

Sir Peregrine was a troubled man. For years he had laboured to keep British public life free from extremism. Every civil servant, every army officer, every MP, every BBC executive whose background betrayed the merest possibility of disloyalty had been quietly blocked from promotion. Now, overnight, all these years of hard work were threatened. Within days the establishment would be crawling with extremists. In Downing Street, the Cabinet Office, the Home Office, the Ministry of Defence, people who until now, thanks to DI5's good work, would not have qualified as doorkeepers in a government department would now be Cabinet ministers. And all because the British public was composed of ignorant clodheads who didn't know what was good for them. Sir Peregrine had never had much time for democracy, but this was the final straw.

By Green Park tube station Sir Peregrine crossed the road and turned right into Bolton Street. Those who did not know better might have assumed that this well-dressed, solitary gentleman was on his way to Shepherd Market where expensive ladies have long been known to provide a wide range of unmentionable services for the upper classes at all times of the day and night. In fact Sir Peregrine was on his way to the DI5 Registry: a seven-storey, fortress-like building of Second World War vintage in Curzon Street, called simply Curzon Street House. Apart from the heavy lace curtains which are features of most secret service décor, there is nothing to indicate what goes on behind the solid walls of Curzon Street House. Those who get as far as the reception will notice only that the internal telephone directory is stamped 'Secret'. In the street directory the building is listed simply as 'central government offices'.

Sir Peregrine entered by the glass doors at the front of the building. Behind these was a steel portcullis with a small door and beyond a reception desk manned by a security officer. Briskly acknowledging the man's attempt at pleasantry, Sir Peregrine went straight to the lift. He emerged on the second floor, turned right and walked a few paces down a carpeted corridor to an unmarked door. Taking his wallet from an inside pocket, he withdrew what appeared to be a plastic banker's card and fed it into a slot in the wall. There was a muffled click as the machine checked the pass code and then, from the door, came the sound of a lock automatically disengaging. Sir Peregrine returned the pass to his wallet, turned the doorhandle and entered.

His office was a large and comfortable room. Wine-red velvet curtains were matched by thick Tibetan rugs. The walls were hung with Vietnamese watercolours and on a table by a lampshade stood a Burmese Buddha: reminders that Sir Peregrine had seen service in the East in his Foreign Office days.

The desk was a large Queen Anne affair, empty save for a tea mug full of felt-tip pens, a teak letter-opener and a framed picture of his wife and daughter. To one side, within easy reach of his swivel chair, stood a visual display unit, still encased in the blue plastic cover in which it had arrived five years ago. Sir Peregrine had only to tap the requisite code into the keyboard of the VDU in order to summon instantly to the screen the most intimate secrets of any one of the two million or so people said to be on the Curzon Street computer. He had only to tap another button and a print-out would slide silently from the belly of the machine.

Gone were the days when clerks and secretaries commuted between the principal floor and the basement of Curzon Street House. Gone were the days of filling in requisition forms, frantic telephone calls to the Registry demanding reasons for delay. Today, on the application of a few simple codes, the secrets of the Curzon Street computer were instantly available.

Not that Sir Peregrine had much time for technology. He was one of the old school, trained in the days of triplicate memoranda and beige files. He had never made any serious attempt to master the VDU and so it stood unused, spurned, beside his desk, an incongruity among the Vietnamese water-colours and the Burmese Buddhas.

Sir Peregrine pressed a buzzer and immediately a side door opened to admit a sharp-featured young man wearing a dark suit and a blue and white striped shirt. This was Fiennes, personal assistant to the Director General. Fiennes was a high-flyer plucked straight from St Antony's College, Oxford, on the recommendation of his tutor.

"Things not going too well, are they, Fiennes?"

"No, sir."

"What have you got for me, then?"

"Actually, sir, there is not very much." He handed Sir Peregrine a beige file labelled 'Perkins, Harold A., Member of Parliament (Labour)'. The file contained about 200 sheets of computer print-out, including records of telephone conversations, photocopies of letters and details of Perkins' voting record on the Labour Party National Executive. There were also some photographs taken at demonstrations. On the top was a short summary of the contents, typed by Fiennes. Sir Peregrine read this and then looked up. "Is this the best you can do?"

"Seems to be all we have, sir."

"What about his sex life?"

"Not married, sir."

18

"Precisely. The man must have buggered or screwed some-body at some time or other."

"Not to our knowledge, sir. Lived with his mother in Sheffield until she died about ten years ago. Then he moved to London and bought a flat near the Kennington Oval. Leads a fairly humdrum sort of life." Fiennes flicked a lock of his blond hair away from his forehead.

"What about East European embassies? Surely he's in and out of those all the time. Most of these lefties usually are."

"Perkins never seems to have been much of a one for freebies, sir."

"Well, we are going to have to do better than this." Sir Peregrine closed the file and handed it back to Fiennes. "When the new Cabinet is announced I want you to go through their files with a fine-toothed comb. And not just the Cabinet. Every minister of state, every under-secre-tary and, above all, any political advisers they bring in with them."

"Yes, sir," Fiennes was heading for the door. "And there is one other thing, sir."

"What's that?"

"Ebury Bridge Road have been on. They want to know if they're to keep the phone taps on Perkins and the other Labour people."

Sir Peregrine smiled. "Why not? Since the Prime Minister or the Home Secretary are theoretically our authority for tapping phones, Perkins and his men will be in the unusual situation of authorising taps on their own phones. I think that's rather amusing, don't you?"

Around the corner from Curzon Street, almost within sight of DI5 headquarters, the nightshift were reporting for duty at Annabel's. Annabel's was not the sort of place where Harry Perkins had a big following.

"Why doesn't someone turn that rubbish off?" A slick young man in a red velvet dinner jacket gestured to the colour television set on the bar which was displaying the beaming features of Prime Minister-Elect Perkins.

"Sarah couldn't come tonight," said a girl in a light blue jumpsuit. "Her father said if she didn't go down to Sussex and vote Conservative he'd stop her allowance."

"Oh, the beast. Poor Sarah."

"Brilliant idea of Charlie's to come on here. We'd have been cutting our throats with depression at the Cavalry Club. Who's for a drink before we start noshing?" The young man in the velvet dinner jacket reached for his wallet.

At the bar a woman strung with pearls the size of gobstoppers was saying she was too depressed even to *think* about food.

Someone hung a gravy-stained napkin over the television screen, obscuring the view of Perkins.

"Simply frightening that a man like that could become Prime Minister," said a slightly balding young man parked next to a bottle of champagne. "Shows how low the country's sunk." He was addressing nobody in particular.

"That's Roddy Bluff. He's microchips. Frightfully rich," whispered a slim blonde girl in a Fiorucci skirt. Lady Elizabeth Fain was the daughter of a Somerset landowner. Although she had left a fashionable girls' boarding school in Sussex at sixteen, and her higher education consisted of a finishing school in Switzerland, she knew more about the world than most girls of her background. For a start she read newspapers, a habit that made her unusual among the female clientele of Annabel's. She had also travelled, with a girlfriend, around India and Thailand, staying in cheap hotels and using only public transport. She even had friends who were left-wingers.

One in particular, Fred Thompson, was a journalist working for an impoverished publication called the *Independent Socialist*. Fred often joked that she was his one contact in what he called the master race. "I'm relying on you to use your influence to get me out when the coup comes," he used to say.

They had last met about three weeks ago, just as the

election campaign was getting under way. Fred had been in a serious mood. "They'll never let a Labour government headed by Harry Perkins take power," he told her.

"Who're 'they'?" she had asked innocently.

"Your friends in the City, the newspaper owners, the civil servants, all them sort of people."

Elizabeth had laughed at him. "You socialists are all the same – paranoid. Always thinking somebody's tapping your phone or blaming all your troubles on the capitalist press. Of course Perkins will take power, if he wins the election."

"I don't mean he'll be chucked in jail or anything crude like that," Fred had countered. "They'll do what they did at first in Chile. Slowly strangle us by cutting back trade and investment and delivering us into the hands of the IMF and the World Bank. I wouldn't be surprised if our ruling class don't team up with the Americans to help de-stabilise us.

"This is Britain, not Chile," Elizabeth had responded firmly, "and Britain is a democracy. That sort of thing will never happen here."

Sitting in Annabel's with the television pundit now predicting a Labour majority of 100 seats, she reflected on her argument with Fred. She had not taken him seriously at the time because, quite apart from the fact that she had been brought up to believe that parliamentary democracy was the greatest thing since sliced bread, it never really occurred to her that Harry Perkins would win. After all, he was an extremist, and she had also been brought up to believe that the British people would never vote for an extremist.

On the night of the Labour landslide in the 1945 general election a woman at the Savoy Hotel is reputed to have said: "My God, they've elected a Labour government. The country will never stand for it." And now at Annabel's on this fateful night history was repeating itself. "The trouble with the socialists," intoned the lady with the pearls, "is that they don't give a damn for the ordinary people of this country. Like us. They dish out wages to the unions all right, but what about the ordinary people of this country?"

Nearby a straight-faced waiter was presenting a folded bill

to a young man sprawling shoeless on a pile of floor cushions. His girl-friend was glued to the television and eating chocolate peppermints. "Con Hold? Julian, where's Con Hold?"

Outside there was a slight drizzle and the young man in the red velvet dinner jacket was puking in Berkeley Square.

Harry Perkins first entered the in-tray of the American President at about 8.30 pm Washington time. The President was giving a dinner party for the executive members of the John Birch Society and their wives when an aide came to whisper the news.

"Jeeeesus Christ," hissed the President, his cigar quivering in sympathy and causing ash to spill on to his lapel. Those mother-fuckers in the CIA had screwed it up again. For months they had been telling him not to worry. This Perkins fellow did not stand a cat in hell's chance, they said. Trust our boys in London, they said. Never been wrong yet. Until tonight.

The President stayed just long enough to make a short speech to the John Birchers, who had made some generous contributions to his campaign funds. Then without going into details he referred to a threat to the Free World which required his urgent attention and headed for the elevator with a posse of secret service agents in tow.

By the time the President reached the Oval Office the head of the Central Intelligence Agency, the chairman of the Joint Chiefs of Staff, the Secretary of State and the President's National Security Adviser were already waiting.

"Okay, George," the President addressed the CIA chief, George McLennon, "how do you explain this one? Only two days ago your people were assuring me that Perkins was a busted flush. Now it seems he's going to be around for some time."

"Sorry, Mr President," stumbled McLennon who was already dreaming of the arses he was going to kick when he got back to Langley. "All I can tell you is what the British boys have been telling us and they've been saying everything

22

was under control."

"That'll teach you guys to take any notice of what that pack of amateurs in London have to say," said the President with venom. Then he nodded towards a man with white cropped hair and cold blue eyes. "Anton, what's your assessment?"

Anton Zablonski, National Security Adviser, an old school world conspiracy man, big on bombing and direct action. Zablonski looked the President straight in the eye, "Mr President, this could be bigger than El Salvador. Perkins' boys have been talking about making Britain a neutral country. That means withdrawing from NATO, kicking out our Third Air Force and doing away with their nuclear submarines. We also lose a base for our cruise missiles. In budget terms Britain is the biggest contributor to NATO, but the main effect would be political, not military. Without Britain the whole alliance could disintegrate."

Despite forty years in the United States Zablonski had not lost his thick Polish accent. The more doomladen his pronouncements, the thicker it became. "Italy's always been wobbly," he went on. "France opted out years ago and the Dutch have never taken the Soviet menace as seriously as we have. Until now Britain has always been our strongest ally, almost a sort of satellite state. We only had to say jump and they jumped."

"Vernon?"

The President had turned to Admiral Vernon Z. Glugstein, chairman of the Joint Chiefs of Staff, the man who had once described 'peace' as the most dangerous word in the English language. Glugstein gave a deep sigh before speaking. "I agree with Anton, Mr President. For all practical purposes Britain's gone over to the other side. Neutrality and Communism are the same thing in my book."

"Easy, Vernon," McLennon interrupted, "it's early days yet. The British Labour Party's notorious for saying one thing in opposition and doing the opposite in government. Let's wait and see what happens."

"Nobody's suggesting we should rush into anything," said the President, "but we'd better make darn sure we're prepared. I don't want any more fuck-ups. The future of Western security is at stake. George, what have we got on the files for de-stabilising Britain?"

"Nothing much, I'm afraid, Mr President. Last thing I can find is dated July 1945. Apparently the Defense Department threw together a plan for a full-scale invasion if the Attlee government went too far. All looks a bit crazy to me."

"Perhaps I can help," interrupted Marcus J. Morgan, the Secretary of State, a corporation lawyer, very fat and very rich. "I had the backroom boys at the National Security Council throw together some options."

"Go ahead, Marcus."

"The key is the British economy. It's in pretty bad shape and not in a position to stand up to much pressure. The first point is, we own about ten per cent of it. Bought it up cheap, after the war. We could easily persuade one or two of the bigger corporations to pull out. Some of them want to anyway."

He was interrupted by the rustle of silver paper. The President was unwrapping a spearmint chewing gum. The President was big on spearmint chewing gum. "Go on Marcus, go on."

"Secondly, there's trade. We account for about twelve per cent of Britain's exports and, if necessary, we could go elsewhere. Thirdly, there's the IMF. Britain is running a very big balance of payments deficit and before long they are going to have to look for a loan. Since we are the biggest contributors to the IMF, we're in a strong position."

The President palmed the silver paper into a neat ball and, with expert aim, lobbed it into a wastepaper bin by the door. Morgan turned the page of his NSC brief and continued. "Fourthly, there's sterling: the United States and the oil-producing countries hold large deposits in London banks. We could start selling and persuade the Arabs to do likewise. We'd have them by the balls, if we did that. Finally, there's covert action: our embassy in London has a few small programmes running. We could expand these. Buy up a few trade union leaders, some Labour MPs, that sort of thing . . ."

"We gotta be careful, Mr President," cautioned McLennon, a veteran of too many failed State Department spectaculars to want to be rushed into a new one. It was always the same. A Secretary of State whose knowledge of the geography was largely gleaned from a *Time-Life* Atlas and the currency markets. A President who wanted to be seen acting tough. And when the whole thing blew up in their faces, nobody would want to know. The CIA would be left to take the rap.

"Britain's not some third-rate banana republic," said McLennon. "If we move too fast, we could create a backlash and turn the other European allies against us."

"Sure, George," said the President irritably. Deep down he knew the CIA Director was right. But just now George McLennon was not his favourite person. "What I want to know," said the President, "is can we expect any help from the inside?"

"I reckon we can, sir." McLennon had perked up a bit. "Fact is there are going to be a lot of very unhappy people in Britain after tonight. A lot of very important persons are about to get their toes trodden on and they aren't going to like it. We can expect to find friends in the top levels of the armed forces, the business community and the civil service, not to mention our cousins at DI5. As far as propaganda goes, we can start the fightback right now, since most of the British press is in friendly hands – although Perkins has said he's going to do something about that."

There was a brief silence, broken only by the sound of the President chewing, then he summed up: "Right, gentlemen. Agreed we wait and see how things turn out. Meantime, George, get your people in London to take some soundings and find out who our friends are going to be. Marcus, you get the NSC boys to put some flesh on that de-stabilisation blueprint. And, very discreetly, sound out the rest of the Alliance to see who we could take with us if the worst comes to the worst."

The President paused, took a deep breath, and looked in turn at each man. "Let's be clear. The election of Harry

Perkins could be the biggest threat to the stability of the Free World since Joe Stalin. We have to do everything possible to keep him in his place. Everything short of landing the Marines at Dover.''

2

Harry Perkins did not intend to become a Labour MP. Having left school at fifteen he followed his father into Firth Brown, the Sheffield special steels plant. From the start he was active in the union, first as assistant branch secretary and later as treasurer.

After five years at Firth's the union paid for him to go on a scholarship to Ruskin College, where he gained a first class honours degree in politics and economics before returning to Sheffield. Before long he was elected convener for the whole plant, which made him chief negotiator for the union side in all dealings with the Firth management. His relations with management were cordial, but not matey. The managing director once remarked, "If I stepped under a bus tomorrow the mills would still be rolling the next day, but if Harry went under a bus the whole place would grind to a halt."

"So long as you realise," Perkins had responded cheerfully.

One evening after he had been back from Ruskin for four years, there came a knock on the front door. It was the secretary of a constituency Labour party on the other side of Sheffield, where a by-election was pending. "We want someone local, someone who knows about steel and who's on the left. So far all we've got applying are bleeding London barristers and sociology lecturers. Some of the lads thought you might be interested."

Perkins was not keen. His father had been dead twelve years and his mother was getting on in life. Who was going to look after her if he was running up and down to London all the time? But Mrs Perkins, when consulted, said she rather fancied the idea of her Harry being an MP.

Then there was the union, what about the union? They hadn't wasted all that precious money sending him to Ruskin just so he could be a Labour MP. But a phone call to the district secretary confirmed that this was exactly what they had in mind.

Perkins said he'd think about it. He thought for two days before agreeing to let his name go forward. The selection was a walkover; as for the election itself, in Sheffield they weigh the Labour votes. His majority was massive. Next morning his workmates from Firth's turned out in force at the station to see him off to London.

Like many working men who find themselves catapulted into Parliament, Harry Perkins let the place go to his head a little. Although he stayed out of the bars and ate mainly in the Strangers' cafeteria the House of Commons brought out a streak of vanity which had hitherto lain dormant. As time passed he lost the ability to concentrate on what other people were saying. His appreciation of events began to revolve around the part he had played in them. His eyes would start to wander during conversation or he would butt in before the other person had finished speaking.

By parliamentary standards it was nothing serious. Indeed, the trait was almost invisible to anyone who did not know Perkins well, but in Sheffield some of his old friends did remark quietly that Parliament seemed to be going to Harry's head. Even so, no one questioned that Perkins was doing a splendid job of shaking up the parliamentary establishment. For a while he became the scourge of the Tory front bench at question time and on occasion did not hesitate to tear a strip off the Labour front bench as well.

Like many before him, however, Perkins soon realised that wherever power lies in Great Britain it is not in the chamber of the House of Commons. Thus he began to concentrate on leading the fight outside Parliament. For three years there was hardly an invitation to speak which he turned down. The more meetings he addressed, the more the invitations multiplied. Gradually, the rise of Harry Perkins had begun.

When Labour was returned to government Perkins was asked to be Secretary of State for the Public Sector, a new post designed to make the nationalised industries accountable to Parliament. It was a meteoric rise for someone who had never been so much as a junior minister. With no love lost between Perkins and the Labour leadership, he was under no illusions as to why he had been offered the job. "They're just trawling for a left-winger to make the régime look respectable," he told his friends. All the same, he accepted.

Perkins' spell in government was dominated by what was in later years to become known as the Windermere reactor affair. As Secretary of State for the Public Sector he was responsible for the Central Electricity Generating Board. The Board was in the process of choosing the type of nuclear reactor for a series of new power stations which would generate enough electricity to meet demand until well into the next century. By the time Perkins took office the decision involved a straight choice between a water-cooled reactor made by the Durand Corporation, an American multinational with a reputation for hard sell, and a gas-cooled reactor to be made by British Insulated Industries, a corporation with its head office in Manchester. To the winner the contract was worth a billion pounds.

Every day delegations of hard-nosed businessmen and learned scientists filed through the Secretary of State's second floor office at Millbank. Behind them they left abstruse memoranda setting out their case. The Americans said their version was cheaper. The men from British Insulated claimed they could get back their costs by selling reactors to the Shah of Iran (whose demise at that time was but a twinkle in the eye of the Ayatollah). The Americans said their version was already in use and had proved as safe as houses. British Insulated brought in experts who alleged that it was not.

And so it went on day after day, week after week. Each night when Perkins boarded a number 3 bus he took back to his flat in Kennington red despatch boxes brimming with memoranda arguing the comparative merits of water-cooled and gas-cooled reactors. There were times, as he sat up late into the night poring over papers he could scarcely comprehend, when he wished he was back at Firth Brown's. Alone in the living room of his three-room flat in the small hours of the

29

morning, the absolute self-confidence he carried through life deserted him. This was no job for a Sheffield steel worker. More than once he reflected on the irony that he, a product of Parkside Secondary School who had barely scraped an 'O' level in Physics, was in a position to over-rule the finest minds in the scientific establishment.

In the end that is exactly what he did. Against the advice of his own civil servants, the Atomic Energy Authority and the CEGB itself, Perkins ruled in favour of British Insulated. The first reactor would be built on the shore of Lake Windermere. The recommendation went to the Cabinet and he talked it through in the face of bitter hostility from his own civil servants. So committed had they been to the American reactor that they refused point blank to provide him with the necessary briefing papers for the Cabinet. Instead he had to commission a report setting out the case for the British reactor from outside academics.

For Perkins the deciding factor was jobs. It was no secret that British Insulated was on the edge of ruin. If they lost the contract a string of factories from Portsmouth to Port Greenock would close. The union men had been to see him. Delegations of shop stewards from every British Insulated factory in the country. In Greenock alone thirty per cent of the town's labour force were employed at British Insulated. Perkins had no desire to be remembered as the man who closed down Greenock. Having satisfied himself that there was nothing to choose between the two reactors on safety grounds, he opted to buy British.

"If you don't mind my saying so, Minister," said Sir Richard Fry, the Permanent Secretary, "I think you have made a big mistake."

"Time will tell," Perkins had replied.

Time did tell. Several years later at Three Mile Island in Pennsylvania an overheated uranium core in a water-cooled reactor led to a radiation leak and the evacuation of a large number of people from their homes. Shortly after the incident Perkins, who had long since returned to the backbenches, received a hand-written note in an envelope bearing the seal of the Public Sector Department. The note, in elegant italic script, said simply: "You were right. We were wrong." It was signed Richard Fry.

Perkins had the letter framed and hung it on the wall of his room in the House of Commons.

It was during the reactor negotiations that Perkins first met Molly Spence. The managing director of British Insulated had come to see Perkins at the Department. He had brought with him his head of research and development, two scientists to advise on safety aspects and a striking blonde girl who took notes. She was aged twenty-seven, her nose was lightly freckled and her expensive accent had a trace of Yorkshire.

Mid-morning they broke for coffee. Someone from the private office produced a packet of digestive biscuits and the girl took hers and walked over to the window. Perkins followed.

"I like your view," she said, indicating the River Thames. She was standing sideways on to the window, half looking at Perkins, half at the river. The light on her face made her eyes gleam.

"I don't get much chance to look at it," said Perkins, drawing alongside. A convoy of red buses passed over Lambeth Bridge and below, on the river, a barge passed on its way to Hammersmith.

"What's that?"

"What?"

"That sort of castle on the other side of the bridge."

"Lambeth Palace, where the Archbishop of Canterbury lives."

"He's done all right for himself." She smiled lightly.

"Aye," said Perkins, "the Church of England's worth a bob or two."

They were interrupted by a private secretary who came with letters to be signed. Perkins took a fountain pen from his inside pocket and signed, scarcely glancing at the letters. The girl waited in silence, staring out at the river. It was Perkins who broke the silence. "Sounds like you're a Yorkshire lass."

31

"Sheffield," she said.

"That's where I'm from."

"I know," she said.

Before he could speak again the private secretary was back. "Minister, I think we ought to make a start. You have the Select Committee at noon." There was a clinking of crockery as a lady with a trolley collected the cups. They turned and walked back to the conference table and she said, almost in a whisper, "I think you knew my dad."

"Did I?"

"Jack Spence, works manager at Firth Brown."

"Good heavens," said Perkins, "is he your father?"

She nodded. They did not get a chance to talk again, but when British Insulated came back to the Department two weeks later, Perkins slipped her an envelope. He tried to do it discreetly so that the private office would not gossip, but he had been seen. David Booth, a young high-flyer on secondment from the Treasury to the nuclear division of the Public Sector Department saw the girl put the envelope in her handbag. At the time he thought nothing of it. The girl was beautiful and the Secretary of State was unmarried. He might have done the same himself had Perkins not beaten him to it.

Molly was dying to open the envelope. On the way out she excused herself and disappeared into the ladies. She cut along the top of the envelope with a nail file. Inside was a single sheet of notepaper which at the top bore the legend "From the Secretary of State". The message inside written in red ink simply said: "Lunch Sunday? Ring me at midnight." And then a telephone number.

There was nothing else. The envelope did not even bear her name. Afterwards it occurred to Molly that this was because Perkins did not know her name. Trembling slightly she stuffed the letter into her handbag and went to catch up with her boss who was waiting in the main reception. That evening, at midnight precisely, she telephoned to say "Yes."

Where women were concerned, Harry Perkins was a late developer. He passed through Parkside Secondary School without ever giving the girls in his class a second glance. It was not that he didn't have friends. There was Nobby Jones whose father was a signalman on the railway. Bill Spriggs, who lived in Jubilee Street, which backed on to the same alley as the Perkins house. And Danny Parker, whose father also worked at Firth Brown. They were all in the same class and went around together. At weekends and during school holidays Nobby's father would sometimes smuggle them into his signal box, where they would sit for hours, with notepads and pencils, jotting down engine numbers. Sometimes when it rained they would go back to Perkins' house and play cards, gin rummy usually. They used to sit round the dining-room table, each with a heap of used threepenny stamps as the stake. Harry never had much luck with cards and very often his supply of used stamps was cleaned out by the end of an afternoon. "Never mind, Harry," Mrs Perkins used to say, "unlucky in cards, lucky in love."

As it turned out Perkins didn't have much luck with love either. By the time they reached the fourth form the other lads had lost interest in train-spotting and gin rummy. Instead they took up girls and pop music.

It was in a rather downmarket coffee bar called Brady's that romance first blossomed. Bill Spriggs and Nobby Jones both did paper rounds and so they could afford to spend the after-school hours sitting round Brady's formica-topped tables tapping their toes to music from the juke box and making a single cup of Brady's awful coffee stretch out over two hours. Occasionally Perkins went with them, but his shilling-a-week pocket money did not run to many cups of coffee, let alone allow for feeding the juke box. Besides, he was not much interested. By the time he was fourteen he preferred to spend an hour browsing through the newspapers in the reading room of the city library. It was the time of the Korean war. Day by day in the *Daily Worker* young Perkins would follow the progress of MacArthur's army as it inched its way up the Korean peninsula towards the border with China.

One evening in Brady's he tried to interest Danny Parker in Korea, but all Danny could talk about was a third-form girl called Lucy Marston whom he had just taken up with. "Last night she let me feel her tits," exulted Danny.

Perkins was disgusted. "Here we are with the world about to blow up and all you're interested in is Lucy Marston's tits." That was the last time he went to Brady's. Most weekends he stayed at home reading. Now and then he would go with his schoolmates to see United play; sometimes a crowd of them would go to the cinema. Danny and Nobby would bring their girl-friends along, but Perkins always played gooseberry. Once they passed themselves off as sixteen year olds and got into an X film called *Flood of Tears*. It was set in America, about a dam that burst and in the floods that followed prisoners escaped from the local jail. Two of the convicts, a murderer and a rapist, end up trapped by the rising waters and seeking refuge in a house with a beautiful girl. What followed was Perkins' introduction to sex. It was pretty tame stuff by today's standards, but for the next few years it was all he had to go on.

Gradually he saw less and less of his schoolfriends. After classes they would go their own ways. Perkins to the library, the others to Brady's. Sometimes on Saturday afternoons, they would meet up at a football match, but that was all they had in common.

Four weeks after Perkins' fifteenth birthday his father was killed in an accident at work. Two steel ingots being loaded by crane on to a lorry fell on him when a cable snapped. But for the accident he would have stayed on at school. His teachers tipped him as Parkside's first candidate for university. Instead he left to take his father's place at Firth Brown.

Perkins' first real girl-friend was Anne Scully. A small, neat girl who was receptionist at the district office of the engineering union. He had been four years at Firth's and met her when he went to pay in the subscriptions from his branch. Anne was quite unlike Perkins. She liked dancing and Buddy Holly and had never read a book – at least not through to the end. That summer they went for long walks in the Pennines and Perkins tried explaining about imperialism (it was the year of Suez) and the goings-on in his union branch. Anne tried hard to understand, but was happier gossiping about who was marrying whom and who was having babies. "You're so bloody serious, Harry Perkins," she scolded him, "always got your head stuck in a newspaper. Why can't you just relax and enjoy life for a change?"

Those days with Anne were the nearest he ever came to relaxing. The high spot of their relationship was a camping holiday in the Lake District. That was in the summer of 1956. For ten days the sun shone brightly. The days they would spend ambling hand in hand along the shore of Lake Windermere, the evenings singing songs with the locals in a pub called The Water's Edge, and the nights snuggled up in the warmth of a single sleeping bag, borrowed from Anne's brother-in-law who ran a camping shop.

They went steady for the best part of three years, until Perkins went to Ruskin. "That'll be the end of us," said Anne sadly. "You'll meet all kinds of fancy people in Oxford and forget about me."

"Don't be daft," he tried to reassure her, but he knew she was right. It was not so much the fancy people, as the distance. At first he hitch-hiked home nearly every weekend. Once Anne came to stay in his digs at Oxford, but the landlady soon put a stop to that. After a while the visits got fewer. The gaps between letters grew longer. In the end they just drifted apart.

By the time he left Ruskin, Anne was married. Perkins got no sympathy from his mother. "That girl was the best thing that ever happened to you," she told him. "If you had any sense, you would have married her while you had the chance." As he passed the years alone he began to think that his mother had been right. Until he met Molly Spence.

"My Dad used to think you were a bit of a bastard," said Molly as she helped herself to salad dressing.

"Between you and I," said Perkins, winking at her, "I was a bit of a bastard."

Molly had never been to lunch with a Cabinet minister before. For the occasion she wore a cotton skirt patterned with red tulips which descended to mid-calf and swirled when she turned suddenly, and a white blouse which did justice to her breasts. Perkins had opened the door to her in his shirt sleeves and a pair of worn brown corduroys.

She was surprised at where he lived. It was a street of late Victorian houses five minutes from the Oval tube station. Perkins' flat was on the third floor. The living room was tastefully, but not extravagantly furnished. Shelves lined with books of Labour Party history and political memoirs. The fireplace had been bricked off, but the mantelpiece remained. Upon it stood a framed photograph of Perkins surrounded by a cluster of small oriental gentlemen.

"Taken in Hanoi," said Perkins when he saw Molly examining the photograph, "two years ago with a delegation."

"And this?" Molly fingered the white bust which sat on the mantelpiece beside the photograph.

"That," said Perkins in a slightly patronising tone, "is J. Keir Hardie."

"Oh," said Molly, none the wiser.

"I don't suppose they taught you anything about him at school."

"Not that I remember."

"Keir Hardie was the first Labour MP," he said, pulling the cork from a bottle of Côte du Rhône.

He poured two glasses and passed one to Molly. "Your health," he said, raising his glass.

"Yours," said Molly, her blue eyes looking straight at him.

They sat at the oak dining table eating the steak that Perkins had just grilled. A Handel organ concerto played on the stereo. They talked about Sheffield. About Firth Brown. About Molly's Dad and Mum who lived in Hallam, on Sheffield's posh side. Perkins told her about the life of a Cabinet minister. Up at six. In the office by eight. Home at midnight. About the red despatch boxes full of letters to sign, memoranda to digest and reports to read. About the time he sat next to the Queen at a lunch for some Arab potentate.

After the steak they had Marks and Spencer's cheesecake and then Perkins suggested a stroll in Kennington Park.

That was how the affair began.

Before she went to bed with Harry Perkins, Molly first looked him up in *Who's Who* to see if he was married. Not that she would have been especially upset if there had been a Mrs Perkins. She just thought she ought to know. Molly was one of those girls who only seem to attract married men. She did not go out of her way to find them. It was just that in the circles in which she moved she had lost the habit of talking to people of her own age.

Affairs with married men had schooled Molly in the art of discretion. At the time the newspapers were engaged in one of their periodic anti-extremist campaigns and Perkins was a prime target. Had Molly been seen with him she would certainly have found her picture on the front page of the popular dailies. The idea appealed to her, but she knew it wouldn't appeal to Perkins.

Molly came once a week, usually on a Sunday. Perkins spent Friday nights and most Saturdays in Sheffield and when he returned he brought with him a pile of constituency mail to be dealt with. More than once Molly arrived expecting to make love and instead found herself sitting up into the small hours typing out what Perkins insisted were urgent letters urging the Home Office not to deport one of his constituents.

From the start Perkins knew there was no future in it. He sensed that she knew too. He was a lonely man, but he had long since reconciled himself to loneliness. Marriage required concessions which he was not prepared to make. He would have had to sacrifice time to small talk and to take an interest in things that bored him stiff. Marriage meant children. Children meant disruption of a life that was already spoken for. There was a time when he might have married. Maybe when he was at Firth Brown. Even perhaps in the early years in Parliament, but not now. Although Perkins would have argued that his life was dedicated to the service of others, it was also a selfish existence in which there was no room for full-time residents, only the occasional guest. That was where Molly came in.

She made no demands on him. Usually she arrived after dark to avoid the prying eyes. In the lighter summer evenings she would ring first from the Oval tube station and he would go downstairs and open the front door to minimise the risk of alerting the neighbours. The routine rarely varied. There would be a record, usually Brahms or Handel, on the stereo. The table would be set for two. The Sunday newspapers, half read, would be scattered near a floor cushion by the window. Red despatch boxes were stacked in the hallway awaiting collection by a Ministry chauffeur. Another stood open on the writing desk in the corner with half its contents still awaiting attention in a neat pile.

If Perkins was cooking, the meal would be simple. Pâté, a Marks and Spencer pie, vegetables, and a bottle of not very expensive wine. If, as was more often the case, Molly was cooking, the meal might run to a joint of lamb. Since Perkins didn't have time to shop, she would bring the food with her in a wicker basket. He would always insist on repaying her, usually by cheque since he never seemed to have the time to go to a bank.

Conversation centred around what Perkins had been up to in the previous week. Sometimes they gossiped. Molly liked discussing the private lives of public figures. Inside information, however trite, gave her a small thrill. Occasionally Perkins would regale her with an account of a little coup he had scored at a Cabinet sub-committee. Now and then they would discuss politics. Usually it was fairly basic stuff. He would talk of kicking out the American nuclear bases and she would say, "What about the Russians?" They would argue for perhaps five minutes before Perkins gave up, feigning disgust. "You sound like the bloody *Daily Mail*," he would say half seriously. She would kiss him and they would go to bed, leaving the washing up in the sink.

It wasn't much of a love affair and by Molly's standards the Secretary of State was not much of a lover. Her other lovers wooed her with flowers, dinners in West End restaurants and expensive presents. The only present she ever received from Perkins was a copy of *The Ragged Trousered Philanthropists*. In the front he had written with a red felt pen, "To a slightly Tory lady in the hope that she will see the light." It was signed, "Love, Harry" and followed by three kisses. She struggled through the first fifty pages and then gave up. Molly had never had much time for books.

After about a year Molly stopped coming. Her disappearance was announced in a note which was only a little longer than the one with which Perkins had first brought her into his life. It read: "Dear Harry, on Saturday I'm getting married so we'll have to call it a day. Please understand. Good luck. Molly." For about an hour Perkins was devastated. He made himself a cup of tea and paced his modest living room composing a reply which in the end he did not send. He toyed with the idea of telephoning, but rejected it on the grounds that the telephone might be answered by Molly's prospective husband. Instead he placed the note in his in-tray along with a pile of other unanswered correspondence. A few days later he filed it away in a green folder together with a postcard she had once sent him while on a skiing holiday in Austria and several notes, none more than half a page long, which mainly concerned arrangements for their Sunday night rendezvous and who should get the shopping. He labelled the folder 'Molly' and placed it between similar files labelled 'Micro-chips' and 'Multinationals' in a steel filing cabinet in the spare bedroom. His only other souvenirs were a yellow plastic bathing cap and a Wisdom toothbrush which she left behind in the bathroom.

Perkins had been in the Cabinet for three years when the government started to close down steel mills. He resigned at once to take part in the resistance. The following year he was swept on to the Labour Party National Executive. Three years later he was topping the poll. Looking back, his election as leader of the Labour Party seemed inevitable, but at the time it took everyone by surprise.

3

By the time Harry Perkins became leader of Her Majesty's Opposition, Labour had been out of power for a decade. Although the National Unity government had brought inflation under control, it had only done so at the cost of massive unemployment and great social violence.

The inner city riots which began in the summer of 1981 grew steadily worse as the decade wore on. Shopkeepers began to evacuate. The buses stopped operating after dark when the police said they could no longer guarantee the safety of the bus crews. Brixton High Street became a corridor of estate agents' fading signs and chipboarded shop fronts smeared with graffiti. "Avenge the Railton Five," said one in a reference to five West Indian youths killed in Railton Road when police opened fire on a crowd of petrol bombers. Another said simply: "Burn Brixton," but it had already been overtaken by events.

Gradually, the inner cities were abandoned to roaming bands of unemployed youths and more and more police were required to stop them breaking out into the suburbs where owner-occupiers with jobs lived. In ten years the police budget had doubled. In Brixton, Toxteth, Handsworth, Moss Side and the Gorbals police in armoured cars and bullet-proof jackets patrolled the streets. Around the city centres special units of riot police on permanent stand-by sat fidgeting with their new, lethal nightsticks, imported from America.

In February 1988 Trotskyism had been banned by legislation rushed through Parliament in three days. This had followed the discovery of an arms cache in a derelict house in Islington, said to be used by the International Marxist Group. Some said the guns had been supplied by the IRA, others said they had been planted by the police. No matter, Trotskyism was now illegal. Army camps on Salisbury Plain were filled not only with rioters, but suspected Trotskyists, too. Under the new law only a single witness, usually an anonymous member of the Special Branch, was needed to secure a conviction for Trotskyism.

The mid-1980s were also the time in which the long struggle between industrial and financial capital was finally resolved in favour of the financiers. For decades successive British governments had pursued policies of high interest rates and manipulation of demand, designed to favour those engaged in speculation rather than production. In these circumstances the only worthwhile investments were short-term ones promising high returns. Even industrial companies already profitable were advised by their accountants to 'go liquid' and hold their assets in cash, gold or oil paintings rather than in new plant and equipment.

As if this were not serious enough, exchange controls (removed by an earlier Tory government) had never been restored thereby making possible what one industrialist, in the privacy of his boardroom, called a 'scorched earth policy'. As the crisis grew worse, the outflow of capital increased.

On the Clyde and the Tyne shipbuilding all but disappeared. A few rusting hulks remained in the yards, half completed at the time British Shipbuilders was allowed to go under. Asset strippers, sharp young men who came from London in Rolls-Royces, wandered among the ruins buying up at bargain prices the cranes and any other movables which they sold at large profits to yards in Spain and France. The hulks that remained were decaying monuments to an industry which had consumed generations of engineers, boiler-makers, welders and fitters. Those who were young enough moved south in search of work. Some went to work in Arabia. Those who were too old or too set in their ways to move stayed put and went down with their ships.

The fishing industry had long since disappeared. In Aberdeen, Fleetwood, Grimsby, Hull and Lowestoft a few rotting trawlers bobbed idly at anchor. They were all that remained of the proud fleets that once roamed the North Sea from the

English Channel to the Arctic Circle. One or two more enterprising skippers had converted their trawlers into pleasure boats taking day trippers for rides along the coast during the summer, but it was no way to make a living. The trawlermen blamed the Common Market for their ruin.

In Yorkshire and Lancashire the textile industry finally succumbed to cheap and inferior imports from Taiwan and South Korea. Calls for import controls, delegations to ministries and mass lobbies of Parliament fell upon deaf ears. Men from ministries on index-linked pensions came and looked at the books. It was, they said, a tough old world. If textile workers in Bolton could not compete with those in Taipei and Seoul they would have to go down the plughole.

There was some brave resistance. Scattered work-ins, here and there attempts to set up a co-operative, but there was never really any hope. In the end the textile industry followed shipbuilding and fishing into history.

This did little to damage the political base of the National Unity government. Textiles, ships and fish were the products of Labour strongholds. Elsewhere the belief was widespread that only the inefficient, the idle and the greedy were unemployed, a belief fostered by the popular newspapers. For a time one of Sir George Fison's newspapers even ran a 'Scrounger of the Week' competition, urging people to spy upon unemployed neighbours and offering cash prizes to those who could uncover the most outrageous fiddles.

The collapse of British Leyland was the beginning of the end. Leyland had been the country's biggest export earner and largest employer. One November morning the chairman of Leyland had appeared at the Department of Industry to tell the Secretary of State that his company could no longer service its debts, never mind finance further investment. He needed an extra £500 million immediately and probably the same again next year.

There were emergency Cabinet meetings, a frantic round of negotiations with a Japanese corporation, but in the end the cupboard was bare and most of British Leyland was allowed to go to the wall. The bus and truck company was sold to the Japanese. The Rover plant went to Volkswagen of Germany who promptly turned it into an assembly plant for one of its own models. The collapse of Leyland also triggered off a wave of bankruptcies which swept through components firms in the Midlands. At last the crisis began to lap at the edge of the Unity government's political base.

The third element in the disaster which overtook Britain in the late 1980s was that North Sea oil began to dry up. For most of the previous decade Britain had been self-sufficient in oil. This meant that, besides not having to spend precious foreign exchange importing oil, the government also received huge revenue from the taxes on the profits of the oil companies. In a sane world this temporary good fortune might have been used to provide industry with the investment funds so badly needed. However, most of the oil revenue was squandered on tax cuts designed to buy favour with the electorate.

As domestic oil supplies dwindled Britain was obliged to go back on to the world markets to purchase oil again. It is true that by this time scientists had succeeded in converting sugar cane and other vegetable matter into a substitute for oil, but it was not yet being produced in anything like commercial quantities. Britain's import bill began to increase dramatically. A balance of payments crisis meant that the foreign holders of sterling would start selling. So too would domestic holders, since they were no longer bound by exchange controls.

For those engaged in certain forms of non-productive activity life had never been so good. As money poured out of manufacturing industry, more became available for speculation in commodities, property and works of art. Because the supply of these was relatively limited and the amount of cash chasing them was for all practical purposes unlimited, what went up was not supply, but prices. The value of gold soared; coffee, rubber, tin and a host of other commodities fluctuated wildly as fortunes were won and lost by those who could afford to gamble in futures.

Property boomed, fuelled by the pension funds – the accumulated savings of millions of citizens. The London docks were filled in and replaced by skyscrapers bearing names such as Hay's Wharf Towers and West India House. The names offered the only clues to what had gone before, in the days when Britain had been a trading nation. The 1980s property boom, the craziest of all time, was still in progress when Harry Perkins came to power.

For most of the decade that preceded the election of Perkins and his government the orgy of speculation which lay at the heart of the British disease was, in the minds of many people, camouflaged by the view that political extremists and greedy workers were to blame. By the end of the 1980s, however, certain weaknesses had become apparent in that line of thinking. Real wages had fallen, public spending had been cut back drastically, the trade unions had been neutered; yet still the slide into ruin continued. By the end of the decade the huge campaign to pin the blame for Britain's ills on extremists had finally run out of steam.

The newspapers received the elevation of Perkins with unprecedented hysteria. "Go Back to Moscow," screamed the *Sun*, unable to come to terms with the fact that 'Red Harry' (as the papers insisted on calling him) had never actually set foot in Moscow. "LABOUR VOTES FOR SUICIDE," raged the *Express*, and *The Times* ran a long leading article which argued that the election of Perkins spelled the end of the two-party system since the British people would never be foolish enough to vote into office a government headed by such a man. Even the *Daily Mirror*, traditionally loyal to Labour, thought the choice of Perkins was the end.

Despite their firm belief that a Labour Party led by Perkins stood no chance of winning an election, the press barons took no chances. No one had done more to alert the British people to the perils of extremism than Sir George Fison (indeed, he had been awarded a knighthood for his services in this regard). But the general election of March 1989 was his finest hour.

Day after day in the run-up to polling Sir George's newspapers published lists of 'Communist-backed' Labour candidates. By way of evidence they offered an article in the *Morning Star* or a platform shared by a Labour MP and a member of the Communist Party. A week before election day Sir George's newshounds 'discovered' documents purporting to show that four senior Labour leaders were paid-up members of a Trotskyist cell.

Not to be outdone, the *Express* took to publishing a picture of Perkins daubed with a Hitler moustache, and words such as 'mugging' and 'terrorism' began to creep into discussion of what life in Harry Perkins' Britain held in store. One leading article was headed "Perkins, the demon mugger unmasked." *The Times*, now owned by an American computer company, provided its readers with a slightly upmarket version of the same: claiming at one stage to have discovered a plot by Trotskyites to blow up the Cenotaph in the event of a Labour election defeat. Another paper splashed on its front page an internal Labour Party document outlining plans to abolish tax relief on mortgages and confiscate all personal wealth over £50,000. Enquiry revealed that the document was a forgery, but the retraction was tucked away at the bottom of an inside page.

Only the *Guardian* and the *Financial Times* conceded that there were any issues to be debated and even they concluded that the election of Perkins would be a catastrophe. One commentator went so far as to speculate that this could be the last free election which the British people would enjoy for many years. Events were to prove him correct, though for reasons rather different from those inferred at the time.

But Harry Perkins had no inkling of what was to come as he set out by train for London on his first glorious morning as Prime Minister of Great Britain.

4

Perkins arrived at St Pancras a little after 10 am. He was bearing exactly the luggage with which he had departed for Sheffield on the final morning of the election campaign two days earlier: a British Airways bag containing two shirts and a change of underwear and a rather battered briefcase embossed with his initials – a present from his constituency party on the tenth anniversary of his election.

He had hoped to occupy the journey down sketching out details of his Cabinet and the host of other appointments he would have to make, but from the moment the sleek Advanced Passenger Train glided out of Sheffield he had been harassed by newspaper men who had chosen to ride down with him. For a while bedlam prevailed as reporters, photographers, camera crews, autograph hunters and assorted well-wishers fought to get near. It was not until the train passed Leicester that the ticket inspector, with the aid of a steward from the dining car, was able to restore some sort of order. Perkins began to realise why Prime Ministers did not travel second class.

In the end, all he managed was a glance at the newspapers purchased on the platform at Sheffield. They were mainly early editions and although by the time they had gone to press Labour appeared to be winning, the scale of the victory was unclear. Considering the onslaught to which Perkins and his party had been subjected before the election, newspaper treatment of the impending Labour victory seemed almost generous. "IT'S HARRY," proclaimed the *Daily Mirror* over a large picture of Perkins casting his vote at Parkside Junior School. "PERKINS BY WHISKER," said the *Express* over a report by the paper's political correspondent predicting a 'wafer-thin' Labour majority which, the correspondent added, "should prevent Perkins and his gang from getting up to any of the mischief outlined in Labour's loony manifesto." Perkins could not resist a chuckle as he pictured the scene on the *Express* editorial floor now that the full result was known. *The Times* tried to set the minds of its readers at rest by recalling the fate which had overtaken previous radical Labour programmes "once the Party's leaders had to face up to the realities of office".

On inside pages the popular press regaled readers with a hurried cuttings job on Perkins' career from his days as a schoolboy at Parkside Secondary School. The picture libraries had been trawled for a class photograph, taken when he was a weedy, freckled youth of fourteen. There was even a picture of young Perkins, aged five years, taken with his mother and father in the back yard of their terraced house in Brightside just before they were bombed out in the second world war. Where the devil did they rake that up from, he wondered.

At St Pancras there were more reporters, photographers and television men with lightweight cameras. Everybody was talking at once. How was he feeling? Who was going to be Foreign Secretary? What did he have for breakfast? And so it went on as Perkins pushed through the throng towards the distant ticket barrier, taking care as he went not to tread on prostrate sound recordists.

After he had fought his way no more than twenty yards, the scrimmage halted. There was a pause and then, as with the crossing of the Red Sea by the Israelites, the ranks of the assembled pressmen suddenly parted to make way for a man in pin-striped trousers and a dark jacket, his cuffs protruding a full three inches from the sleeves and joined by jade links. A silence fell over the assembled multitude, then the man spoke: "Mr Perkins," he said in a voice that rang with self-assurance, "Mr Perkins, my name is Frederick Porter. I have come to take you to the Palace."

Sir Frederick Porter was the King's private secretary. Perkins had been told to expect him at St Pancras. The previous day Downing Street had been on the line to him in Sheffield and explained the procedure for the transfer of power. At the time the votes had still to be counted, the pundits had still been predicting a Tory victory and yet the man from Downing Street had spoken as though a Labour victory was already a fact. Telepathy? Perkins had wondered. Or just the establishment hedging its bets? In the event Downing Street's caution had proved justified and now the well-oiled machinery for ensuring a smooth transfer of power was in motion. First there was an audience with the King, morning dress optional. He would ask Perkins to form a government. From that moment on he was Prime Minister and he would be taken from the Palace in a Downing Street car. The outgoing Prime Minister would leave Downing Street by a rear entrance. They would not meet, but it was normal practice for the incoming Prime Minister to make Chequers available to his predecessor.

Perkins put down his briefcase and advanced towards Sir Frederick, hand outstretched. Eton, Balliol and the Guards had taught Sir Frederick to display a stiff upper lip in the face of adversity and as he took Perkins' hand his face betrayed no trace of his inner anguish.

"I have a car, sir," said Sir Frederick, indicating with a sweep of his hand the general direction of the Euston Road.

"Car?" said Perkins. "What's wrong with a bus? Number 77 runs down Whitehall from here." Perkins made a fetish of travelling by public transport. Many were the anxious moments chairmen, presiding over mass rallies, had spent looking at their watches because their Party leader's bus was running late. Perkins had resolved that even when he was Prime Minister he would stick to public transport.

For one-hundredth of a second Sir Frederick's face registered dismay, but when he spoke his voice contained precisely the right blend of firmness and humility. "Sir, His Majesty is waiting."

Perkins might have replied that it would do His Majesty no harm to be kept waiting for once. He might even have said that His Majesty could get stuffed. History records, however, that he simply shrugged, handed his bag to the chauffeur and climbed meekly into the back of the car drawn up in the forecourt of St Pancras station.

They drove to Buckingham Palace in silence. As they passed down Kingsway Perkins reflected wryly that he had suffered his first defeat at the hands of the establishment – and he was not yet Prime Minister.

The King and Queen breakfasted together in the private apartments in the north wing of Buckingham Palace. The crockery was Doulton. The cutlery, Louis XIV. The marmalade, Rose's Lime. The Regency windows looked out over verdant lawns. In the distance a gardener crouched planting polyanthus.

The young Queen gazed first across the gardens and then turned to her husband. "I do hope," she said firmly, "that you are not going to go about repeating the sort of things you were saying last night."

The King looked surprised. "I meant every word. This Perkins fellow will be the ruin of us."

"Do be careful, my love. You know the trouble your father used to get into every time he sounded off about politics."

The King sighed. It was not the first time they had had this conversation. "You do exaggerate, darling. Perkins would never dare close us down. He'd have an uprising on his hands."

"He'll be here in two hours. You must bring yourself to be nice to him." With that the Queen buttered a finger of toast and resumed her gaze across the lawns.

Without another word the sovereign placed his napkin on the table, rose and left. A footman glided noiselessly among the tea cups. He had heard nothing.

After seeing the King, Perkins was driven to Downing Street. The car sent by Number Ten to collect him from the Palace was waiting in the inner courtyard. Sir Frederick Porter stiffly ushered Perkins from the private apartments and handed him into the custody of a man in the full uniform of the middle rank civil service. A blue striped shirt, pin-striped trousers and a dark jacket. The bowler hat and umbrella were visible on a shelf through the rear window of the car.

"Prime Minister," said the man, proffering a manicured hand, "my name is Horace Tweed. I am your principal private secretary."

And with that he opened the rear door of the car, a blue Mercedes driven by a woman in a green uniform (since the Leyland collapse Mercedes had replaced Rovers in the government car pool). Perkins scrambled inside. Tweed closed the door after him, walked round the back of the car and climbed in through the door on the other side. The car slid out of the courtyard. As they passed, the sentries in their lofty bearskins presented arms.

"When I was a kid," said Perkins, "I wanted to be a soldier with one of those hats."

Tweed looked at him blankly. When he was a kid he probably never wanted to be anything but private secretary to the Prime Minister, thought Perkins.

Leaving the Palace they ran a gauntlet of photographers, some of them running out into the road alongside the car. A police car materialised, as if from nowhere, and preceded them down the Mall, its headlights on full beam, despite the daylight.

Tweed was saying something about sterling and the Governor of the Bank of England wanted an appointment, but Perkins was reflecting on his audience with the King. It had gone well. With apparent sincerity the King had congratulated him on his party's victory and charged him with forming a government. After formalities they had indulged in a few minutes of small talk, mainly about football and gardens. Perkins said he had never lived in a house with a garden. The King said he would show him his and Perkins had departed saying he would take up his offer some day.

By the time they reached Downing Street, Tweed was saying something about a phone call from the President of the United States. But Perkins could see only the crowds which spilled out into Whitehall and along the pavement outside the Cabinet Office. As the car turned into Downing Street he glimpsed a young woman in a white raincoat pressed against the barrier. Her long blonde hair was tucked into the collar of the raincoat; her cheeks were lightly freckled and as he passed she smiled a small, discreet smile. Perkins had scarcely time to think that she reminded him of Molly Spence before the thought was lost amid the cheering of the crowd.

A stone's throw from Downing Street, by a quiet terrace of Queen Anne houses overlooking the south-west corner of St James's Park, a Rolls-Royce was disgorging the portly frame of Sir George Fison. Waiting at an open doorway to greet him was a languid figure swathed in a red corduroy smoking jacket – Sir Peregrine Craddock.

"So good of you to come, George."

"Least I could do in the circumstances, old boy."

In the oak-panelled dining room a maid was clearing away the remains of Sir Peregrine's late breakfast. A pile of newspapers had been cast unread into an armchair; the morning sun streamed in through a bay window overlooking the park; through the plane trees the Treasury edifice was just visible.

Sir Peregrine poured two black coffees from a silver pot, waited until the maid had gone and then spoke quietly. "No doubt you've guessed why I asked you in. At a time like this it's important that those of us who care about civilised values stick together."

"Couldn't agree more," nodded Fison, who had flopped into an armchair by the window. The daylight from behind illuminated his bald crown, creating a kind of halo effect. Sir Peregrine, who was seated facing into the light, was obliged to squint to catch the expression on Fison's face.

The clock on the mantelpiece registered a quarter past the hour in unison with Big Ben, the distant chimes of which were just audible. Sir Peregrine took a sip of coffee and then resumed in the discreet tones he reserved for distasteful subjects: "In order to help people see sense we may have to cut a few corners, if you get my meaning. Float the odd rumour, organise the occasional punch-up." The expression

51

'punch-up' tripped uneasily off Sir Peregrine's refined tongue and he winced as he pronounced it.

"Absolutely," said Fison, slapping his knee with the flat of his podgy hand. Fison came from a tougher school than Sir Peregrine. He knew exactly what was required. He had started life as an East End barrow boy and a follower of Oswald Mosley. He even had a couple of convictions for incitement under the 1936 Public Order Act. That was a long time ago, of course, but when it came to a bit of bother George Fison could mix it with the best of them. Not that this stopped his newspapers taking a hard line on law and order.

Fison's obvious relish made Sir Peregrine unhappy. "Obviously one doesn't like to think in these terms," he said quickly. "We are supposed to be a democracy and all that, but it's important that people realise what's at stake. Not just the national interest, but the future of the Western alliance." Sir Peregrine's voice rose. He was happier talking global strategy.

Fison slapped his knee again. "Entirely agree, dear boy." The 'dear boy' was an affectation. People didn't speak like that where he came from, but it had been forty years since he moved from Stepney to Chelsea and Fison had been working ever since to adopt what he believed to be the mannerisms of a gentleman.

Sir Peregrine paused to light a pipe. His first of the day. When the blue smoke cleared he continued. "To start the ball rolling, what I had in mind was, I hesitate to use the word," he resumed the *sotto voce* reserved for distasteful subjects, "a smear campaign." He drew on his pipe and then breathed out again, emitting more blue smoke. "Nothing too heavy at first. Just enough to sow the seeds of doubt in the public mind about Perkins and his gang. For the time being we will lay off Perkins himself. His popularity is running high and anything we try to stick on him could blow up in our faces." He looked across at Fison who was nodding intently. "To start with we must concentrate on ministers and advisers. That way we can discredit Perkins without attacking him directly."

With graceful movements of his left hand Sir Peregrine brushed tobacco ash from the lapels of his smoking jacket. He wasn't keen on Fison. The man lacked breeding. He was crude and unsubtle. It stood out a mile. Still, one couldn't choose one's friends in a situation like this. He went on, "I've got a team of chaps standing by and the moment we get details of ministerial appointments they'll be going through the files looking for anything that may be useful. Shady business deals, illicit love affairs, trips to Moscow, articles in the *Morning Star*. Naturally we'll pass everything over and you and the other Fleet Street boys can take it from there."

Sir Peregrine stretched his legs, sank back into the armchair and puffed his pipe. The smoke mingled with the incoming rays of sunlight and caused a cloud to form between himself and Fison. When it cleared he went on, "Normally we'd just shove this sort of stuff in plain brown envelopes and stick it in the post to a few reliable old hands, but this time we want something bigger. That's where you come in." He looked across at Fison, through the haze. Fison was already composing the lecture he was going to give to his senior editors. The nation, he would tell them, was facing catastrophe. In the battle that was to come there were only two sides. Anyone with doubts about which side they were on could collect his cards now. Fison smiled inwardly. He was sure that his services would not go unrewarded. At the very least he was expecting a peerage to provide the final seal of respectability he craved.

The pipe was now clamped between Sir Peregrine's teeth, causing him to speak through the side of his mouth. As he did so the end of the pipe wobbled. "I want you to get together a few proprietors, editors and senior journalists whom we can absolutely count on. You should meet regularly to co-ordinate coverage. As things get hotter, and believe me they will, we're going to need people we can rely on. Can you manage?"

"No problem," said Fison, "no problem at all."

"What about the journalists? Bound to have some trouble with them if we lay it on too thick."

Fison wiped his lips with the back of his hand. "I promise you," he said slowly, "there won't be a peep out of anyone."

"Very embarrassing to have journalists whining on about ethics and press freedom just as we get a decent campaign going."

"My dear boy," Fison leaned towards Sir Peregrine, "take it from me, most Fleet Street journalists wouldn't recognise a real live ethic at five paces. Why do you think we pay them so well?"

"Good, that's settled, then," said Sir Peregrine, rising. He placed the pipe, by now extinct, in an ashtray on the mantelpiece. "One other thing. Very important you don't breathe a word of this conversation to anybody. Nothing we send you must be traceable to us. If Perkins gets a whiff of what's going on, we'll all be in the excreta up to our necks."

Gripping both arms of the chair, Fison heaved himself to his feet, panting slightly with the exertion. He drew himself rigidly to attention, a fitting posture for a man about to serve his King and country, "Don't worry, Peregrine, you can count on me."

Perkins crossed the threshold of Number Ten Downing Street to find the entire staff, private secretaries, clerks, telephonists, footmen and garden girls from the downstairs typing pool lining the corridor that leads to the Cabinet Room. As he entered they applauded. Not entirely spontaneously since many of them confidently expected to be sacked. Only an hour had elapsed since they had gathered on the same spot to applaud the outgoing Prime Minister who had departed by a back entrance.

Guided by the omnipresent Tweed, Perkins crossed the black and white marble tiled floor of the entrance lobby and passed down the corridor to the Cabinet Room, nodding to the right and left in acknowledgment of the applause. He paused respectfully at the entrance to the Cabinet Room as a Catholic might pause in the entrance of a church to cross himself with holy water. Even for a Sheffield steel worker, born and bred with a healthy disrespect for tradition and the trappings of power, the Cabinet Room had something of a presence. Within these walls the British government had first heard of the loss of the American colonies, plotted the downfall of Napoleon, the Kaiser and Hitler and granted independence to India. Now these same walls were to bear witness to the rise, and perhaps the fall, of Harry Perkins.

He entered diffidently and stood at the top of the long table, down either side of which were arranged chairs covered in red leather. Each place at the table was marked with a leather-bound blotter and crystal decanters of water. Perkins made one slow circuit of the table, peering cautiously out of each window overlooking the garden. When he had completed his lap of the room Tweed gestured that he should sit. Perkins sat.

"One or two things we must attend to immediately, Prime Minister."

"Don't I even get to wash my hands?"

"This won't take a moment," said Tweed.

Three private secretaries had now filed into the room and they stood in a crocodile behind Tweed, waiting to be introduced. The first bore a letter from Perkins to his defeated predecessor, placing the Prime Minister's country residence, Chequers, at the disposal of the outgoing Prime Minister until he had made arrangements to go elsewhere. "Just a formality," said Tweed: "Sign here, Prime Minister." Perkins signed.

The second private secretary presented figures showing that three cents had been wiped off the value of sterling in the two hours since the London market opened. Heavy selling was also reported from Hong Kong and Tokyo. "The Governor of the Bank wants an appointment as soon as possible." One was agreed for the afternoon at five o'clock. The Cabinet secretary also wanted an appointment. He was told to come at six.

The third secretary said that the White House had telephoned. The President wanted to congratulate Perkins personally and it had been agreed that the Prime Minister should receive the call in his study in three hours' time.

Formalities complete, Perkins was shown to a small lift in the rear of the building which conveyed him up two floors to the attic flat built into the roof of Number Ten. "This will be your private quarters," said Tweed, as he unlocked the door. "You are planning to live here, of course?"

"Not likely," said Perkins.

"But, Prime Minister, we've already brought your wardrobe here." Tweed ran a manicured hand through his thinning hair.

"You what?"

"We got the key to your flat from your secretary and I sent someone round this morning."

"Then you can just send them back again."

Although it was scarcely an hour since the flat had been vacated there was no trace of the previous occupant. No hint of cigar smoke from the night before. No sign of the whisky bottles that had littered the hearth as the outgoing Prime Minister, surrounded by his closest aides, watched his majority crumble. Before departing for the Palace, Tweed had given instructions that not a trace of the old régime was to remain. The thick carpet had been scrupulously vacuumed. Windows had been flung open. The bed linen and the curtains changed. Even the David Hockney that hung above the fireplace had been replaced by a Lowry print of a Lancashire fairground which Tweed had brought up from the basement. The private office thought of everything.

In a wardrobe in the main bedroom Perkins found his suits, all neatly pressed, in accordance with Tweed's instructions.

"My goodness, you lads work fast," said Perkins.

While he was changing there came a knock on the bedroom door. "Inspector Page and Sergeant Block of the Special Branch," intoned Tweed, who was still loitering in the living room. "These gentlemen will be responsible for your safety from now on."

"That's right, sir," said Page. A thickset, balding man with a Zapata moustache and a face like a closed book. "Sergeant Block and I will take it in turns to accompany you at all times of the day and night outside of Downing Street and the House of Commons. Naturally we will try to be as unobtrusive as possible."

Perkins nodded as he selected his brightest tie from a rail along the inside of a wardrobe door.

"One other thing, sir. I understand that you're in the habit of travelling around on buses."

"That's right, Inspector."

"Is that strictly necessary, sir? Makes life very difficult for Sergeant Block and me."

"I am afraid it is necessary, Inspector. You see, my party wants to phase out the private motor car in cities and encourage people to use public transport instead. If we want to be taken seriously, then I've got to set an example.'

"I see, sir," said Page, who clearly didn't see. Not one of my voters, thought Perkins as the Inspector and the Sergeant withdrew. As they left, a private secretary entered to say that the Governor of the Bank had been on again. "He says sterling's going down fast. Can't wait till five o'clock. Must see you immediately."

Lady Elizabeth Fain slept until nearly noon in her mews cottage near Sloane Square, a twenty-first birthday present from her father. Still clad in her nightdress she tripped downstairs to the kitchen, raised the blind to let in daylight and opened the back door to let her dog, a cocker spaniel called Walpole, out into the tiny garden.

She was pouring a glass of grapefruit juice when the phone rang. It was Fred Thompson. "Hi, Lizzie, just called to see how my friends in the Master Race are coping with the revolution."

'Actually, I've just slept through the first ten hours of revolution."

"Don't worry, the tumbrils will soon be rolling through Sloane Square, but I'll see you're okay," said Fred with a chuckle.

"You should have heard them at Annabel's last night. Anyone would have thought Harry Perkins was going to send us all to Siberia the way some people were carrying on."

"There are some people I wish he would send to Siberia."

"Such as?"

"Such as that man Fison, for a start. He was on the radio half an hour ago prattling on about the threat to press freedom. Thinks Perkins is going to nationalise his newspapers."

"Isn't he?"

"Course not. All we promised to do was look at alternatives to leaving the newspapers in the hands of fat slugs like Fison. Trusts, co-operatives, that sort of thing. That's not state ownership, is it?"

"If you say so, Fred." At this point Walpole the spaniel passed through the kitchen on his way to the hall and returned with the mail between his teeth.

Telephone in hand, Elizabeth stooped to extract the letters and continued, "I must say that for someone who only last week was predicting a coup if Perkins became Prime Minister, you're sounding remarkably cheerful this morning."

"I never said anything about a coup," protested Fred. "Only that we are going to get a lot of shit from the Americans and your friends in the establishment . . . Anyway, that's not what I rang about. I wondered if you want to come to a party on Sunday. We're celebrating the election result."

"Frightfully sorry, Fred, I'm going to the country this weekend."

"Too bad. You'd have enjoyed it. Lots of left-wing extremists coming."

"No left-wing extremists where I'm going," said Elizabeth. "Chap who's invited me is an army officer, his brother is a Tory MP and his father was something big in the City. They've got a huge house in Oxfordshire."

"Sounds fascinating," said Fred.

"Don't worry, I'll tell you all about it when I get back – providing you manage to keep the tumbrils out of Sloane Square."

At noon precisely Fiennes of DI5 strolled into the coffee shop of the Churchill Hotel in Portman Square. Under his arm he was carrying a folded copy of the *Financial Times*. He glanced to right and left until his eyes came to rest upon a clean-cut man in his late thirties, in a white, open raincoat.

"Ah, there you are, Jim." Fiennes approached and sat down opposite the man in the raincoat. They shook hands over the table. "Guess you know what I've come about," said Fiennes.

"Sure do." The man's accent was East Coast American.

"Thought we ought to meet on neutral territory. Not wise for me to be seen at the embassy."

The American lit a cigarette without offering one to Fiennes, who went on, "The Old Man thought we'd better liaise directly with your people instead of going through DI6. In any case they'd only balls it up."

"Okay by me." The American took a drag of his cigarette and placed it on the edge of an ashtray. A waiter approached and they ordered two black coffees. "Now what are you guys planning to do about Perkins?"

"The Old Man thinks we ought to take it easy at first. Just feed out a little dirt to the newspapers. Let the civil service and the City do the rest, for the time being."

"What dirt you got on him?"

"That's the problem. There's nothing on our files. We were hoping you might have something."

"Nope. He's clean at our end too. I had the boys at Langley run him through the computer last night. Clean as a whistle."

"Should have more to go on when he starts naming ministers and camp followers," said Fiennes.

"We'll run 'em all through the computer and anything we get we'll pass over to you."

"Better be discreet. No point in going through the usual channels or we'll have DI6 whining to be let in on the act."

"Anything we get I'll hand over personally to you."

The waiter came with the coffees and the bill. They drank in silence. Fiennes paid the bill with a pound note and some coins and got to his feet. "Keep in touch, Jim."

"Sure will."

*

59

Perkins took the call from the President on the scrambled line in the Prime Minister's study.

"Harry."

"Mr President."

"Harry, I just wanted to congratulate you personally on your magnificent victory."

"Very generous of you, Mr President," said Perkins, reflecting that a flair for hypocrisy was going to be one of the specifications of his new job.

"Harry, we ought to get together just as soon as possible to iron out any little points of difference that may arise between your government and mine."

"Early days yet, Mr President. I've only been in this job three hours so far and as yet I don't have a government."

"Of course, of course, Harry. What I had in mind was to send my Secretary of State, Marcus Morgan, over for a chat as soon as possible. Some time next week, perhaps?"

"Okay by me."

"Fine, Harry, fine. I know how much you share my desire for world peace and I reckon we're going to work together real well. Like you, I have spent my life fighting oppression and exploitation, so you see we got a lot in common."

Perkins listened patiently as the President elaborated on his lifelong crusade for freedom. The conversation, or rather monologue, was finally brought to a close with the President saying that he had to go because he was keeping 'some general from Paraguay' waiting outside the Oval Office.

Scarcely had Perkins replaced the receiver when he was interrupted by a call from the private office to say that the Governor of the Bank of England was at hand.

This was Perkins' second conversation with the Governor that day. The first had taken place in the small hours of the morning – minutes after the outgoing government conceded defeat. Perkins had been in Sheffield town hall when he heard the news and immediately went in search of a telephone. Since the Mayor's parlour was locked up and the Mayor nowhere to be found, Perkins had had to telephone the Bank of England from a coinbox next to the porter's lodge. Having obtained the Governor's home telephone number from an astonished night duty officer Perkins had proceeded to rouse the Governor from his bed and order him to reimpose exchange control instantly. By moving so swiftly he had hoped to mitigate the impact of his election on the delicate constitution of the foreign exchanges, but it was not to be.

The Governor did not waste time on pleasantries. "Prime Minister, I have bad news."

"Surprise me, Governor." Perkins was given to mild bouts of irony.

"The pound has fallen four cents in as many hours. If it carries on like this, we'll have a slide of catastrophic proportions on our hands."

"Who's selling?"

"Everybody's selling. The Arabs, the Americans, the oil companies. Everybody."

"So what are you proposing?"

"Prime Minister, it is my duty to tell you that the markets need reassuring. Frankly, they are worried that they are going to get a government of . . ." The Governor hesitated.

". . . extremists?" suggested Perkins.

"Something like that."

"In other words," Perkins was looking straight at the Governor, "you are asking me to let a crowd of speculators dictate who I should appoint to my Cabinet."

"Not exactly, no."

"What, then?"

"Only that you take account of feeling in the City."

"And if I don't?"

"Prime Minister, I could not be responsible for the consequences."

"Now let's get one thing straight." Perkins spoke quietly, but firmly. "As long as you are Governor of the Bank of England you *will* be responsible for the consequences. You and your friends in the City may not have noticed, but there has been an election. *My* side has won and *your* side has lost. What's the point in having general elections if, regardless of the outcome, a handful of speculators in the City of London and their friends abroad continue to call the shots?"

The Governor was taken aback. Accustomed as he was to being the bearer of bad news to a succession of Prime Ministers, he was unused to plain speaking.

Perkins, who had been seated next to the Governor in the semi-circle of armchairs at the end of the study, rose and went over to the windows. They overlooked St James's Park and were half covered by green bullet-proof glass. With his back to the Governor, Perkins continued, "Perhaps you could tell me how much the Bank has spent defending sterling today?"

"Nothing yet," the Governor said, almost under his breath.

"Nothing," said Perkins.

"Nothing," repeated the Governor.

"Why not?"

"Prime Minister, I was advised . . ."

"Don't give me that crap." Still Perkins did not raise his voice. "I'll tell you why you haven't intervened. Because you thought you'd give me a bit of a scare, didn't you? 'New Prime Minister with all sorts of crazy Socialist ideas. We'll soon teach him a lesson.' That's what you thought, isn't it? Let sterling slide for a few hours and then rush round to Downing Street with a list of demands in return for calling a halt."

Perkins turned to face the Governor. "Those days are over. If you know what's good for you, you'll get back in your Rolls-Royce, return immediately to your office and start buying. Fast. If the pound hasn't gained two cents by close of business, I want your resignation."

With that Perkins strode over to the double doors and pulled them open, indicating the exit with a gesture of his left hand. The Governor, his face drained of colour, swept past and on to the landing. He went down the main staircase almost at a trot. Past the portraits of former Prime Ministers, through the entrance lobby with its bust of Disraeli and into the back of his green Rolls-Royce.

By close of business sterling had recovered 2.16 cents against the dollar.

5

Fiennes was pouring himself a coffee from the office percolator when the telex machine in the far corner came to life. Coffee cup in hand he went and stood over the telex. It was the Downing Street press office with the details of Perkins' Cabinet.

As the machine tapped out the first name Fiennes gave a low whistle. The Lord President of the Council and Leader of the House was to be Jock Steeples. Steeples was a former East End docker and veteran left-winger. Despite his undoubted ability he had never been given office of any kind during his thirty years in Parliament, largely because DI5 had fingered him as a possible Communist agent. Steeples would be in charge of pushing the new government's programme through Parliament.

Next out of the machine was the new Chancellor of the Exchequer, Lawrence Wainwright. Wainwright was Oxford educated and had once been a merchant banker. Not an obvious choice for a left-wing government. Fiennes was pleasantly surprised. Maybe Perkins was going to play safe after all.

Any illusions about Perkins being overcome by a sudden fit of moderation were, however, quickly dispelled by his choice of Home Secretary, Mrs Joan Cook. Mrs Cook was one of only a handful of women MPs, an honorary vice president of the National Council for Civil Liberties. She had campaigned for greater public control of the police and the intelligence services. DI5 also suspected she was a crypto Communist. Fiennes groaned.

The Foreign Secretary, Tom Newsome, had been a Yorkshire schoolmaster. DI5 had a file an inch thick on him. In 1968 he had led the huge march to the American embassy in Grosvenor Square. He had been Chairman of the Chile Solidarity Campaign and led numerous deputations to the

Foreign Office to protest against just about every military régime with which Britain traded.

Fiennes placed his coffee cup on the windowsill and with unnecessary vigour ripped the first page of the telex from the machine.

The Defence Secretary headed the second page. This was to be Jim Evans, a Welshman with a fine line in fiery rhetoric. Evans had been a ban-the-bomber since the early days of CND. By now Fiennes was beside himself. This was it. The revolution was unfolding before his very eyes.

So it went on. Four pages of new appointments. Extremists almost to a man. The Northern Ireland Secretary was known to favour British withdrawal. The Minister of Agriculture was a former farm labourer.

"This will send the pound through the floor," said Fiennes half out loud as he tore the final sheet from the telex. He had to restrain himself from running as he went to tell Sir Peregrine the awful news.

Sir Peregrine was composing a memorandum when Fiennes entered. He always composed in long hand, using a blue felt-tipped pen, and he did not like being interrupted. "Yes, Fiennes, what is it?" The irritation in his voice was barely concealed.

"The new Cabinet, sir."

"Oh, yes; bad as we thought?"

"Worse," said Fiennes, handing over the sheaf of telex pages.

There was a full minute's silence as Sir Peregrine ran his eyes slowly down the list. When he looked up there was no hint of dismay in his voice. "Well, Fiennes, we've had a stroke of luck."

"Luck, sir?"

"Wainwright, the new Chancellor. He's on our payroll. We signed him up soon after he got into Parliament. He's been reporting to us ever since."

With a flourish Sir Peregrine returned the telex pages to Fiennes and added, "Perkins has made his first mistake."

*

Fred Thompson was already in bed at his flat in Camden Town when the phone rang. Putting on his dressing gown he stumbled into the living room.

"Sorry to ring at this hour," said a cheerful Yorkshire voice at the other end of the line.

Suddenly Thompson was wide awake. "Harry, or should I say *Prime Minister*?"

"Never mind about that, lad. Listen, I've got a job for you." Perkins paused and then went on, "How would you like to work in my Private Office? I need someone to keep an eye on all these damn civil servants."

For a moment Thompson was stunned into silence. "Will you or won't you?" said Perkins impatiently.

"Of course, Harry, I'd be delighted. What do you want me to do?"

"Just answer a few letters and generally keep your eyes open. I'll tell you more when you start on Monday."

"Monday? But what about the *Independent*? I've got to give notice."

"I've already had a word with your editor. He says he's been trying to get rid of you for years," said Perkins drily.

"What time on Monday?"

"If you come to Downing Street at 8.30 in the morning we can have a cup of tea and I'll show you what's what."

"Okay, Harry," said Thompson, who could think of nothing else to say, so overwhelmed was he by the dramatic change in his circumstances.

"Right, lad, see you Monday." And with that Perkins was gone, leaving Thompson still holding the receiver.

Fred Thompson was one of those journalists who hover on the fringe of the big time, but never quite make it. He had started out on one of George Fison's provincial papers and drifted in the general direction of Fleet Street via a publication called *Municipal News* which operated out of two rooms in Chancery Lane and which folded six months after he joined the staff. After a spot of freelancing, a euphemism for the dole, Thompson landed a poorly paid job with the *Independent Socialist*. It was the sort of journal that everyone had heard of, but nobody seemed to read. If long-serving members of its staff were to be believed, there was a time when the *Independent* had been required reading for every serious left-winger, but those days were long passed. By the time Thompson arrived it was tired and clapped out, snapping harmlessly at the ankles of the parliamentary establishment.

His first encounter with Harry Perkins had been inauspicious. Perkins had telephoned to lambast the editor for transposing a paragraph in an article he had contributed the previous week on the steel industry. In the absence of the editor he lambasted Thompson instead. Next thing he knew Perkins had invited him for a drink at the House.

It was a hot summer evening six months after Labour's second successive election defeat and they sat on the terrace supping half pints of Guinness. Perkins did most of the talking. He was seething with anger at the way the election had been handled. "Serves us bloody right." His brow glistened in the last rays of the sun. "We offer the electorate a choice between two Tory parties and they choose the real one. Now we find ourselves back in the wilderness for five years and the country's going down the plughole." For a moment they sat in silence looking out over the river. A police launch sped past throwing a cloud of spray in its wake. Perkins rested a hand lightly on Thompson's arm in the manner of someone about to impart a great secret. "You mark my words, lad, come the conference heads will roll."

Six days later Perkins announced his intention to challenge the leader. The media had a minor bout of hysteria. Most of his colleagues were mildly amused. For some reason Perkins had never been taken seriously by the clever young lawyers and polytechnic lecturers who seemed to account for about half the Parliamentary Labour Party. In any case, it was whispered that the trade union leaders had met the Shadow Cabinet and agreed to back the status quo.

But if there had been a stitch-up, it came unstitched. Looking back it was amazing that no one saw it coming. Not until the Transport and General Workers' Union delegation met on the morning of the election and threw out the recommendation of their executive, was it clear something was up. In the hours that followed, at delegation meetings in clubs and hotel suites all over Blackpool, the block votes began to shift. By evening Perkins was home and dry. In the elections for the National Executive Committee which followed, the left cleaned up. Heads had rolled, just as Perkins had predicted. From that day on he was taken very seriously indeed.

Fred Thompson was the only journalist to tip a victory for Perkins. Week after week the *Independent Socialist* had carried articles documenting the rising tide of anger in the constituencies and at the lower levels of the trade unions. Since no one took the *Independent* seriously, it was not really surprising that Thompson's articles had gone unnoticed. Unnoticed, that is, by all save Perkins.

For some time before he became Labour leader, Perkins had been employing Thompson for occasional bits of research. It was not uncommon for Thompson to spend a morning burrowing in the House of Commons library for figures on West German coal subsidies or imports of special steels from Scandinavia. More and more they would be seen talking earnestly over a cup of coffee in one of the Commons cafeterias or poring together over notes in one of the dark recesses of the Committee Room corridor. After he became leader Perkins gradually came to look more and more to Thompson as his eyes and ears in the party. It was not uncommon, after a ten o'clock division, to see Thompson making his way across the Star Chamber court to the leader of the opposition's rooms for a late-night whisky and a chat about the way the world turned round. So frequent a visitor had Thompson become that the policemen on duty in the lobbies no longer bothered to ask for his pass.

The arrangement was never formalised but by and by it came to be taken for granted that if you wanted access to Harry Perkins, Fred Thompson was the man to speak to. This being so, it should have come as no surprise to Thompson to be awakened from his bed in the early hours by a telephone call from the Prime Minister with an offer of a job in Downing Street. Nonetheless Thompson was surprised and trembled slightly as he replaced the receiver and went back to bed. It was nearly dawn by the time he fell asleep.

The sun shone brightly over Chelsea as Lady Elizabeth Fain left for her weekend in the country. On the back seat of her new Volkswagen (assembled by robots at the old Rover plant in Solihull) was a small blue suitcase containing two changes of clothes and an evening dress. Beside the case a wicker shopping basket covered by a teacloth contained an apple pie she had baked herself and a bottle of Beaujolais. Walpole the spaniel was upright on the front passenger seat.

Kensington High Street was jammed with Saturday shoppers, but the traffic flowed smoothly. Within twenty minutes Elizabeth was through Hammersmith and on to the M40 motorway. As grey suburbs turned into green countryside she found herself thinking of Fred. On paper at least he was not her type. Had a bit of a chip on his shoulder; always going on about his being working class and how he came from another planet from the one on which she lived. She had a very easy life. Like most of her friends she had a private income and only worked when she felt like doing so. Now she came to think about it, she hadn't a single friend, apart from Fred, who would answer to the description of 'working class'.

Fred was always going on about how corrupt and violent the police were. She had protested that all the policemen she had ever met were kind and courteous. He had replied that the police existed to protect people like her from people like him. At the time she had laughed at him, but as the riots crept closer to Sloane Square she began to think that there might be a grain of truth in what Fred had said.

Walpole curled up on the front seat and fell asleep. Elizabeth exerted pressure on the accelerator. The motorway cut a swathe through lush Oxfordshire pastureland sloping away to a river valley and, beyond, a clump of forest which parted to reveal a country house not unlike the one in which her parents lived. What a contrast with life in one of the great grey skyscrapers in Battersea, where she had once worked for six months in a private nursery school. Somehow people in

Battersea even looked different from those she mixed with. The women were pale, pasty, often with unwashed straggly hair and tired eyes. Girls her own age were weighed down with children and shopping baskets and push chairs. Was that what being working class meant? Would she have been like that if she had been born on a council estate in Battersea instead of a country house in Somerset?

About ten miles from Oxford Elizabeth left the motorway at an exit signposted to Watlington. Before reaching the village she turned into an avenue marked 'private'. The avenue was lined on either side by beech trees which united overhead to form a long tunnel. After a thousand yards it swerved sharply right and, suddenly, there was the house.

Watlington Priory was the seat of the Nortons, an ancient Catholic family which traced its ancestry back to the time of King John. The house was a Tudor mansion with two main wings branching off from a centrepiece to which clung several centuries' growth of ivy. The Volkswagen crunched across the gravel forecourt and came to a halt by a walled vegetable garden. As it did so two golden labradors came bounding from the house and rushed in excited circles round the car. From the passenger seat Walpole eyed them cautiously.

The labradors were followed by a young man in faded levis and a tweed jacket with patches on the elbows. "Elizabeth," he called, "how lovely to see you."

Elizabeth had by this time emerged from the car and was being mobbed by the labradors. "Roger," she beamed.

"Jackson, Johnson, get down," the young man bellowed as though giving orders on a parade ground. Instantly the dogs obeyed.

By now Roger stood face to face with Elizabeth. He placed a hand on each shoulder and kissed her on both cheeks. Then, turning, she reached into the car and pulled out first the suitcase and then the wicker basket.

"You shouldn't have bothered," said Roger when she showed him the apple pie and the wine. Taking her case, he ushered her towards the main door of the house. Walpole and the labradors had in the meantime disappeared.

Roger Norton was a major in the Coldstream Guards, his father's old regiment. Home on leave after a spell in Oman. His elder brother, William, the brains in the family, was Conservative Member of Parliament for Banbury. "William's coming for dinner this evening," said Roger as he showed Elizabeth up the creaking staircase to her room in the west wing, "so's Uncle Philip; I think you'll find him interesting."

They dined on roast duck, taken from a deep freeze stocked by Roger in the shooting season. Apart from the presence of Elizabeth it was a family affair. Mrs Norton did the cooking; Mr Norton, a retired banker, carved. Uncle Philip poured the wine. They ate around a large trestle table in the sixteenth-century banqueting hall lit only by candles which cast long shadows.

At first the conversation was dominated by Roger, who regaled them with tales of his exploits in Oman 'bopping the wogs', as he put it.

"Bloody lucky we're there, if you ask me," said Roger, helping himself to more sprouts. "Somebody's got to stick up for democracy, even in that fly-blown dump."

"I thought it had more to do with oil than democracy," said Elizabeth, trying to sound as though she was making an enquiry rather than an assertion.

Roger was taken aback. He didn't have much experience of being contradicted, let alone by a woman. "What do *you* know about Oman?"

"Only what I read in the papers." Elizabeth sipped her wine. She wasn't looking for an argument. Roger was a friend, not a lover. He had been a classmate of her brother's at Eton and they had kept in touch ever since. There was a time when Elizabeth had been attracted by him, but nowadays the more she saw the less keen she was.

It was Roger's brother, William, who first brought the conversation round to the home front. William was in his late thirties, young for such a safe seat as Banbury. Like his father he had started in merchant banking. Folding his napkin and placing it on the table he leaned back and said firmly, "Won't be long before we need someone to stick up for democracy here."

"Ah," said Mrs Norton with relish, "I was wondering how long it would be before we got round to Harry Perkins."

William warmed to his theme. He spoke with the sort of loud self-confidence learned at public school debating societies and rugby club dinners. "Harry Perkins will be the ruin of this country. Nobody in his right mind would invest a penny piece here while he and his shower are in charge. Pound's already going down the chute. Americans are being told to clear out and leave us to the mercy of the Russians. There's even talk of muzzling the press."

"The question is," said Mrs Norton, "what are we going to *do* about it?"

"No good looking to us chaps in the House of Commons," sighed William. "Morale on our side's pretty low. I've never known it so bad."

"Come now, William, dear boy." It was Uncle Philip who until now had hardly spoken. "Picture's nothing near as bleak as you make out."

Uncle Philip paused to cut the end from the cigar he had taken from his top pocket, but no one interrupted. "It's not as though Perkins has got a free hand. Any day now he's going to have to go to the International Monetary Fund for a socking great loan and they aren't going to part with that money without attaching a few strings."

He leaned forward to take them into his confidence. "Between you and me, the chaps in the Treasury are already having a quiet word with their opposite numbers in the finance ministries of the other IMF countries. Do you know what the Treasury chaps are saying? 'Don't bale the bastards out,' that's what they're saying. Let Perkins and his crew stew in their own juice for a while."

Uncle Philip paused again to light his cigar. He went on, "As regards the Americans. If you think they'll just pack their bags and go just because Brother Perkins tells them to, you're quite mistaken. Of course, if the worst comes to the worst they may make a show of leaving, taking a few aeroplanes and soldiers home, but they've got billions of pounds worth of equipment invested in British bases and they aren't going to abandon it. They'll do a deal with the British military to keep it on ice for a while until we get a government with some sense. Then they'll come back and take over where they left off."

Uncle Philip had everyone's attention. The candlelight made the shadows flicker. He took a puff on his cigar and still no one else spoke. "If you ask me," he went on, "Perkins isn't going to make it to the next election. I'd give him a year, maybe two."

"Surely you aren't suggesting someone's going to bump him off?" asked William.

"Not literally, no, but there's other forms of assassination." He tapped the ash from the end of his cigar into a saucer. "Character assassination, for example. You never know what the boys in the media will dig up."

Elizabeth thought she saw a twinkle in his eye, but it may only have been the candlelight.

"Your Uncle Philip seems very sure of himself," she said later as Roger showed her to her room.

"So he should be. Don't you know who he is?"

"Should I?"

"Uncle Philip is the Co-ordinator of Intelligence in the Cabinet Office. The link man between the Prime Minister and the spooks."

On Monday morning Fred Thompson arrived at Number Ten Downing Street at 8.30 sharp. The policeman on the door was expecting him and he was taken immediately up the main staircase to the Prime Minister's study.

"Ah, there you are, lad," said Perkins, stretching out his hand.

"Nice place you've got here, Harry."

"Comes with the job." Perkins gestured Fred towards an easy chair at the near end of the room. "Tea or coffee?"

"Coffee," said Thompson, expecting the Prime Minister to pick up a telephone and order coffee for two. Instead Perkins walked to the far corner of the study and plugged in a kettle which stood on a formica-topped surface behind the writing desk. As the kettle boiled he scooped spoonfuls of Nescafé into two coffee mugs. One of the mugs bore the slogan "Harry for Prime Minister."

"A present from one of the lads at Firth's," said Perkins when he noticed Thompson straining to read the inscription.

The kettle had boiled and Perkins was pouring the steaming water into the mugs. "About this job." As he spoke he stirred in milk from a half empty bottle that stood beside the kettle. "Officially, you'll be in charge of replying to correspondence from party members and trade unions."

Perkins did not ask about sugar. He just plopped two lumps into each cup and carried them back to where Thompson was sitting. He was still wearing a red carnation in his buttonhole. When he was seated in the armchair opposite Thompson he took a sip of his coffee and then resumed in a low voice.

"Unofficially, I want you to keep an eye on the civil servants." He lowered his voice. "To be honest, Fred, I don't trust the bastards an inch. When things hot up, we can expect ferocious opposition to our policies from the Treasury, the Foreign Office and the MoD. I want you to keep your ear to the ground for any underhand tactics. Leaks to the press, withholding information, that sort of thing."

Perkins drained his mug and placed it on the low table by his chair. "I've told the Cabinet Secretary in words of one syllable that we don't want any of the nonsense we had to put up with last time Labour was in government. And I told him to pass the word around."

The Prime Minister stood up and walked to the door. Thompson followed. "Where will I be working?" he asked.

"Follow me and I'll show you."

They turned right outside the study and walked until they came to the staircase at the front of the house. Perkins took the stairs two at a time. On the second floor he opened a door leading from the landing. Inside there was a small room with a low ceiling. The walls were bare except for a Tory Central Office calendar left over from the previous régime and a copy of the fire regulations. The front wall sloped inwards in line with the angle of the roof. "Used to be the servants' quarters," said Perkins.

Thompson walked to one of the two box windows that protruded from the roof and peered out. The view below was of Downing Street and opposite, the huge metal gates barring the first of a series of archways through the Foreign Office and beyond the Treasury.

"Doesn't catch the sun much, I'm afraid," said Perkins, who had half seated himself on the grey metal desk that stood by the left-hand wall. The wall bore traces of a bricked-up fireplace.

The surface of the desk was clear apart from a Philips word processor and a wire rack containing Downing Street writing paper and envelopes. On the floor by the desk was a table lamp with a long flexible arm, but minus a light bulb.

"Functional, that's the word," said Perkins, who was by now seated on the desk with his feet no longer touching the floor. "Still, I expect you'll brighten the place up a bit. Stick up a few CND posters. That'll give them heart attacks downstairs." He gave a little chuckle. Thompson smiled too.

Outside on the landing Perkins indicated another door to which was glued a hand-painted wooden sign which read: Church of England Crown Appointments Commission. "Your neighbours for the time being," said Perkins, raising his eyebrows. "You should have heard the fuss when I said I was asking the Archbishop of Canterbury to find them a place at Lambeth Palace. Anyone would have thought I'd ordered them to demolish Westminster Abbey."

Thompson moved closer to the door so that he could read the sign. "What on earth are they doing here?"

"In theory the Prime Minister appoints the bishops and all sorts of other worthies." Perkins was now leaning against the wall with one hand in a trouser pocket. "In practice the Archbishop just sends over his nomination and I sign on the dotted line. Ludicrous, isn't it? I haven't set foot in a church since we buried my Mum."

They went downstairs again. This time to the ground floor.

In the entrance hall Perkins introduced Thompson to Inspector Page, who was taking tea with the duty policemen. "This is the gent who keeps me safe from all those vicious Tory ladies." Inspector Page managed only the briefest of smiles as he reached for Thompson's hand.

From the entrance lobby they passed down the long gold-carpeted corridor to the Cabinet Room. Perkins opened the door and they stepped inside. At the far end the early morning sunlight streamed in through the long windows. "This is where it all happens," said Perkins, propping himself against one of the two white pillars which extend from ceiling to floor just inside the door. "The table," explained Perkins, "is shaped like a boat. I sit in the middle" – he pointed to the chair in front of the mantelpiece – "so everyone can see the expression on my face." For a moment they stood in silence and then they turned and left, Perkins closing the door behind them.

The private office adjoins the Cabinet Room. Horace Tweed had just arrived when Perkins' head came round the door. His bowler hat was on a peg by the filing cabinets. He stood as Perkins entered. "Good morning, Prime Minister."

"Mr Tweed, I want you to meet Fred Thompson who is joining my political staff."

"Delighted," said Tweed in a tone of voice that suggested he was far from delighted by the prospect of working with some young Labour Party upstart.

When they were out of earshot Perkins whispered, "Don't forget, Fred, you report to me and only to me. Don't let Tweed or anyone else tell you otherwise." Thompson nodded.

They went back upstairs again to the office that was to be Thompson's. By this time a sack of mail had arrived and was sitting on the floor by the desk. "I assume you'll type most of your own letters," said Perkins, "but if you want any help, the typing pool is in the basement. Garden girls they call them. All twinsets and pearls. That's something we'll have to sort out. Get some of our lasses in." Perkins looked at his watch. He still had some reading to do before the Cabinet meeting.

"Right, Fred, I'll leave you to it. If you want anything, ask Tweed." As he moved towards the door Perkins turned. "There is one thing I should have mentioned." He smiled broadly, causing the lines in his rugged face to sharpen. "You'll have to be vetted by security. To make sure you aren't a threat to democracy."

The Cabinet met at ten o'clock. Ministers arrived at Downing Street on foot as Perkins had given instructions that cars from the government pool were only to be used for emergencies.

In the Cabinet Room Perkins sat with his back to the fireplace in the seat traditionally occupied by Prime Ministers. Above him hung a melancholy portrait of Sir Robert Walpole. Wainwright, the Chancellor, sat on his left. Only a handful of members of the new government had ever held Cabinet rank before and some had never held any government office.

Perkins opened the proceedings with a little homily. "We are about to embark on one of the most exciting programmes any British government has ever dared contemplate. Although we have a clear popular mandate, we can expect to come under the most severe pressure from those vested interests who would rather our programme were not fulfilled. If we are to resist such pressure it is important we should never lose sight of the ideals of the Party that sent us here."

He looked around the table. He had the attention of everyone present. "At the moment we have the advantage of surprise. This will not last long, but while we have it we must use it. As my old Dad used to say, 'Hit 'em hard and when they're down, hit 'em again.' " This elicited smiles from everyone except the Cabinet secretary who sat stone faced.

Item one on the agenda was a paper on the economic situation prepared by the Treasury. Wainwright reviewed the main points and stated his opinion. "They want us to go for higher interest rates and a large IMF loan."

"They don't waste any time at the Treasury, do they?" interrupted Jock Steeples, the Leader of the House. "Before we know where we are they'll be asking for spending cuts and an incomes policy." From around the table there was a sympathetic murmur.

Wainwright ignored the interruption. "As far as the IMF's concerned we don't have much choice. If the pound continues to fall at the present rate our entire reserves will be gone by the end of the month."

Perkins went round the table seeking the opinion of each minister. After each had spoken briefly he summed up, "So we steer clear of the IMF for the moment and talk to the Germans, the French and the Dutch about the possibility of a stand-by credit. If that fails, we'll think again. Meantime interest rates will stay as they are."

The main item was the draft of the King's Speech, which had been cobbled together by civil servants in the Cabinet Office. The law providing for the detention of suspected Trotskyists was to be repealed. A special department, headed by a minister, was to be set up to supervise the reconstruction of the riot-torn inner cities.

All the main manifesto pledges were covered, although one or two had been watered down a little. On the American bases, the draft said simply that "negotiations would be opened with the United States government regarding the future of US military bases in Britain." After some discussion, in which the only strong dissent came from Wainwright, 'withdrawal' was substituted for 'future'.

On British nuclear warheads the draft said simply that they would be phased out. 'Dismantled' was the word the Cabinet preferred.

"Christ Almighty," said Steeples as they filed out into Downing Street two hours later, "the King will have a heart attack when he reads that little lot."

When the details of the King's Speech began to leak sterling went into a nosedive. By the time the markets in New York closed, the pound was a staggering six cents down against the dollar.

6

It was starting to rain when Marcus J. Morgan's bullet-proof Cadillac swept into Downing Street. The Cadillac was preceded by two police motorcycle outriders and a carload of American secret service agents. Behind came a second Cadillac with aides and advisers. Officers of the Metropolitan Police Diplomatic Protection Unit brought up the rear in an unmarked car.

The waiting cameramen scarcely glimpsed the Secretary of State's portly frame as he was propelled through the door of Number Ten surrounded by the secret service men. After him came the American ambassador and a man from the US Treasury.

There was a minor scene in the lobby when Inspector Page told the secret service men that they would not be allowed to accompany their charge to the door of the Prime Minister's study. "If this were America . . ." one of them was heard to say before the inspector cut him short by stating sharply, "This is not America, this is Great Britain and I'd thank you to remember that."

Morgan, happily unaware of the contretemps, was taken to see Perkins. His bodyguards were left pacing up and down in the hallway, chewing gum and muttering curses.

Perkins was waiting on the landing when Morgan, slightly out of breath, reached the top of the stairs.

"Mr Prime Minister," said Morgan without smiling as he extended his hand.

"Mr Secretary of State."

Perkins was nervous. A nerve in the left side of his face twitched uncontrollably and he wondered whether Morgan had noticed. He knew this was going to be an important meeting and he also wondered whether he would manage to conceal his dislike for fat American lawyers. Morgan had a reputation for crudeness and dealing with him might require more tact than Perkins could muster.

Inside the study, Morgan introduced the ambassador and the man from the US Treasury. Perkins in turn introduced his team, Newsome the Foreign Secretary, and Wainwright, the Chancellor.

Morgan seated himself in one of the two armchairs. Perkins took the other. Newsome, Wainwright and the rest arranged themselves in a semi-circle of hard chairs between the Prime Minister and the Secretary of State. An aide of Morgan's placed a small voice-activating tape recorder between the two men. Tweed, the private secretary, did likewise. He then busied himself serving drinks from a cocktail cabinet at the far end of the study. Morgan had a neat whisky, Perkins an orange juice.

Morgan did not stand on ceremony. "Mr Prime Minister, I'm here because the President is very concerned that your government's programme constitutes a threat to the security of the West."

A pained expression appeared on the face of the American ambassador. In the car on the way to Downing Street he had spent ten minutes advising Morgan to warm up slowly.

"According to your programme," the Secretary of State continued, "you are intending to remove all foreign bases from British soil, scrap nuclear weapons and go neutral." Morgan spat out 'neutral' as though he were referring to a contagious disease which, in a manner of speaking, he was.

He was heard in silence interrupted only by the clink of glasses as Tweed served drinks. "Mr Prime Minister," growled Morgan, "I am authorised to warn you that any attempt to detach Britain from the Western alliance would be regarded by my government as a hostile act and one which would have grave consequences for the United Kingdom."

Morgan was not a man of many words and when he had made his point he stopped. Perkins' face remained expressionless. When it was his turn to speak he did so quietly and slowly. "First, I would like to thank the Secretary of State for stating his government's position so frankly. I will now try to state our position with equal clarity."

Perkins' opening remarks were heard in silence. "For a long time the British Labour Party has been of the view that the presence of American nuclear weapons on our soil, far from offering us protection, actually makes Britain into a target for Russian missiles. The pledge to remove nuclear weapons was a prominent part of our election manifesto and it was on the basis of that manifesto that we recently won an overwhelming popular mandate."

At this Morgan's lips moved almost imperceptibly. What he said was only audible to those closest to him, but one of the stenographers said afterwards that it sounded suspiciously like "Popular mandate, my ass." The ambassador's face was white.

If Perkins had seen Morgan's lips move, he gave no clue. He went on speaking quietly, "I therefore take the opportunity to inform you that we will shortly be making a formal request to your government to begin the withdrawal of troops and weapons from British soil." He paused to sip his orange juice. "Obviously the details are a matter for negotiation, but we are thinking in terms of a phased withdrawal over two or three years."

Morgan's cheeks flushed. His eyes dilated. "Prime Minister," his voice had acquired a harder edge, "this is grossly irresponsible." He paused to think of something to add. "It's like telling the Soviets, 'We're coming out with our hands up.'"

Perkins could not suppress a smile. "Nonsense," he said firmly, "we are just telling the Russians and anyone else who cares to listen that we don't wish to be annihilated, and inviting them to follow our example."

"And the West Germans," said Morgan, "what about the West Germans? Are you going to abandon them to the Soviets?"

Perkins was feeling confident now. The nerve in his left cheek had stopped twitching. "The West Germans," he said quietly, "have no more interest in being annihilated than we do. If they want to defend themselves against a possible Russian invasion, they would be wise to develop local militia capable of fighting guerrilla warfare. That is what the Swiss and the Yugoslavs have done and that is how British defence policy will develop in future."

Tweed appeared with the whisky bottle and refilled Morgan's glass. Perkins took another sip of orange juice. Since Morgan had not responded, Perkins added unkindly, "Look at Vietnam. All the nuclear bombs in the world didn't help you there."

At the mention of Vietnam, Morgan's chins began to quiver. He had not come here to have salt rubbed in America's wounds by the leader of some third-rate, clapped-out colonial power. "Prime Minister," he sneered, "I don't think we understand each other very well. Let me spell out our position in words of one syllable."

Tweed lingered in the background, whisky bottle in hand, his ears flapping. The ambassador wished that the ground would open up.

"Let me tell you plain," snarled Morgan. There was a meanness in his voice which had not been apparent until now. "If you kick out our bases, you can kiss goodbye to any help from the United States in putting this ramshackle economy of yours back together again."

Perkins said nothing. Wainwright and Newsome looked blankly at each other. The US Treasury man looked at the floor. The ambassador fidgeted. No one seemed to know what should happen next. Morgan solved the problem. Heaving himself to his feet, he towered over Perkins for a few seconds, then he turned and lumbered towards the door. The man from the US Treasury followed. The aide with the cassette recorder paused only long enough to scoop up his machine. The ambassador, without speaking, stayed to shake hands with Perkins and then scurried after the Secretary of State.

Surrounded by secret service men Marcus J. Morgan climbed back into his bullet-proof Cadillac and was swept away to the ambassador's mansion in Regent's Park. In place of a press conference, scheduled for noon at the American embassy, a statement was put out saying simply that the Secretary of State and the Prime Minister had a frank exchange of views.

When they heard the King's Speech the executive of the Confederation of British Industry went into special session at its tenth floor offices in Centre Point. Two hours later a statement was issued saying that government plans to force the pension and insurance funds to invest in manufacturing industry would lead to a final collapse of confidence in the currency. They begged the government to think again.

The newspapers next day were rather more forthright. "Recipe for Ruin", screamed the front page headline on the *Daily Mail*. "Downright looney," said the *Sun*. The *Guardian* agonised for ten column inches before concluding that, although Labour's plans made sense, "Now was not the time." Perkins' honeymoon with the press was over. It had lasted just six days.

The weekly meeting of permanent secretaries takes place in the boardroom of the Cabinet Office overlooking Horseguards' Parade. As the senior civil servants in charge of each of the main Whitehall departments, they meet, in theory, to co-ordinate government policy. In practice they also sometimes co-ordinate resistance to government policy.

The Cabinet secretary, Sir Richard Hildrew, was a Balliol man. He had a first in classics and had spent most of his career at the Treasury before taking charge of the Cabinet Office three years previously. "Obviously," Sir Richard was saying, "they can't carry on like this. It's only a matter of time before we get a U-turn. Our job, meanwhile, is to minimise the damage."

"Peter," he turned to a man in a double-breasted, chalkstripe suit seated on his right. "Peter, any news of the stand-by credit yet."

"Nothing final." This was Sir Peter Kennedy, permanent secretary at the Treasury responsible for overseas financial relations. "My chaps have been on to Bonn and Paris and they seem most unlikely to stump up the funds. The Americans have been putting the screws on and urging them not to co-operate."

"Hardly surprising after yesterday's débâcle." The new-comer to the discussion was Sir Michael Spencer, who was in charge of Defence. Although none of the permanent secretaries had been present at the meeting between Perkins and the American Secretary of State, every one of them knew exactly what had taken place. News travels fast on the Whitehall network.

Spencer paused from doodling logarithms on his blotter: "As I see it we have at least six months before we have to start giving the American bases the heave-ho. By that time the government will have had a taste of the real world and may be in a mood to think again."

"The IMF loan is going to be the key." It was Kennedy of the Treasury again. "With any luck the terms will be so stiff that the foreign bankers will do our job for us."

Outside, the rain had stopped for the first time in two days. Shafts of sun streamed through the Regency windows to form puddles of light on the floor in front of each window.

Sir Richard gathered his papers into a neat pile. "So we're agreed, then, gentlemen." He glanced around the table. "No one does anything precipitate until we see which way the wind blows. Delay is our strategy."

In the distance the chimes of Big Ben could be heard striking eleven o'clock. From nearby came the clip-clop of horses' hooves at the Changing of the Guard.

"Three Communists, one Trotskyite and a queer." Fiennes was almost licking his lips as he placed the last beige file on the desk in front of Sir Peregrine. The other files, about twenty in all, were arranged in three piles. "Not to mention that His Majesty's Foreign Secretary seems to be screwing some ripe little twenty-one year old from Hampstead Labour party."

Sir Peregrine leaned back in his chair. "Not the sort of stuff that brings down governments," he sighed.

"Surely, sir, three Communists?"

"But that was thirty years ago, Fiennes. People do all sorts of silly things at university." He picked up one of the files and flicked through the pages of computer print-out. "In any case we can't make too much of the Communist angle. One of them was Wainwright and he's ours now."

"How about the Trot?" Fiennes passed another file.

Sir Peregrine opened it and read aloud: " 'Ted Curran, aged sixty-two, Minister for Overseas Development, until 1962 a member of the Socialist Review Group, a forerunner of the Socialist Workers' Party.' " He looked up at Fiennes. There was the merest hint of a smile on his lips. "Nineteen sixty-two; that's leaving it a bit late to go respectable. What have we got in the way of pictures?"

A pile of full plate black and white pictures lay on the desk beside the files. Fiennes picked them up and quickly leafed through them. "This one's not bad. Taken at a CND demonstration in the late Fifties." He passed the picture to Sir Peregrine. "Curran's in the donkey jacket on the left, the fellow next to Jim Thomas. Today he's National Secretary of the SWP."

Sir Peregrine held the picture close to his face while he studied it carefully. "Hmm, promising. Even shows the SWP banner in the background." He laid the photo on the desk. "Any evidence that Curran is still in touch with Thomas?"

"Not as far as we know."

"Pity. Still, we can't have everything."

Fiennes stood up and gathered an armful of files. "Shall I pass this on to Fison?"

Sir Peregrine thought for a moment. "No, I wouldn't do that. A cheap rag like his is a bit too obvious for this sort of thing. How about *The Times*? We've got a man on *The Times*, haven't we?"

"Yes, sir."

"And while you're about it," Fiennes was almost at the door when Sir Peregrine spoke again, "why don't you check out that girl Newsome's sleeping with?" He smiled thinly.

"Quite a turn-up for the books, if we found the Foreign Secretary sleeping with a Trot."

By the end of his first week in Downing Street, Fred Thompson was only halfway through the backlog of mail. It was mostly letters of congratulation. Requests for interviews he passed on to the press secretary who had an office off the main hallway. Invitations to speak at Labour Party or trade union functions were passed to Perkins' personal secretary, Mrs Kendall, a plump, greying lady in her late fifties who had worked for Perkins since he entered Parliament. She took the invitations through to the Prime Minister and he would simply write 'Yes' or 'No' in the top right-hand corner. Mrs Kendall would return them to Thompson and he would reply accordingly. Abusive letters he filed without replying. Threatening letters were passed to the Special Branch.

If a letter was received from a trade union general secretary, a Labour Member of Parliament or a personal friend of Perkins, Thompson would draft a reply and take it to the Prime Minister for signature. Usually Thompson would take the letters for signing to the Prime Minister's study in the early evening, after Perkins had returned from the House of Commons. Before setting out Thompson would buzz Mrs Kendall and she would tell him if the Prime Minister was free. Sometimes Perkins would make them both a cup of Nescafé, using the kettle behind his desk, and then they would sit and gossip for ten minutes.

During the day Thompson saw little of Perkins. Once, after he had been in Downing Street three days, Perkins had put his head round the door and enquired how he was getting on. The Prime Minister's flat was on the same floor, but since he was still living in Kennington he only used it as a changing room.

The attitude of Tweed and the other private secretaries towards Thompson can best be described as 'correct'. They were never rude, but never went out of their way to be helpful. The men from the Church of England in the office next door gave Thompson little more than the time of day. He assumed they were sulking over their impending eviction and after the first day he gave up trying to make friends with them.

To Thompson's surprise the garden girls were on the whole friendly. Since they had worked for the previous régime they knew their way about and Thompson went to them when he needed help.

Mrs Kendall was a dear. She was always neatly turned out and with long grey hair tied in a bun at the back of her head. She had strong political views of her own and was, if anything, to the left of Perkins. She did not hesitate to tick him off if she thought he was pulling his punches. Thompson got on well with her and since she was on better terms with the private office he channelled requests for such things as filing cabinets through Mrs Kendall.

On his first morning Thompson was given a long form to complete and return to a box number in the Ministry of Defence. He was asked to list every address he had lived at over the last ten years, the names of any Communists, Trotskyites or Fascists with whom he had ever had dealings, and to give two referees.

Two days later a Special Branch man with a rolled umbrella and a navy blue Marks and Spencer mackintosh came to see him. An ex-CID sergeant in his fifties who had been pushed sideways, he was bitter at never being made inspector. "My job is to make sure there are no subversives in Whitehall," he said without a trace of humour.

"According to the newspapers the place is crawling with subversives," replied Thompson mischievously. "Only problem is they're all elected."

The Special Branch man did not attempt a smile. He refused an offer of coffee and sat down without so much as unbuttoning his raincoat. "You in debt to anyone?"

"No."

"Have you a girl-friend?".

"Several."

Solemnly the man recorded each answer in his standard

issue notebook. "Which system do you support?"

"I beg your pardon?"

"Our system or theirs?" There was irritation in his voice. Thompson was not treating him seriously.

"What do you mean, *ours*?"

"The King, Parliament . . . "

"And *theirs*?"

"The Russians."

Thompson struggled to keep a straight face. The man sat waiting, biro poised, for an answer. "I am a member of the Labour Party. There's all sorts in the Labour Party."

"Which sort are you?"

"Is that really relevant?"

The man's voice hardened. "I'll decide what's relevant and the longer you piss about the longer this will take."

It took two hours and as he left the man did not attempt to conceal his annoyance. Civil servants treated the Special Branch vetting with respect because their careers depended on security clearance, but political appointments were made by ministers who usually did not give a toss what the Special Branch dredged up. Thompson could afford to be cocky.

"You'll be hearing from us again," said the Special Branch man as he departed, but he knew he was wasting his time.

When Thompson left Downing Street, it was already getting dark. He walked up to Whitehall and took a number 24 bus back to his flat in Camden. Indoors he switched on the kettle for a cup of tea and just caught the headlines at the end of the radio news. Sterling was still sliding. That day it had dipped under two dollars for the first time since the early 1980s.

Before the kettle had boiled the phone rang. It was Elizabeth Fain. "Fred, at last. I've been trying to get you all week."

Thompson told her about his new job and then asked about her weekend in the country. She sounded agitated. "That's what I want to talk to you about. It's important."

"Fire away."

87

"No, Fred, not on the phone."

"Now who's paranoid?"

They met that evening in a Holborn wine bar. At eight o'clock next morning Thompson saw Perkins alone in his study.

7

Every morning at ten a blue Mercedes deposited the Chancellor of the Exchequer, Lawrence Wainwright, at the main entrance to the Treasury. Despite the Prime Minister's memorandum ordering ministers to limit their use of government cars, Wainwright insisted on being driven the 300 yards from Number Eleven Downing Street. Not that Wainwright was lazy or incapable of walking. On the contrary, he was a man of iron constitution. He insisted on being driven to the Treasury each morning only because Perkins had asked him not to. It was as simple as that. Had Perkins insisted ministers go by car, Wainwright would probably have walked.

Wainwright was a bitter man. By rights he and not Harry Perkins should have been in Number Ten. At least, that was what he told himself. That was also what the newspapers said. And so did a surprising number of Labour MPs in the privacy of the tea rooms. Wainwright knew that had history taken its natural course he would have been leader of the Labour Party. It was no secret that a comfortable majority of Labour MPs would prefer him to Perkins any day of the week. But just as Wainwright had been poised to enter upon what he regarded as his rightful inheritance, the rules had been changed. Instead of leaving the choice of leader up to the MPs, the party had set up this damn fool electoral college. The result was Harry Perkins.

Wainwright had toyed with the idea of leaving politics, of taking a job with the World Bank or NATO and coming back to haunt Perkins in a new incarnation. There had been no shortage of offers, but in the end he had decided to stay. For one thing it was only a question of time before Perkins and his friends ran into deep trouble. When that happened there might well be a role for Wainwright. He might be just the man to step in and fill the breach when Perkins ran aground. This was what Wainwright's friends were saying. Stick around,

Lawrence, they said. We may need you soon. So Wainwright had stuck around. The result was an offer of a senior Cabinet post.

At first Wainwright had been surprised when Perkins offered him the Chancellor's job, but the more he thought about it, the more he realised he was doing Perkins a favour by accepting. Firstly, because he probably represented more of a threat outside the government than inside. Second, because his contacts in the City were impeccable. In opposition Wainwright had accepted directorships on the board of a leading merchant bank and a multinational chemical company. He had of course to resign the directorships when he went back into government, but the contacts were still there. Wainwright moved very easily in the world of high finance. Being the only moderate in the Cabinet he was virtually a prisoner. The more he thought about it, he was an obvious choice for Chancellor.

The Treasury was a gloomy place. The building was designed originally for the British Raj in New Delhi and intended to exclude the Indian sunlight. For some reason it ended up being built in Whitehall rather than Delhi and excluding British rather than Indian sunlight. The corridors are built around a circular courtyard and account for more than a quarter of the entire surface area. They are wide enough to accommodate six people walking abreast and all day long messengers pushing little wicker baskets ply back and forth.

The Chancellor's office is on the second floor overlooking King Charles Street. Sir Peter Kennedy, the senior permanent secretary, was waiting when Wainwright arrived.

"Bad news, sir." Kennedy's eyes betrayed a tiny gleam of satisfaction as he spoke. "No go with the stand-by credit. The Americans didn't want to know. The Germans said only if the Americans co-operate and the French said 'Get stuffed'. Only the Dutch seem prepared to lend a hand."

Wainwright placed his red despatch box on the oak desk, walked to the other side and sat down. "Do the markets know?" he asked Kennedy.

"Not yet, sir, but it's only a matter of time," said Kennedy, affecting regret.

"When they do, I suppose they'll wipe another billion off sterling." Wainwright was toying with a paper knife.

Kennedy did not reply, but remained hovering like an obsequious butler. "I told the Cabinet," said Wainwright self-righteously, "I told them we were wasting our time even asking, but they would insist." He placed the paper knife by the base of a large lampshade on the right hand corner of the desk. "That only leaves us one option, the IMF."

That was Kennedy's cue. "I've already been on to Washington," he said quickly. "They say they could have a team here by Wednesday."

"Wednesday?" Wainwright raised an eyebrow. "They don't waste any time, do they?"

"Actually, sir," said Kennedy with a smile, "we did warn them we might be calling." And then he added hastily, "Unofficially of course."

"Of course," said Wainwright, who knew very well that behind his back the Treasury mandarins were in daily contact with the IMF. For all he knew they may even have agreed the conditions. Probably all that remained was to get the Chancellor's signature on a letter of application.

He looked up at Kennedy. The man never put a foot wrong. Yet everyone in the Treasury knew that it was he and not Wainwright who was boss. Long after Wainwright had gone from the Chancellorship, Kennedy would still be steering the British economy.

"We'll need a summary of our financial position to show the IMF."

"There's a draft in your tray, sir."

"And a position paper for the Cabinet."

"The first draft is being typed now," said Kennedy, clasping his hands and tilting his head to one side. Will that be all? he seemed to say.

"I'd better tell Perkins." Wainwright pressed a button on the intercom connecting him to his private office. "Get me the PM," he said.

Marcus J. Morgan was back in his Washington office when he heard that the British were sending for the IMF. He thumped the desk in triumph. "Now we'll screw the bastards."

Morgan was a mean man and he was proud of being mean. "I didn't get where I am today by helping old ladies across the street," he was fond of telling subordinates.

That night top secret cables went out from the State Department to American ambassadors in Nigeria, Saudi Arabia, Kuwait and other countries holding reserves in sterling. The cables instructed the ambassadors to apply *all legitimate pressure* to persuade the governments to which they were accredited to start converting their reserves into any currency but sterling. Legitimate pressure included offers of increased military aid.

The British were on the run. Morgan planned to make them run even faster.

Sir Philip Norton, the Co-ordinator of Intelligence in the Cabinet Office, had just returned from lunching at the Reform Club when he was summoned by the Prime Minister. "PM's in a bit of a flap," said Tweed as he ushered Sir Philip into the presence.

"Ah, there you are, Norton," said Perkins, indicating the seat in front of his desk. "I've got a little job for your fellows."

Perkins paused to take off his reading spectacles. It was the first time Sir Philip had seen Perkins wearing glasses. They made him look more of an intellectual than his public image suggested. "I've had reports," Perkins went on, "that civil servants in the Treasury have been privately advising foreign finance ministries not to provide the stand-by credit we have been trying to negotiate. Do you know anything about that?"

Inwardly Sir Philip was aghast, but his face betrayed not a flicker of emotion. "New one on me, Prime Minister."

Perkins placed both hands palm downwards on the desk. "As far as I am concerned there is one word to describe a situation where a servant of His Majesty's government conspires with officials of a foreign government against the British national interest: *treason*." Sir Philip winced at the word. Really, this was laying it on a bit thick. "Tell DI5 I want the names of those involved. Tap the phones at the Treasury if necessary." Perkins paused and then added with a smile, "About time DI5 had something useful to do. A change from photographing CND demonstrators and spying on trade union officials."

Sir Philip did not share Perkins' amusement.

"May I enquire what your source is for this information, Prime Minister?"

"The source is my affair, but you can take it from me it's reliable."

Too damn reliable, thought Sir Philip.

"While you're here," said Perkins, "perhaps you can tell me, do DI5 keep files on members of my government?"

"These days, Prime Minister, it's all on computer. Curzon Street will have something on every Member of Parliament. Mostly just name, age, school, assets. Standard procedure."

"How do I get at them?" Perkins took a Kleenex tissue from a box on his desk and started to clean his glasses.

"I beg your pardon, Prime Minister." Sir Philip was sitting bolt upright.

"The files, tapes or whatever you call them. How do I get them? It's the ones on Cabinet ministers I'm interested in." He breathed on the lenses of his spectacles, causing them to mist over.

"Prime Minister, I must advise you that it would be most irregular for any member of the government to see those files."

Perkins cocked an eyebrow. "But I thought the Prime Minister is supposed to be the head of the security services. Surely I can see what I like?"

In eight years as Co-ordinator of Intelligence and before that as head of DI5 Sir Philip had served three Prime Ministers and four Home Secretaries. Never had any of them asked to see files except on the recommendation of the security chiefs. Sir Philip was embarrassed, but firm. "Prime Minister, there is a convention that ministers do not concern themselves with particular cases. It was set out in a directive by the former

Home Secretary, Sir David Maxwell Fyfe, in 1952. I can provide you with a copy."

Perkins was incredulous. "You are not seriously suggesting I should be bound by a memorandum from some Tory Home Secretary nearly forty years ago?"

Sir Philip wrung his hands. That was precisely what he was suggesting.

"Because if so," Perkins replaced his glasses and leaned across the desk, "you are quite mistaken. I want copies of everything that damn computer has on members of my Cabinet. And I want it today."

Four hours later Tweed wheeled in twenty-four small bundles of computer print-out. One for each Cabinet minister. Perkins sent each minister his own and asked for comments. What he did not know is that before parting with print-outs, DI5 had carefully weeded out juicier snippets such as the Foreign Secretary's affair with the girl in the Hampstead Labour party. The reference to the photograph of the Overseas Development Minister marching alongside the National Secretary of the Socialist Workers' Party was also missing. It turned up a few weeks later on the front page of *The Times*. The photo was published under the headline "A Trot in the Cabinet" and the story underneath went on to imply that he was just one of many. *The Times* had even managed to dredge up a couple of Curran's old SWP colleagues who reminisced at length about the minister's days as a revolutionary Marxist.

The story caused a mild flurry in the popular newspapers and the *Daily Telegraph*, and Tory backbenchers had some fun at question time in the House. By and large, however, the only people who were shocked were those who wanted to be, since Curran had never made any secret of his political past.

"That'll do for starters," said Sir Peregrine when Fiennes placed the press cuttings in his in-tray. Then he added, with the nearest he ever came to a smile, "Next we'll give the Foreign Secretary's love life an airing."

*

The first thing Sir Philip Norton did when he got back to the Cabinet Office was to ring his brother. The phone rang for a full minute before a refined voice said, "Watlington Priory."

"Andrew." As Sir Philip spoke his secretary placed a cup of tea on the desk in front of him. "Andrew, I wanted to thank you for that awfully nice dinner the other evening."

From the other end of the telephone came a couple of minutes of "Jolly decent of you to come, old boy . . ." Sir Philip clasped the telephone receiver with one hand, stirred his tea with a spoon in the other, and, occasionally, uttered a "Yes" or "No". When the babble at the other end subsided, he replaced the teaspoon in the saucer and came to the point. "Who was that girl with Roger?"

"What girl? Oh, you mean Elizabeth? Fain's girl. Charming . . ."

Sir Philip had taken from an inside jacket pocket a gold-topped fountain pen. *Fain* he wrote on a sheet of Cabinet Office notepaper. "Any idea what she does for a living?"

"Not a clue. Father was an equerry to the King." There was a silence at the other end of the phone and then, "I say, old boy, nothing wrong?"

"Of course not. Just curious, that's all." Sir Philip laid the pen on the desk and reached for his tea. "Sorry Andrew, must rush. Thanks again for dinner."

He replaced the receiver and put the top back on his fountain pen which he returned to his inside pocket. On the Cabinet Office notepaper Sir Philip had written under *Fain* the words *Equerry* and *King*.

His next call was to Sir Peregrine Craddock to whom he related the details of his conversation with Perkins. When that was done he flipped a switch on his desk intercom. "Get me some background on Lady Elizabeth F-A-I-N," he said into the machine. "And when you've found out where she lives tell Ebury Bridge Road to put a tap on her phone."

The men from the IMF arrived two days later. They checked into Brown's Hotel in Mayfair under assumed names. Their anonymity did not last long. A story in the *Financial Times* the next day blew their cover. News of their arrival caused the pound to rally by half a cent, but the recovery did not last long.

There were five of them: an American, a Dutchman, a Japanese, a German and an Englishman, Bill Whittaker, a former deputy chief cashier at the Bank of England. Whittaker was a hard, humourless man, who had not come to look up old friends. He was here to look at the books and offer a diagnosis. He was not concerned with the political consequences of this diagnosis, only with the facts. The facts in this case were that Britain was asking for the biggest loan in the IMF's history. Inevitably the price would be high.

Everywhere the IMF team went they were trailed by pressmen. Photographers were waiting outside the Treasury, the Bank of England and Downing Street. As if to underline the gravity of the mission, rain started soon after the IMF team arrived in London and continued almost without respite until they left. Every day the newspapers published pictures of five unsmiling men in mackintoshes, getting in and out of chauffeur-driven cars, king-sized umbrellas held aloft. And with every day that passed the pound continued to fall until the reserves were nearly exhausted.

Only a three per cent increase in Minimum Lending Rate staved sterling's complete collapse.

One rain-sodden night after the IMF team had been two weeks in Britain a Royal Air Force DC10 took off from Northolt in Middlesex. On board were three men whose identity was known only to the captain and the steward who were sworn to secrecy. The three passengers boarded the plane after darkness from a car which was driven to the aircraft steps. The DC10 left Northolt at 2100 GMT and flew west over the Atlantic until it was well clear of European airspace. Then it veered south, skirting Spain and Portugal. Just before the Canary Islands the DC10 turned east towards Morocco. It crossed Morocco behind the Atlas Mountains and then turned north east. At 0130 GMT the DC10 landed at Dar El Beidah airport, Algiers.

The plane taxied to a dark corner of the airport and stopped. Two black Mercedes, one containing a high official of the Algerian government, were waiting. Even before the engines were switched off, a gangway was in place. The doors opened and the three passengers emerged, each carrying a briefcase and a small suitcase.

While a chauffeur put their luggage in the boot of the first Mercedes the three men each shook hands with the Algerian official. Then they climbed into the car and were driven away to a secluded villa on the Mediterranean coast. The crew of the plane followed in the second Mercedes.

The three Englishmen were the Foreign Secretary, Tom Newsome; his parliamentary private secretary, Len Fuller; and a political adviser, Ray Morse.

In London the IMF team were commuting between the Bank of England and the Treasury. At the Bank they talked about interest rates and devaluation. At the Treasury they discussed the Public Sector Borrowing Requirement and income policies.

Between officials at the Bank, the Treasury and the men from the IMF there was little disagreement about what was necessary. They had all been brought up to believe that borrowing was basically immoral and should be heavily penalised. They believed that government spending was far too high and that free trade was sacred. The only problem was how to convince the government. As Sir Peter Kennedy said, "The government has just won a huge election victory based on exactly the opposite analysis of the situation."

When, after two weeks of deliberation, the IMF men unveiled their terms for a loan, even Wainwright was taken aback. They wanted £10,000 million off public spending in two years. Even on Treasury estimates that would add another million to the dole queues. It would also require a rigid incomes policy, something the government was pledged not to introduce. On top of this the IMF also wanted guarantees that the government would not introduce import controls

97

or any other restrictions on free trade. "I'll never get that through the Cabinet," Wainwright told them.

"Your problem, not ours," said the American member of the IMF team, and it was he who did most of the talking. He went on, "We're bankers, not politicians. We don't make any distinction whether we are dealing with British social democrats or Turkish Generals."

"All very well," replied Wainwright, "but Turkish Generals have ways of dealing with public opinion that aren't open to British social democrats."

At 0800 GMT (ten o'clock local time) Tom Newsome had an audience with the Algerian President at the Casr Es Shaab Palace. Later he spent an hour with the Prime Minister and the Finance Minister after which he was driven to the airport. At noon local time Newsome was airborne again, this time bound for Tripoli.

In London Annette Newsome phoned the private office and said that her husband was unwell and would work from home. She added that since he had lost his voice he could not be contacted by telephone. Arrangements were made for the red despatch boxes to be delivered by car to his home in Camberwell.

The Foreign Office press department issued a short statement saying that the Foreign Secretary was indisposed and had cancelled all engagements until further notice.

When the IMF terms were put to the Cabinet there was uproar. "What do they think we are, some banana republic?" raged Jock Steeples.

"Tell them where they can stuff their bloody money," said Jim Evans, the Defence Secretary.

The Home Secretary, Mrs Joan Cook, was more rational. "Even if we wanted to, we couldn't get a package like that through the Parliamentary Labour Party, let alone the National Executive Committee," she said quietly.

In the end it was agreed to defer any decision until Wainwright and the Prime Minister had had another talk with the

IMF. If necessary the managing director of the Fund was to be invited over from Washington.

Evans was asked to prepare a paper outlining drastic cuts in Britain's NATO budget, including the complete withdrawal of the British Army on the Rhine. News of this decision was to be leaked to the lobby correspondents when Perkins had them in for an off-the-record briefing later that day. As Perkins told Fred Thompson over a whisky in the Prime Minister's study that evening, "When our friends in NATO realise that defence will be the first casualty of any cuts, they may take more interest in getting the IMF off our backs."

In Libya Newsome lunched with the young colonel who had succeeded Gaddafi in a bloody coup two years before. Then he was driven back to the airport by the colonel's personal chauffeur. There was an awkward moment when it was discovered that the British ambassador was there seeing his wife off to London on a shopping trip. Fortunately the ambassador did not notice the DC10 with British markings parked a discreet distance from the terminal buildings. Heaven knows what he would have said had he known his Foreign Secretary was hiding from him in the Men's lavatory of the VIP lounge.

By 1500 GMT Newsome was en route to Baghdad.

8

Fourteen direct telephone lines connect the office of the Chancellor of the Exchequer with the outside world. They lead to Number Ten Downing Street and to each of the main government departments. Two lines connect with the official residence of the Chancellor at Number Eleven Downing Street (one to the sitting room and the other to the study). But the most important line connects the Chancellor's office with the Bank of England, which is obliged to clear with the Treasury every £10 million of reserves spent defending the value of sterling.

All the telephone lines pass through a concentrator in the Chancellor's private office. Incoming calls are indicated by a light flashing above the appropriate line on the concentrator. During a sterling crisis the light above the Bank of England line flashes with increasing frequency. Every time that light flashes everyone in the private office knows that the Bank has kissed goodbye to another £10 million.

When word reached the foreign exchanges that negotiations with the IMF had broken down the light above the Bank of England line to the Chancellor's private office began to flash every fifteen minutes. Tiny beads of sweat formed on the brow of the normally imperturbable Sir Peter Kennedy.

"Reserves down to £500 million, sir," said the junior private secretary who took the last call from the Bank. He handed Sir Peter a scribbled note with the latest details. The Bank was spending £30 million an hour from the reserves. At that rate they would be bankrupt in two days.

Kennedy crossed the red lino corridor which separated his office from the Chancellor's. He entered without knocking. Although Wainwright's desk was by the window most of the light was excluded by the Foreign Office building opposite. On the wall behind Wainwright hung an oil of the Relief of

Lucknow. Sepia was the predominant colour and it only added to the gloom.

"The Saudis and the Nigerians are selling," said Kennedy, his voice doomladen. "We're down to $1.47 and the cupboard's almost bare."

Wainwright was already preparing his alibi. "I told them," he said, "but they wouldn't listen."

"Couldn't you try the PM again?" Kennedy pleaded. "Something's got to give soon."

"I had Perkins on ten minutes ago. All he could say was we should keep our nerve." Wainwright did not attempt to conceal the contempt in his voice. "Seemed to think something would turn up by the special Cabinet tomorrow morning."

Kennedy withdrew shaking his head and mumbling to himself. He now seemed certain to go down in history as the permanent secretary who had presided over the collapse of the currency.

In the private office the intervals between the calls from the Bank of England grew shorter. And every time the light flashed on the concentrator apprehension shivered through the inner sanctum of the Treasury.

The DC10 bringing Newsome and his two colleagues from Baghdad touched down at Northolt at 0932 GMT. The Cabinet was due to meet at ten o'clock and the London foreign exchange market opened at the same time.

An official Mercedes was waiting to take them to Downing Street. Newsome sat in the front passenger seat; Len Fuller and Ray Morse in the back. Although tired the three men were exhilarated.

As they were passing through Willesden, Newsome dialled Downing Street on the radio telephone. "He's just gone into the Cabinet." It was Tweed's voice on the other end.

"Then get him out," said Newsome.

There was a delay of about forty-five seconds, most of which was spent waiting for traffic lights in Willesden High Street, before a voice said, "Perkins here."

"Harry, we've got it," Newsome was hardly able to contain his excitement.

"Everything?"

"Everything."

"Well done, lads," said Perkins. "How quickly can you get here?"

Newsome consulted the driver. The traffic was bad, but he said he knew a short cut through St John's Wood.

"About twenty minutes."

"I'll put the kettle on," said Perkins.

Newsome replaced the receiver on its rest between himself and the driver. Then, reaching in his briefcase, he took out a small battery operated shaver and began to shave.

Ministers were glum as they arrived for the Cabinet. Everybody knew this was the crunch. Batteries of television cameras waited outside.

"It's so unfair," said Mrs Cook to Jock Steeples, as they went in. "We never even had a chance."

Sir Peter Kennedy had been busy overnight preparing a brief outlining in the direst terms the consequences of a crash. By eight o'clock that morning every permanent secretary in Whitehall had a copy of the document in their hands. By 9.30 every Cabinet minister had been briefed on the alternatives facing them: the IMF or bankruptcy.

Jock Steeples came prepared to resign rather than accept the IMF terms, but he was in a minority. In the face of three days' intense pressure the majority against the IMF at the last Cabinet had melted. They had only been in office six weeks and already the hope that had attended their election was about to evaporate. The bankers had outwitted them in record time. They felt ashamed.

Only Perkins had a spring in his step when he returned to the Cabinet room after taking the telephone message in the private secretary's office. "What's he so cheerful about?" whispered Jim Evans, the Defence Secretary, to his neighbour as the Prime Minister sat down. He didn't have to wait long to find out.

"Comrades." The Cabinet Secretary winced at the use of the word. Such language simply was not used in Downing Street. "Comrades," repeated Perkins, "I have an important announcement."

They listened, not expecting to hear anything that would make the day more bearable. "Half an hour ago the Foreign Secretary arrived back in this country after a visit to Algeria, Libya and Iraq." Jim Evans' eyes widened. It was only half an hour since he had phoned Tom Newsome to find out if he would be well enough to make the Cabinet. Newsome's wife had said he was propped up in bed inhaling Friar's Balsam.

Perkins went on, "The Foreign Secretary has concluded an arrangement with these countries to make available to us a standby credit of up to £10,000 million on very generous terms."

From around the baize-covered table there was an audible gasp. First of disbelief, then relief. A miracle had happened. "The cunning old bugger," said Steeples. It was not clear whether he was referring to the Prime Minister or the Foreign Secretary.

Perkins allowed a few seconds for the good news to sink in and then tapped his pen on the table to call order. "The Foreign Secretary will be here in fifteen minutes and he will then be able to fill in the details."

When Newsome came through the door the Cabinet stood and applauded. Like the use of the word 'comrade' to address Ministers of the Crown, standing ovations are not a common feature of Cabinet meetings. Only the Cabinet Secretary remained in his seat.

Newsome outlined the details briefly. The new credit facilities would be available for an initial period of two years, renewable for a further two should the need arise. Interest payable at ten per cent annually on any money drawn.

Questions about the terms went on for twenty minutes. "What did you give away on Israel?" asked Wainwright, his voice betraying a note of sourness. He, after all, should have been told what was going on.

"Only what's in our programme." Newsome smiled benignly. "A homeland for the Palestinians."

"And what did you tell them about our relationship with the Americans?" persisted Wainwright.

"Told them we were going to kick out the bases," said Newsome looking round at his colleagues. "We are, aren't we?"

"You bet your life," growled Steeples.

From around the table there was a murmur of assent.

After the Cabinet, Newsome was driven home to Camberwell where he kissed his wife on the forehead, bathed, changed his clothes and left again. By three o'clock he was on his feet in the House of Commons.

The Chancellor's statement drew prolonged cheers from the Labour benches. The only note of dissent came from the Zionist lobby who feared that Israel had been sold out, but their doubts were swept aside in the general euphoria.

Scenting blood, the Conservatives had turned out in droves for the Chancellor's statement. They were stunned by the announcement. Questions to the Prime Minister followed. Perkins rubbed in the news. "You can tell your friends in the City," he roared at the subdued Tories, "that their attempt to subvert the democratically elected government of Great Britain has failed."

News of the Arab loan came too late in the day to have much effect on the London exchange, but by the time it closed at 4 pm the slide had eased. When the New York market closed five hours later the pound was one cent up on its value at the start of business.

As the Far East markets opened buying was feverish. The Arabs and the big corporations appeared to be leading the spree. The value of sterling began to climb fast. By the end of the week it had passed $1.60 and was still rising. Disaster had been averted.

*

The mandarins were less than overjoyed to see the government get off the hook so easily. At their weekly meetings in the Cabinet Office the permanent secretaries indulged in a fit of collective pique.

"You should have heard them crowing," said Sir Richard Hildrew, the Cabinet Secretary. "Actually stood up and applauded him there and then. Have you ever known government ministers who behave as though they are at a football match?" He shook his head wearily. What was the country coming to?

Sir Peter Kennedy had made a complete recovery from the prospect of going down in history as the permanent secretary who presided over the collapse of the currency. Now the threat had receded, his mind was turning to another vexing question. "Why wasn't the Treasury told? That's what I want to know." He stabbed the air with the forefinger of his right hand. "Not even Wainwright knew. No one even told the Chancellor."

Sir Cedric Snow, Foreign Office, was even more indignant. "I was told that Newsome was ill in bed at home when all the time he was gallivanting around the Middle East. Lied to by my own minister." He stressed the word *lied* as though it was the first time in the history of diplomacy that a lie had ever been told.

"Anyone would think," Sir Cedric went on, "that this government doesn't trust its own civil service."

A full thirty seconds elapsed before anyone else spoke.

When Marcus J. Morgan heard the news his chins began to quiver. He had barely finished reading the cable from the London embassy when the scrambled telephone on his desk began to bleep. It was the President, wanting to know "How the hell can a British Foreign Secretary travel 6,000 miles to three Arab countries and meet three heads of state without the CIA or the State Department picking up even a whisper?"

Morgan didn't know, but he was sure going to find out. "Meantime, Mr President, it's back to the drawing board."

*

Sir Peregrine Craddock was putting golf balls into a horizontal Nescafé jar as Fiennes entered with news of the Arab loan. He was in mid putt when Fiennes began describing the Foreign Secretary's secret visit to Algeria.

"Algeria?" He looked up just as the putter made contact with the ball. Fiennes was forced to side-step to avoid obstructing the ball as it rolled towards him, missing the Nescafé jar by more than three feet. Sir Peregrine now stood erect, brandishing the putter as though it were a sword. "Fiennes, do you mean to tell me that the Foreign Secretary has spent the last thirty-six hours in Algeria and that those nitwits in DI6 didn't even get a sniff?"

The ball had come to a halt just short of the doorway that led to the outer office. Fiennes shifted uneasily. "And Libya and Iraq," he said quickly.

Sir Peregrine leaned the putter against his desk. In silence he walked around the desk and settled himself in his swivel writing chair. It was a full minute before he spoke again. Fiennes wondered whether his presence was still required. At length Sir Peregrine looked up; his hands were joined beneath his chin as if he were in prayer. "Fiennes," he said slowly, "the time has come to sort out the Foreign Secretary's love life."

9

Maureen Jackson preferred older men. She was the youngest of the three daughters of a Politics professor at the London School of Economics. When she was still a third former at Camden School for Girls she was going to parties with her sisters, borrowing their clothes and reading their books. She was fifteen when she read *Fanny Hill*.

Maureen had little to do with boys of her own age. Her first lover was a third year student of her father's who came to their Hampstead house for tutorials. She was sixteen at the time.

By the time she was twenty, Maureen was working as a reporter on the *Hampstead and Highgate Express* and going out with men ten years older. She had wide eyes, perfect teeth and a complexion that rendered make-up superfluous. Although abnormally intelligent she did not get good enough 'A' levels to go to university. Her poor results were put down to her active social life and the amount of time she spent working for the local Labour Party. At least that is what she said she had been doing. Her mother had doubts.

Her parents took a tolerant view of their daughter's sex life. Both Maureen's elder sisters had been allowed to bring steady boyfriends home for the night. Even when her mother came home unexpectedly one weekday afternoon and found Maureen in bed with a man the fallout need not have been too disastrous.

Except that the man was His Majesty's Foreign Secretary.

Tom Newsome first met Maureen Jackson when she came to interview him for her newspaper. At the time Labour were in opposition and he was a junior foreign affairs spokesman. If he had known that in a year's time he would be the Foreign Secretary, he might have resisted getting involved. But Newsome had always had an eye for the ladies. As a schoolmaster in Yorkshire he had flirted with the young female teachers, but it was not until becoming a Member of Parliament that he realised the possibilities.

Power, as Dr Kissinger once said, is a great aphrodisiac. Not that backbench MPs have any power, but as Newsome quickly discovered, dinner in the Members' Dining Room of the House of Commons, followed by a drink on the terrace (weather permitting) did go down well with the ladies.

For his first five years in Parliament his wife, Annette, remained in Leeds looking after their two sons. When the sons left home Annette moved south and they bought a house in Camberwell. For a while Newsome behaved himself. He and Annette were a good team. Their politics were the same and she helped him with his constituency work.

Not until that spring morning when Maureen Jackson walked through his front door was Newsome again tempted to stray from the straight and narrow.

They chatted for two hours. Much of the time he spent interviewing her. By the time she left he knew where she lived, that she didn't have a steady boyfriend and what she thought of nuclear weapons.

That evening he rang Maureen from the House. He knew he should not, but he could not resist. Did she fancy a spot of dinner? When? Central Lobby at eight o'clock. After that it was back in the old routine. A meal in the Members' Dining Room, a drink on the terrace, even a stroll after dark round the lake in St James's Park.

The next day in the lobbies they were ribbing him. "Who was that young floosie I saw you with last night, Tom?" asked a Member from South Wales with a wink.

"Just some journalist in for an interview," said Newsome, trying to sound casual.

After that he was more discreet. Maureen never came to the House again. Usually they met in one of the parks. When they started sleeping together it was in a cheap hotel in Pimlico, booked under the name of Mr and Mrs Murray. But anyone could see at a glance that she was young enough to be his daughter. In fact one of his sons was older than Maureen. There was a knowing look in the hotel receptionist's eye.

All very sordid, but what else could he do? They couldn't go to his home because Annette was there. They couldn't go to her place because she still lived with her parents.

Then came the election. Labour won. Newsome to his astonishment became Foreign Secretary. Overnight his life was transformed. Cabinet meetings, state receptions, overseas tours, private secretaries to organise every detail of his life and everywhere he went he was followed by the red despatch boxes.

There was scarcely any time for Annette, never mind Maureen. The affair should have ended there and then. More than once he was on the point of ringing her and ending it, but he could not bring himself to. Newsome was in too deep.

Then came that awful September morning. He had given the private secretaries and the red despatch boxes the slip. "Come back to my place," she had said, "Mum's out all day."

He must have been mad, but he went. It was the first time he had ever been home with her. They were in bed within half an hour. Their love-making was just reaching fever-pitch when Maureen suddenly went rigid. He looked up and found himself looking Mrs Jackson straight in the eye at five paces.

She never said a word. Just stood there staring straight at him. For nigh on a minute the only sound was the ticking of the clock on the dressing table. Then she turned and was gone. They heard the front door slam behind her.

Foreign Secretaries are not supposed to panic, but this one did. His hands were shaking as he pulled on his trousers. "Oh, Christ, Maureen, maybe she's gone for the police."

"Don't be silly, Mum would never do anything like that. It's not as if I'm under age." Young Maureen remained as cool as a cucumber.

Newsome was out of the house within minutes. He glanced to right and left but there was no sign of Mrs Jackson. Then he practically ran all the way to Hampstead Underground station.

For days afterwards he held his breath and waited for the storm to burst. But life went on. Maybe Mrs Jackson hadn't recognised him? A moment's thought told him this was inconceivable; his photograph had been everywhere since the Arab loan triumph. Yet there was not a whisper in the newspapers. Nothing from DI5 or the Special Branch. His secret seemed safe.

Maureen didn't contact him for two weeks. For all she knew his phones might be bugged (they were, as it turned out). They met in a café at Euston at eight in the morning and after a quick conference decided to carry on. But one problem remained. After a row with her parents Maureen had decided it was time to leave home. The simplest solution would have been for Newsome to rent her a small flat but Maureen rejected the idea, saying that she was not going to be a kept woman. Instead she moved into a girl-friend's flat near Chalk Farm. Maureen failed, however, to tell Newsome that her friend was a member of the Workers' Revolutionary Party.

Sir Peregrine's face lit up when he saw the file. "How about that?" he kept repeating as Fiennes showed him the photographs of the Foreign Secretary walking hand in hand with the lovely Maureen.

"Shot with a 300 mm lens in Kew Gardens," said Fiennes.

"And these?" Sir Peregrine's eyes lingered over a 10″ × 12″ of Newsome planting a kiss on Maureen's right cheek.

"Euston at eight-fifteen in the morning. Our chaps had to get up early for that one," smirked Fiennes.

Sir Peregrine placed the prints on the desk and looked up. Fiennes had never seen the old man looking so happy. "Quite a turn-up for the books, that she should be sharing a flat with a Trot," said Sir Peregrine. "An unexpected bonus."

He thought for a moment. "There are two ways we can play this. We can either throw it to the press and let public opinion do the rest. Foreign Secretary in blackmail situation. Threat to security and all that. Or . . ." He tapped the desk with the flat of his hand. ". . . or we can go to Perkins and demand the resignation of Newsome on security grounds. Then we can leak it to the press anyway."

Sir Peregrine revolved his desk chair towards the window.

"I think we'll take the second option. That way we get the best of both worlds."

He spun back towards Fiennes again. "Does his wife know?"

"Not a dicky bird."

"In that case," said Sir Peregrine, "she's in for an unpleasant surprise."

Not every visitor to the Prime Minister enters Number Ten Downing Street through the front door. Certain very important persons, whose existence is not officially acknowledged, enter by way of the double doors leading from the Cabinet Office. Sir Peregrine Craddock and Sir Philip Norton were two such persons.

Walking one behind the other and led by a private secretary bearing the key, the two men walked in silence. They passed through the Cabinet Office to the sturdy door leading into Downing Street. The private secretary unlocked the door and they passed through, still without speaking. Tweed was waiting on the other side. Behind they heard the key turn in the lock.

"The PM is in the study," said Tweed as he led them up the main staircase. Still they walked in single file, still without speaking. A solemn little procession, in keeping with the distasteful task they had to perform.

Perkins was waiting for them in one of the armchairs just inside the door. "Sit down, gentlemen." He gestured to a settee in the centre of the room. "What can I do for you?"

Sir Philip looked over his shoulder to check that Tweed had withdrawn. Then he told the Prime Minister about Tom Newsome and Maureen Jackson and the flat she shared with a girl from the Workers' Revolutionary Party. Sir Peregrine sat in silence, his face shrouded in a funereal expression.

Perkins listened with his chin resting in his right hand and his elbow on the arm of the chair. As he listened he sank deeper into the armchair. Having outlined the facts Sir Philip went on to review the implications. "First, there is the blackmail potential. His wife doesn't know."

It was late October. St James's Park lay under a thick covering of leaves. The sky was cold and clear. The last rays of sunlight filtered weakly through the bullet-proof glass on the windows. "Second," said Sir Philip, "there is the fact that she shares a flat with a Trotskyite."

When he had finished Perkins thought for a moment in silence. A deep melancholy settled over his normally cheerful countenance. At length he raised his chin from his hand and asked, "So what are you advising?"

"Prime Minister," said Sir Philip gravely, "you have no choice. You have to ask the Foreign Secretary for his resignation."

But Perkins did not share his intelligence chief's perception of the threat to the nation posed by one twenty-two-year-old female Trotskyite living in Chalk Farm. "Is there any evidence that security has been breached?" he asked, looking first at Sir Philip and then at Sir Peregrine.

Sir Philip took a deep breath. "With great respect, Prime Minister, that is not the point."

"Very much the point as far as I'm concerned," said Perkins.

"In any case, Prime Minister," Sir Peregrine Craddock was speaking for the first time, "there is still the blackmail question."

"That can be disposed of quite simply," said Perkins. "All Newsome has to do is tell his wife and the threat of blackmail disappears."

Sir Philip tried to conceal his dismay. "Prime Minister, our advice is very strongly that the Foreign Secretary must be asked to resign."

Perkins stood up. The interview was at an end. "Thank you, gentlemen. I shall bear your advice in mind, but my inclination is to call in Newsome and suggest he tell his wife immediately. As far as the girl is concerned, he can either stop seeing her or she can move to a flat without a resident Trotskyite."

Tweed appeared, as if from nowhere. The two security chiefs turned to leave. Perkins walked to the door with them.

"One other thing, gentlemen." The Prime Minister looked first at Sir Peregrine and then at Sir Philip. "I'm not expecting to read anything about this in the newspapers tomorrow morning."

"Too late," said Sir Peregrine gravely, "the affair is already common knowledge in Fleet Street." In fact no one in Fleet Street knew Tom Newsome's secret, but they soon would. DI5 would see to that.

Perkins saw Newsome that evening in the Prime Minister's room at the House of Commons. Newsome reacted calmly to the news that Maureen had been discovered. For months he had lived in fear of being found out and now the time had come he was almost relieved. He asked for twenty-four hours to consider his position. Perkins agreed. "Think carefully, Tom," he said, "you're one of the most valuable members of my team and I can't afford to lose you."

The *Daily Express* got the story first. When the tip-off came the editor sent one of his best photographers, Bill Ham, to sit outside Maureen Jackson's flat with a telephoto lens trained on the front door.

Ham had had to spend an uncomfortable night before his big break came. He could hardly believe his luck when just after breakfast a green Volkswagen drew up and out stepped the Foreign Secretary. Ham was seated in his own car on the opposite side of the street. He wound down the front window. Before Newsome had reached the doorstep Ham was halfway through his first roll of Tri-X.

Newsome was inside the flat for half an hour. Ham was just about to light a cigarette when the front door opened again and there she was, Maureen Jackson in the arms of the Foreign Secretary. They embraced for a full three minutes before finally parting. If Ham had been closer, he would have noticed that Maureen was crying. And if he had been closer still, he would have noticed that Newsome was also crying.

*

After seeing Perkins, Newsome had made up his mind quickly. He would tell Maureen it was all over and then he would drive home and come clean with Annette. The next morning he was out of the house well before eight. He told Annette he was borrowing the car and drove, as fast as the early rush hour traffic would allow, to Chalk Farm. Normally he would have looked around before getting out, but that morning there was too much on his mind. He did not see Bill Ham's Nikon lens pointing directly at him as he locked up the Volkswagen.

The scene with Maureen was heart-breaking. She did not try to talk him into changing his mind. They both knew it had to end. For half an hour they held hands in the living room. An uneaten Ryvita and a cold cup of coffee, Maureen's interrupted breakfast, lay on the table. On the mantelpiece was the gold charm bracelet he had given her on her twenty-first birthday. She had never dared wear it in public in case anybody asked.

He said not to mind about seeing him out, but she followed him downstairs all the same. He was already on the doorstep when she flung herself into his arms. If he had thought for a moment, he would have known it was madness, but then the whole affair had been madness from start to finish.

When at last she let go he kissed her lightly on the forehead and walked away down the garden path. He did not look back, but he knew she was watching because he did not hear the door close.

In the car, driving back to Camberwell, Newsome tried to compose himself. Now he had to face Annette. Truly, he thought as he crossed the river at Waterloo, this must be the worst day of my life. But he was wrong. The worst day of his life was still to come.

The *Express* went to town on the story. Most of the front page was taken up with Bill Ham's exclusive shot of Newsome saying goodbye to Maureen. FAREWELL, MY LOVELY said the headline. The story inside was dominated by a picture of Newsome walking away from the house with Maureen watching forlornly from the doorstep.

To make matters worse she was still in her dressing gown. As well as a close-up of Maureen and a picture of Newsome and Annette taken at an embassy reception a few weeks earlier, there was even a photograph of the girl who shared Maureen's flat. The accompanying story said that "Security chiefs were last night urging the Prime Minister to sack Newsome." It went on to point out that Maureen's flatmate was a member of the Workers' Revolutionary Party. The story had DI5's fingerprints all over it, but no one would ever prove anything.

The first edition of the *Express* arrived at Downing Street within an hour of coming off the presses. Perkins saw it when he returned from the vote at the House. Twenty minutes later the Downing Street switchboard was jammed by calls from other newspapers demanding a statement.

Poor Newsome buried his head in his hands when Perkins showed him the *Express*. "Fancy letting yourself be photographed kissing this lass on the bloody doorstep," said Perkins, but he did not rub it in. Newsome looked as if he were cracking up. He offered to resign there and then, but Perkins refused to discuss the subject. "Go home and see Annette before the rats from the gutter press get to her."

By the late editions the story was leading every front page. The phone started ringing at 10.15 that evening and did not stop until Annette took it off the hook. Newsome arrived home to find a horde of newspapermen camped in the front garden. Annette was in the kitchen with a mug of tea and a cigarette. It was a year since she last smoked. She was wearing the silk dressing gown he had bought her at a recent foreign ministers' meeting in Tokyo. Her eyes were red, but she was not crying.

She made him tea and they sat and talked. He tried to apologise, but in the circumstances it did not seem very adequate. Annette wanted to know about Maureen. When had they first met? How often? Where? She received the information calmly. Sitting on the opposite side of the table, puffing her cigarette and sipping her tea. Never quite looking him in the eyes. Taking care that her feet under the table did not touch his.

He told the story quietly, dispassionately. Giving more detail than was strictly necessary. As the words tumbled out, Newsome was conscious for the first time of the extent of his treachery.

They went to bed around two o'clock. Annette said she preferred to sleep in the spare room and Newsome did not argue. Neither of them slept well. Quite apart from everything else, the doorbell kept ringing.

Newsome got up around seven. Peeping through the curtains he could see that the crowd of pressmen had grown. There were television cameras too. He turned on the radio and the story was leading every bulletin.

At seven-thirty he rang John, his eldest boy who was in his second year at Magdalen. He rented a flat in Oxford with two other students and news of the furore had not yet reached him. Newsome advised him to keep a low profile. He offered to come home at once and fend off the press, but Newsome said that would not be necessary. It would all blow over.

The younger boy, James, was working as a waiter in the South of France. Improving his French before going up to Cambridge next year. Newsome searched in vain for a telephone number. Eventually he gave up. The call could wait a couple of hours. It would be a while before the hacks managed to trace him.

At nine Newsome rang the Foreign Office to say he would not be in. The private secretary did not sound surprised.

All day long the chorus of demands for a statement grew louder. By Prime Minister's questions that afternoon, these had turned into calls for Newsome's resignation.

That evening Newsome saw Perkins alone in the study at Number Ten to hand in his resignation letter. This time Perkins did not demur. They both knew resignation was inevitable. The two men shook hands and then Newsome drove for the last time to the Foreign Office. He planned to clear up his papers and then take Annette away somewhere quiet for a few days to give the uproar a chance to die down.

*

When he got back to Camberwell it had gone eleven. The house was in darkness. He turned the key in the front door and switched on the hall light. Annette's coat was hanging on a peg by the door, so she had not gone out. She must be in bed. Not wanting to wake her he trod lightly on the stairs.

The bedroom door was open. In the light from the landing he could see Annette lying on the bed, fully clothed, one leg trailing over the edge.

"Annette," he whispered, but there came no answer.

He listened for the sound of her breathing, but he could hear nothing.

"Annette," he screamed, jamming on the light.

She lay on the bed. Very pale and perfectly still. On the table by the bedside was a glass half full of water and beside her on the bed an empty bottle. The label on the bottle said, "Maximum dosage: three tablets."

10

The weather in November 1989 was bitter. The lake in St James's Park froze and the keepers had to break a hole in the ice for the ducks. Even the Astrakhan pelicans sought refuge from the cold in the shrubbery on an island in the lake and disappeared from public view.

The weathermen forecast a white Christmas and as the evenings drew in the clear sky turned grey. "What we need now," said Sir Peter Kennedy to Sir Richard Hildrew, as they took a lunchtime stroll across the park, "is a nice long miners' strike."

The trade union leaders filed into the Great Parlour at Chequers and took their seats around the polished mahogany table. Before he sat down Bill Knight of the Engineers' Union caressed the oak wall panelling. "This is what I call *class*," he said and as he spoke his hand drifted to the blue and white porcelain on the mantelpiece. Despite impeccable proletarian origins most union leaders quickly adapted to the comforts of high office.

Chequers, the country residence of the Prime Minister, is a huge Tudor mansion in Buckinghamshire donated to the nation by a patriotic magnate who would no doubt have revolved in his grave if he could have seen Harry Perkins sitting at his dining table.

Or maybe he would not. For Chequers with its galleries and terraces and Old Masters had transformed generations of Labour Prime Ministers into country squires. When he first took office Perkins vowed he would have nothing to do with Chequers, but he was there before the year was out.

"Gentlemen," said Perkins, turning the cover page of the Cabinet Office brief on the table before him. The document was entitled "The first five years," and across the top a private secretary had written in longhand "first draft". The trade union leaders all had copies before them and they turned the cover page in unison with the Prime Minister. "Gentlemen," Perkins repeated, "we are here to reach an understanding between the government and the trade unions on the management of the economy for the remainder of our term of office." As he spoke tea was served by girls in the blue uniforms of the WRNS, seconded to Chequers for such occasions.

Perkins chose his words with care. Every such 'understanding' between a Labour government and the unions had started by embracing prices, pensions, public ownership and a range of other issues dear to the hearts of trade unionists and ended up as a disguised incomes policy. This was a sore point with union leaders and Perkins was keen to reassure them. "Let me be clear," he was saying, "we will deliver our share of the bargain." The government would take control of the pension and insurance funds. Industrial capital would be made available at low rates of interest. There would be quotas on the import of manufactured goods, particularly cars and textiles. He was heard in silence and his pauses were punctuated only by the ticking of the fine grandfather clock in the corner.

Not everyone was listening. Bill Knight of the Engineers' Union was gazing out of the window at the frost-tinted north lawn. Reg Smith, general secretary of the United Power-workers was wondering if the portrait of Oliver Cromwell on the opposite wall would suit the living room of his house in Virginia Water. There are not a lot of power workers living in Virginia Water, but then Smith had come a long way since his days as a stoker in Battersea Power Station.

Perkins stopped and asked for comments. Cups were re-filled and the Wrens wheeled away their trolleys. Knight spoke first. "What about wages. You ain't said nothing about wages."

"That's right," said Smith, "my lads will be asking for fifty per cent." This news was greeted by a low whistle from Jim Forrester, the railwaymen's leader. His lads would be lucky with ten per cent.

Perkins concealed his anger, but his cheeks were flushed. Here were two men who had devoted years to fixing Labour party conferences into voting down just about every progressive demand on the agenda. Now here they were with their hands out at the first opportunity.

"Wages," said Perkins calmly, "will have to be part of the whole package. If we are going to put money into social services and industrial investment, then we have to go easy on wage claims for the moment."

"My members will accept that," said Bob Sanders of the local government workers. Even as he spoke he was nervous. He had seen four Labour governments in his working life. Each one started by promising the moon and ended up turning on the unions. But he would give it a try. He was now a year off retirement and his lifelong dream seemed to have come true. Britain had a real Socialist government at last. He did not want to see it become bogged down by wage militancy. "Providing," added Sanders, "and only providing that the government keeps faith on its share of the deal."

"My members only earn half as much as yours." Sanders was speaking directly to Reg Smith. "Of course they'd like a fifty per cent increase too but they recognise it's a question of priorities. They attach higher priority to reducing unemployment than to higher wages."

"We're here to represent the employed, not the unemployed," snapped Smith. Then he stopped abruptly because he knew he'd gone too far.

"Speak for yourself," said someone at the end of the table.

After that the meeting went more Perkins' way. It was agreed that there would be no limit on public sector wage claims. Trade union negotiators would however be asked to bear in mind that there were other ways of improving living standards beside higher wages. Not everyone went along with this. Smith declared that his power workers would be going all out for as much as they could get. And he was heard to say that, if Perkins did not watch out, he would have a strike on his hands.

*

Sir Philip Norton was casting an eye over the Cabinet minutes when the phone rang. It was Fiennes of DI5. "You wanted some background on Lady Elizabeth Fain."

"At last," said Sir Philip.

Fiennes read from his notes, "Daughter of the fourth Earl. A former equerry to the King, a thousand acres in Somerset, former colonel in the Coldstream Guards. Retired from the army seven years ago."

"Never mind the father," said Norton impatiently, "what about the girl?"

"Aged twenty-five. Private income of £11,500 a year. A mews house near Sloane Square. All fairly predictable really," said Fiennes wearily.

"And the phone tap?" Sir Philip drummed his fingers on the desk top.

"Nothing much. Her life mainly seems to consist of organising dinner parties or being invited to them."

A blind alley, thought Sir Philip. Still, it had been worth a try. He was just about to thank Fiennes for his trouble when Fiennes said, "One curious thing, sir. She has made a couple of calls to a number in Camden. Chap by the name of Fred Thompson lives there. Seems to be that young leftie who works in the Prime Minister's office. Strange, someone with her background mixing with a chap like Thompson."

"Yes," said Sir Philip, "very strange." Thanking Fiennes for his help he replaced the phone. So that was how Perkins knew about the conversation at Watlington. In future he would be more careful. You couldn't trust anyone these days.

The phone rang. It was Fiennes again. "One other snippet that might interest you, sir."

"Go ahead, Fiennes."

"This Fain girl has just started a job as a research assistant in the Shadow Cabinet office at the House of Commons."

"Has she by jove?" said Sir Philip. "We'll see about that."

Fred Thompson was in his Camden flat preparing to set out for the launderette when the phone rang. It was Elizabeth Fain. She sounded upset. "Fred, I've been fired."

Thompson dropped the bundle of dirty shirts he had been stuffing into a pillowcase and sat on the floor by the telephone. "Why on earth . . . ?"

"They said my work wasn't up to scratch, but I've only been there a week and nobody complained until yesterday." Poor Elizabeth. She was almost in tears. Normally she was so composed. "I asked why they hadn't complained before and they came over very funny. Said they had really been looking for someone who knew about economics but they never said a word about economics when I was interviewed." Her voice trailed off.

Thompson was about to commiserate, but before he could say a word Elizabeth spoke again. "Fred, you don't think it has anything to do with what I told you about my weekend in Oxfordshire with the Nortons?"

"How could it? I told no one except . . ." He had been going to say, "except the Prime Minister," but stopped himself just in time. Yes, of course that was it. He knew exactly what had happened.

"Except who?"

"Elizabeth, let me buy you lunch. I'll be over in twenty minutes." Thompson put down the phone and scooped the pile of fifty pence pieces he had been saving for the launderette into the pocket of his raincoat.

Out on the street he hailed a taxi to Sloane Square. They lunched at a bistro on the King's Road and afterwards drove in Elizabeth's Volkswagen to Hyde Park. Walpole the spaniel came too. That afternoon they held hands for the first time.

"Coming on to snow," said Sir Peter Kennedy as he brushed the flakes from his Aquascutum raincoat. The sky was greyer than ever and the lake in the park remained frozen. An old lady was feeding breadcrumbs to the ducks although the sign said she shouldn't.

"No sign of that miners' strike you were hoping for," said Sir Richard Hildrew, as they hurried across the park towards Whitehall.

"No," said Sir Peter, "but looks like the next best thing.

The power workers are threatening a go-slow after Christmas." By the time they reached the steps leading into Downing Street the snow was falling fast.

11

One reason why the British ruling class have endured so long is that every so often it opens ranks and absorbs a handful of its worst enemies. Reg Smith was a case in point.

He was six feet six in his bare feet. His greying hair was closely crew-cut and this, combined with a broken nose and half closed eyes, gave him a somewhat menacing appearance. Out of earshot, he was known to most of his colleagues as Odd Job. Within earshot he was referred to with deference. Reg Smith had presence.

He started life in a crumbling terrace of back-to-back houses in Chester-le-Street, County Durham. But for the second world war he would have followed his father down the pit, but instead he was conscripted into the army at the tail end of the war. A sergeant by the time he was demobbed, he signed on as a stoker at Battersea Power Station.

Chairman of his union branch within no time, after two years he was sent as a delegate to the national conference of the United Power Workers' Union. At about this time he joined the Labour Party and before long he was attending the annual conference as a union delegate. Those with memories long enough recall the day when Reg Smith was at the sharp end of the class struggle. There was even a time when he would not have taken offence at being described as a Marxist.

But times changed. At the end of the 1950s a ferocious battle was taking place to wrest control of the United Power Workers' Union from Communists. Smith saw the way the wind was blowing and weighed in on the side of the moderates. Not long after, a vacancy as a district organiser was advertised in the union journal. Smith applied, got the job and never looked back.

He first came into contact with the Americans at a conference organised by the Ditchley Foundation in the summer of 1981. The Ditchley Foundation is not exactly secret, but nor is it exactly public either. Its purpose, according to the prospectus, is "to provide opportunities for people concerned with the formation of opinion from the United States and Britain . . . to meet in quiet surroundings."

The 'people concerned with the formation of opinion' tend to be mainly bankers, businessmen, politicians and diplomats. Occasionally a right-wing trade unionist is invited to discuss how to keep his members under control. That was where Reg Smith came in.

The 'quiet surroundings' are a magnificent eighteenth-century mansion secluded among oak and beech trees in the rolling countryside of Oxfordshire.

After his first Ditchley conference Smith found that he was plugged into an international network of very powerful people. Like all powerful people they were obsessed with the notion that someone somewhere was plotting to take away the power and status they had amassed.

The American embassy arranged for Smith and his wife to go on an expenses paid tour of the United States to learn about American labour relations. In Washington they even arranged for him to spend five minutes with the President and a photograph of the event occupied pride of place on the mantelpiece of his Virginia Water house.

The powers-that-be knew that one day Reg Smith would come in handy. And with the election of Harry Perkins, Smith's hour had come.

Negotiations between the Electricity Council and the United Power Workers' Union broke down in mid-January. The employers, prompted by the government, wanted to take the dispute to arbitration, but Smith would have none of it. Instead he summoned a special meeting of his executive for the following Wednesday. Item one on the agenda would be a proposal for a work to rule to start forthwith. No one doubted it would be carried. The snow began to settle for the first time that winter.

*

The executive of the United Power Workers' Union met in the seventeenth floor boardroom of the union's smart new premises on the Euston Road. The offices had been an investment by the power workers' pension fund and built on an old British Rail goods yard. The union occupied the top five floors with the other twelve rented out at considerable profit. When they first became public the plans for the lavish new offices had provoked criticism from some members. Several letters were sent to the union journal pointing out that the power workers were supposed to be against property speculation. The letters were not published. Smith saw to that. "Nothing's too good for the working class," he told the critics.

To the south the boardroom overlooked Bloomsbury and beyond that the Thames. The river meandered in a grey ribbon from Tower Hamlets to Wandsworth. St Paul's Cathedral, Nelson's Column and the tower of the House of Lords stood out clearly, and in the far distance, the television mast at Crystal Palace and beyond that the beginnings of the Kent countryside. On a clear day you could even tell the time by Big Ben. Reg Smith enjoyed nothing better than showing visitors the view from his boardroom, particularly after dark when the whole panorama was a mass of twinkling lights. "One word from me," he was fond of telling his guests, "and that lot would be in darkness."

Smith took his seat at one end of the solid oak table in the centre of the room. He brought the meeting to order by slapping the polished surface with the flat of his hand. There was immediate silence. "Brothers," said Smith in an accent that owed more to Virginia Water than the Durham mining town of his birth, "it's very simple. We're asking for fifty per cent and an extra week's holiday. The Board are offering us ten per cent and no extra holiday."

He cast an eye around the table in search of dissenters. There being none he continued, "We have made our position clear from the start. If there is no more money on the table, then we will be forced to take industrial action."

Again Smith scanned the faces. Despite the indignant tone

in which he addressed them, his remarks provoked no nods of agreement. Left to themselves most members of the executive would have settled at ten per cent. They were moderates almost to a man. Indeed most of them owed their seats to the fact that they had featured on a slate of moderate candidates published in certain popular newspapers at the time of the election. Now they were being asked to agree to industrial action in support of a wage demand that most of them privately considered was outrageous. It was a strange old world.

"This afternoon your president," Smith indicated a balding hollow-cheeked man immediately on his left, "and myself went to see the minister at the Department of Employment. All he could offer us was arbitration. We . . ." Smith looked again at the president, ". . . *we* told the minister that arbitration was completely unacceptable and that in view of the government's intransigence we would be forced to take industrial action. To which the minister asked us to spare a thought for the economic situation of the country and the efforts the government was making in other areas. I . . ." Smith paused, ". . . *we* told him that this had no bearing whatever on the merits of our case."

Not everyone could bring themselves to look at the general secretary while he addressed them. When it came to the vote he could count on most of them but their hearts were not in it. Smith came to the point. "I therefore propose that we instruct our members to commence working-to-rule as from midnight tonight." He paused to draw breath. "Any comments?"

Midway down the table a large, debauched looking man raised the forefinger of his right hand. His shirt collar was concealed beneath an overhang of chin.

"Brother Walker."

Tommy Walker represented the north-east division. His support was a certainty. "I agree with the general secretary." He paused to muster synthetic indignation. "I think it is a scandal the way we've been treated. All these years we've been sliding down the pay league and now the time has come to put the power workers back where they belong. At the top." He underlined the last phrase by bringing his hand down with a slap on the surface of the table.

"Thank you, Tommy," said Smith. A man at the end of the table was indicating he wished to speak, but Smith ignored him and scanned the other executive members. No one else indicated and so he returned to the man at the end of the table. "Brother Clwyd."

Barry Clwyd was a younger man than the rest, in his mid-thirties. He represented South Wales. There was no love lost between him and Reg Smith. Smith had been through the rule book in search of reasons to declare Clwyd's election invalid. "What I don't understand," said Clwyd, "is why we can't go to arbitration. Why is the general secretary so keen on industrial action all of a sudden?"

"You're the one that's supposed to be a revolutionary," sneered Smith.

"If you'd let me finish, Brother Smith," Clwyd's lilting Welsh voice contrasted with the harsh tones of the general secretary. "Everyone here knows that if there were a ballot tomorrow our members would vote overwhelmingly against this work-to-rule."

"You're out of order." It was Smith again. "Under the rules a ballot is only required before strike action. A work-to-rule is the responsibility of the executive."

This time Clwyd did not attempt to respond. He knew from experience that it was useless to argue. Few executive members could be swayed by argument. The rest took their cue from the general secretary. Three other members contributed to the discussion. Two for, one against. Then Smith took the vote. There were only three dissenters. "Right then, brothers, that's it." Smith stood up. "We take action from midnight."

Picking up his file he walked to the window. Far below, the lights were coming on all over London. The Euston Road was gummed with traffic. A train sounded its two-tone horn as it pulled into St Pancras. "Pity Downing Street has its own generator," said Smith quietly, "otherwise I'd pull the plug myself."

*

128

After the executive meeting broke up Smith spent an hour dictating a memorandum on the conduct of the work-to-rule for circulation to all district officers of the union. He also issued a terse statement to the Press Association blaming the dispute on the intransigence of the government which, he said, was refusing to allow the Electricity Board to negotiate freely.

He was then driven to Victoria Station. The pavements were thick with snow pounded to slush by the footfalls of rush-hour crowds. Along the Strand an automatic salt-spreader was stuck in a traffic jam. The last of the day's commuters, bent double against a cruel wind, trickled into Charing Cross. Newspaper vendors sought refuge from the cold in shop doorways. At Victoria, Smith dismissed the chauffeur, waited until the car was out of sight then walked briskly away from the station and into Buckingham Palace Road. He crossed the road and continued in the direction of St James's Park, perusing the shop fronts as he went. After about two hundred yards he came to a halt outside a restaurant called Bumbles. Reaching in the pocket of his overcoat he drew out a piece of paper and checked the name against a scribbled address. Then, looking to the right and left, he pushed open the door and entered.

The American, who was already seated at a table towards the rear of the restaurant with an evening newspaper spread before him looked up when Smith entered. He was wearing a white raincoat, open at the front, the one he had worn when he had last met Fiennes of DI5 in the coffee shop of the Churchill Hotel.

"Jim." Smith bore down upon the American, his right hand extended.

"Reg." The American was on his feet now. A waiter took Smith's overcoat and scarf. His heavy briefcase he placed on the floor by the table. "I see you boys are in the headlines." The American indicated the front page of the paper he had been perusing. The headline story was about the impending power dispute. Smith turned the paper towards him and glanced at the story which included a rather unflattering picture of himself taken at a press conference two weeks earlier.

The waiter fussed around them. Did they want apéritifs? The American already had a Scotch and Smith ordered the same. He specified Chivas Regal; nothing was too good for the working classes.

"To victory," said the American raising his glass.

"Victory," said Smith, his heavy jowls emitting a modest smile. Victory over whom or what, they did not say.

The American was Jim Chambers, first secretary, political section, at the embassy. The British Labour movement was his brief. He had a caseload of middle-rank Labour MPs and trade union leaders. His job was to pinpoint rising stars and get in close. It was all above board, so far at least. In the three years he had served in Britain, Chambers had become a familiar face in the bars at Labour party conferences and TUC congresses. Every snippet of information or gossip he had carefully noted and filed away. As a result he had identified the drift to the left in the Labour Party long before it had become apparent to his masters in Washington. At least three members of the new régime were regular guests at the dinner parties Chambers held at his home in Connaught Square. He had entered into the spirit of his job. Many was the drunken evening he had spent with his arm around a Labour politician singing the Red Flag or a chorus of Avanti Popolo.

Chambers was an old hand. His earlier assignments had included spells in El Salvador and Portugal. President Ford had claimed that saving Portugal from Communism was one of the achievements of his presidency. Jim Chambers had played his part.

Now Chambers was in London. He had thought he was in for a quiet life. At least there won't be a revolution in England, they had joked with him in the State Department, when he was posted. Little did they know. But Chambers was ready. He had been one of the few to tip a victory for Perkins. Now he was one of the few to predict that Perkins would not last the course.

Chambers had assembled his British caseload with precision. It offered him contacts in every significant faction of the Labour movement. He even had a contact on the central committee of the British Communist Party. It was he who had set up Reg Smith's visit to the United States three years earlier. He had persuaded Smith to attend the conferences at Ditchley. The beauty of it was that no money had changed hands and no one had done anything they would have to lie about. His only outlay had been the occasional bottle of Scotch, the odd expenses-paid tour of the States and a little harmless entertaining.

They started with oysters washed down with white wine. Duck in orange sauce followed. "What exactly is a 'work-to-rule'?" asked Chambers. "We don't have them on my side of the Atlantic."

"A work-to-rule," said Smith in between mouthfuls of duck and spinach, "means that my members will do exactly what is in their contracts and no more. There will be no overtime worked, all productivity agreements will be cancelled and, if someone is off sick, no one else will do his job."

"How long before it bites?"

Smith wiped a trickle of orange sauce from his jaw with a napkin. "The lights will start to go out within two or three days. By the end of the first week there will be lay-offs in the factories. Within a fortnight the government will have disaster on its hands."

Chambers had finished eating and pushed his plate to the middle of the table. "How long will it last?"

"Until we win."

"Is your executive behind you?" Chambers sat with his forearms resting on the table.

"More or less." Smith served himself another helping of spinach from a tureen in the middle of the table. "A couple of them cut up rough. Wanted to know why I was pushing a strike now when I advised against when the Tories were in."

"What did you say?"

"I gave them the usual." The waiter removed Chambers' finished plate and the vegetable dish. "Five years of restraint under the Tories. Power workers now are well down the wages' league. Time we caught up."

This was not by any means the whole story. The truth was that Reg Smith hated Harry Perkins. For years he and other right-wing trade union leaders had worked to keep the Labour Party in the hands of the moderates. Labour leaders had looked to Smith to deliver a majority of the trade union block vote on crucial issues at the party conference. And for years Smith and his friends had delivered.

The reward for loyal service had been an unending flow of quangos and honours doled out by a grateful Labour Party establishment. For tame trade union leaders there were seats on the boards of nationalised industries and places on the vast array of public authorities, committees, commissions and enquiries that were in the gift of a reigning Prime Minister. The ultimate accolade, and one upon which Smith had set his sights, was retirement to the House of Lords.

The election of Perkins had put an end to all that. Under Perkins the Labour Party was pledged to abolish the honours system and whatever public appointments were going, Smith could not expect to benefit.

Reg Smith was a bitter man and the focus of his bitterness was Harry Perkins. He wanted to see Perkins humiliated, and closing down the power stations seemed the best way of going about it.

"The advantage of a work-to-rule," he said as the coffee arrived, "is that we don't have to cough up any strike pay because our members will still be drawing their wages. If we had an all-out strike, our funds would dry up in two weeks. With a work-to-rule we can hold out indefinitely and inflict maximum damage."

12

Reg Smith proved spot-on in his estimate that the work-to-rule would start to bite within three days. The coal-fired power stations were the first to go out of service. They consumed up to twenty thousand tons of coal a day and required constant maintenance. Each boiler and generator was serviced by a team consisting of a leader, an assistant and several attendants. Under the terms of the work-to-rule, if one man did not turn up, the rest of the team stopped work and gradually the huge boilers became clogged with clinker.

The Littlebrook station on the south side of the Thames estuary was the first to be hit. By noon on the third day the manager reported that his number five boiler had accumulated a thousand tonnes of slag. He would have to close it down. Once the boiler cooled and the slag solidified it would take a team of men with pneumatic drills ten days to clear. Every boiler that closed down meant a 500 megawatt generator out of service and the supply of electricity to the national grid reduced accordingly. Within twenty-four hours of the Littlebrook shutdown, coal-fired stations at Pembroke, Didcot, West Burton and Battersea had each closed down a boiler. By the end of the first week the national grid had lost twenty per cent of its capacity. All that week the temperature hardly rose above freezing. It was the coldest January on record. Demand for electricity had never been higher. Smith could hardly have picked a better time.

As the boilers were closed down, the blackouts began. At the Grid Switching Centre in Streatham sweat was glistening on the brow of control engineer Wally Bates as he snapped out orders to men in white overalls who sat in a circle around the edge of the room before a bank of dials and switches. "Give it back to Lambeth, take out Putney and Southwark." As he spoke he scribbled calculations on a notepad.

One of the four telephones rang. He reached for it without looking up. "Yup," he barked. It was the West London Hospital. They were in the middle of a major operation and having trouble with the emergency generator. Could he spare them for another hour? He promised to do his best and before he replaced the receiver another phone was ringing. It was the Control Centre at East Grinstead. Could he save another fifty megawatts? They were running low. He groaned. Why didn't they ask St Albans? He already had two boroughs in darkness.

He slammed down the phone, tapped a series of numbers into his calculator and entered the answer on a sheet attached to a clipboard in front of him. Then he shouted, "Tell Horseferry Road to stand by for shutdown in one hour." He permitted himself the merest trace of a grin. The Horseferry Road sub-station took in the House of Commons and most government ministries.

The phone rang. It was East Grinstead again. No, St Albans were already taking more than their share. He would have to take out another London borough. More tapping on the calculator. More scribbling on his clipboard. "Tell Wandsworth to stand by in one hour," he barked. Then, drawing a handkerchief from his trouser pocket, he wiped his forehead. "Jesus," he said to himself, "this is only the first week."

The Cabinet went into emergency session the morning after the work-to-rule began. Everyone was agreed that the demands of the power workers could not be met. "We'll have every bleeding union in the country at our throats if we give in to this one," growled Jock Steeples.

The Energy Secretary, Albert Sampson, reported on the likely effects if the dispute dragged on. Sampson was a Yorkshire miner. He owed his place in the Cabinet more to a feeling that the miners ought to be represented than to his ability. Even before the dispute there were those who had questioned whether Sampson was up to the job. "According to my Department," Sampson read ponderously from the

134

brief in front of him, "normal demand at this season of the year is around 50,000 megawatts. So far we have lost about 9,000 megawatts generating capacity. Some of that can be absorbed by surplus capacity but next week we can expect to lose double that."

As Sampson droned on Perkins' attention wandered. He had always regarded Reg Smith as a malicious bastard, but this took the biscuit. In ten years of Tory government Smith had never even threatened industrial action, yet within weeks of a Labour victory he was suddenly posing as a super-militant. Sampson was now listing the emergency measures recommended by his department to conserve electricity. A five-inch limit on bathwater, powers to limit illuminated advertising, shop-window lighting and floodlights at football matches. And if the dispute went into a third week, they would have to put industry on a three-day week.

Outside, the sky was grey. A chill wind whipped up snowflakes which whirled against the windows of the Cabinet Room. Wainwright was calling for a state of emergency. If necessary troops would have to be used to run the power stations.

"Hang on a minute," said Perkins, "if you think I'm flying up to Balmoral to get the King's signature on a bit of paper allowing a Labour government to use troops against the power workers, you can think again. We'd be a bloody laughing stock if we fell for that one." There was a general murmur of agreement around the table and Wainwright, seeing that he was outnumbered, did not press the point.

It was agreed that Perkins should ask the TUC General Secretary to try and bring the power workers' union to the negotiating table. The army would be asked to make available generators for hospitals. The Cabinet Office would be asked to draft emergency legislation giving the government temporary powers to restrict the use of electricity for consideration by the next Cabinet meeting. In the meantime the Civil Contingencies Committee would be asked to advise on further measures.

*

Jonathan Alford was the first to arrive at Sir George Fison's home in Cheyne Walk. A Philippine maid in a black dress answered the door. Alford hovered in the hallway while the maid disappeared with his coat and scarf. "Sir's in the drawing room," she said on her return. Alford followed her up the stairs to the first floor. The wall was lined with prints of eighteenth-century London. There was one of Park Lane in the days when it was a lane and the only traffic were carriages bearing ladies with parasols. Another showed Westminster Abbey viewed from a field in Millbank at about the spot which is now the headquarters of Imperial Chemical Industries.

The maid pushed open the ornate double doors that led from the first-floor landing and then stood aside to let Alford pass. The drawing room, which extended from front to back of the house, was illuminated by table lamps, one on the marble mantelpiece and two on low coffee tables in the left-hand corner. Fison, brandy glass in hand, was standing alone by the front window, apparently gazing at the traffic on the Embankment. He turned as Alford entered and lumbered towards him, hand outstretched.

"You'd be the chap from the BBC," said Fison in his poor imitation of an upper-class accent. Alford nodded. The maid lingered. "Get Mr Alford a drink," snapped Fison in the harsher tone he reserved for addressing servants.

"A whisky and ginger, please," said Alford relinquishing Fison's weak handshake.

"Glad you could come. Peregrine Craddock told me you could be relied upon. Just as well. Reliable chaps are thin on the ground at the Beeb, these days." Alford's chest swelled. He was flattered to think that he should be known to the chief of DI5. The little Philippine maid presented his whisky and withdrew in silence. As they drifted towards the window, Fison rumbled on about left-wing extremists who seemed to be running the BBC these days. Alford contributed only the occasional nod.

Downstairs the doorbell rang again. Fison was still denouncing extremists in the BBC when the maid reappeared to announce the editor of *The Times*. In the ten minutes that followed Alford found himself being introduced to the owners or editors of just about every newspaper in Fleet Street. There was also the chairman of the Independent Broadcasting Authority and the editor of Independent Television News. My goodness, thought Alford, this is for real.

Like his father before him Alford's view of the world was fashioned by Winchester, Oxford and in the Guards. It was at Oxford that he had first become aware of the extremist menace. He saw how Communists and Trotskyites wormed their way into the Oxford Union. How they used the union debating society as a platform for promoting their extremist views and how easily ordinary students were misled by smooth-talking agitators. It was at Oxford that he first resolved to do whatever he could to resist the rising tide of extremism. Alford's opportunity came when his tutor offered to put him in touch with "someone in the right line of business".

The result was an interview with a man from London who gave his name as Mr Spencer and who left a telephone number where he could be contacted at any time. The number connected with the switchboard at the Department of Trade, but led in fact to an office in the West End. Alford used to ring the number about once a month with snippets on who was organising meetings on Ireland and demonstrations against the military régime in Chile. He also reported on Iranian students organising opposition to the Shah.

Alford had never lost touch with the secret world. Soon after obtaining his commission in the Guards he was seconded to Military Intelligence. He did a spell in Ireland, mainly desk work evaluating reports from agents in the field. The Ireland tour ended abruptly when two of his agents were assassinated by the IRA.

There followed a year in Hereford teaching political theory to SAS recruits until one May morning in the early Eighties he was summoned to Curzon Street and asked how he felt about leaving the army for a career in Civvy Street. "As what?" he had asked. "Television," they said. "Job coming up at the Beeb. Nothing very taxing. Just want you to keep the airwaves clean for us." There followed a crash course in journalism at a polytechnic in Harlow and six months in the Ministry of Defence Information Department until the BBC advertised for a Defence Correspondent. Alford was told to apply and was boarded for an interview. "A formality," said Curzon Street. Sure enough, Alford was appointed. Now, still only in his late thirties, he was Editor News and Current Affairs, and responsible for every syllable the BBC addressed to its subjects on the state of the nation and much else besides.

"Gentlemen, if I could have your attention?" Fison was tapping a wine glass with the blunt side of his fish knife. They were seated around a polished oblong table which fitted together in three sections. Including Fison, there were a dozen of them. The maid had withdrawn, leaving them alone with the port and the cheeseboard. "You all know why I invited you here," said Fison. "We've got to decide what we're going to do about this damn government."

The cheeseboard reached Fison and he lopped off a generous portion of Stilton. "In the coming months," he continued, "things are going to get pretty rough. Perkins has already made it clear that he intends to evict the American bases, and that will destroy the Atlantic alliance and play straight into the hands of the Russians."

There was a "Hear, hear," from Lord Lipton swathed in cigar smoke halfway down the table. The Lipton Corporation's holding included over one hundred provincial newspapers, a merchant bank, a chain of wine merchants and four oil tankers.

"Withdrawal from the Common Market," Fison went on, "will be the end of Britain as a trading nation." He paused for a sip of port. "There is even talk of a plan to dispossess the owners of our national newspapers which would be the end of the free press we all cherish." Fison was playing on home ground here. There was a sustained outbreak of "Hear, hears".

He cut himself a sliver of Stilton and munched as he spoke, "What we are engaged upon is a battle for survival. No holds barred. We have to recognise that in the task that lies ahead of us old-fashioned concepts like free speech and democracy might have to be suspended." The editor of *The Times* shuffled his feet. What Fison was saying might be a necessary expedient, but did it have to be stated quite so boldly? Fison's voice rose as he reached his climax. "This government has to be brought down. Those of us who control public opinion have a special part to play in bringing the nation back to its senses."

Amid the cheese, the cigars and the port there followed a discussion of what was to be done. Lord Lipton took the hardest line. He said the armed forces must resist withdrawal from NATO but did not specify what form the resistance should take. The editor of *The Times* advised caution. He was sure that once Perkins had taken stock of what he called "the hard realities", he would do a U-turn. Everyone agreed that Newsome's downfall had been an unexpected bonus and Fison was indiscreet enough to hint that DI5 might have had a hand in the affair. It was at this point that Alford came in. "What we have to do," said Alford, "is to drive a wedge between the government and its support in the country. In that sense this dispute with the power workers is a god-send. We have to back the power workers and lay the blame for this dispute squarely on the government."

This was too much for Lord Lipton. "Since when have we ever backed strikers?" he interrupted.

"Poland," interjected someone at the end of the table.

"Quite different," snapped Lipton.

"On the contrary," said Alford. "The analogy with Poland is very helpful to us. We backed the Polish strikers because they were striking against a Communist government. It didn't matter that some of their demands were ridiculous. The point was they were attacking Communism." He stressed this point with a wave of his finger. "Since Perkins and his government are Communists for all practical purposes, it follows that we should be backing the power workers and anyone else who cares to strike against the government."

It was generally agreed that Alford had a point. Stories about old ladies dying of hypothermia and denunciations of the strikers for greed and heartlessness would have to be played down. Instead every effort would be made to present the power workers' case as a good one. Emphasis would be placed on the importance of the service they provided and how undervalued their services were. If the power workers extracted a decent settlement, that might spark off a rash of extravagant wage claims which would bring the government into conflict with its trade union base. It was quite the opposite of the line newspapers normally took on wage claims but then, as Fison drily remarked, "A little inflation is a small price to pay for bringing down a government of extremists."

It was after midnight when the party broke up. This was only a beginning, Fison said as they departed. The removal of Perkins and his government was in the national interest. Since between them, they controlled access to just about all the information in the country, they would play a vital rôle. In view of what was at stake they could not afford to be too scrupulous. It was, he said, the end that mattered, not the means.

As January turned into February the snow had turned to sleet. The demand for electricity remained constant, but the supply declined. One by one the great power station boilers clogged with clinker and generators went out of service. By now every major city was without electricity for at least two hours a day. Where possible the Electricity Board tried to give notice by publishing a roster of areas to be hit, but with the amount of electricity in the national grid declining hourly notice was not always possible.

The House of Commons debated the crisis in a Chamber lit by paraffin lamps. The opposition wanted to know why Perkins hadn't declared a state of emergency? Why weren't troops being used to run the power stations? Did he have any figures for the number of old people who had died of cold? How much production was being lost? What steps was he taking to settle the dispute? Perkins was less than impressive. He fumbled his lines. He contradicted himself. On the possibility of a settlement he was evasive.

In truth there was absolutely no sign of a settlement. Reg Smith wasn't budging at all. He had refused arbitration and rejected the good offices of the TUC General Secretary. He had not even scheduled a meeting of his union's executive to discuss terms for negotiation.

The newspapers carried stories of residents in high-rise flats marooned by the failure of power to the lifts. In Coventry a thirteen-year-old girl was killed in an accident at traffic lights which were not working during a power-cut. In Glasgow a man on a kidney machine had to be rushed to hospital when the power failed without warning. The Volkswagen plant at Solihull was working mornings only.

By the end of the second week public opinion was turning ugly. Bricks were being thrown through electricity board showroom windows. A farmer who had lost one thousand baby chickens when his incubators were cut off, drove into Whitehall and dumped the corpses at the end of Downing Street. Perkins had to abandon his daily practice of arriving at Downing Street by bus after a passenger tried to assault him and was only prevented by the speedy intervention of Inspector Page.

The Civil Contingencies Committee, CYI as it was known in Whitehall jargon, met in the Cabinet office every morning at ten o'clock. The Secretaries of State for the Home Office, Energy and Defence were present, together with their permanent secretaries and the army Chief of Staff, General Sir Charles Payne. Even Perkins created a precedent by attending.

From day one the permanent secretaries and Sir Charles were pressing for a state of emergency. The permanent secretary at the Home Office, Sir Oliver Creighton, appeared one morning waving a draft Order in Council which he proceeded to try and sell to the committee like a salesman promoting some cure-all wonder drug. "Valid for seven days without the approval of Parliament," enthused Sir Oliver. "His Majesty's signature is all that's necessary."

"Then what?" asked Perkins, his voice betraying a hint of sarcasm.

"Then you simply order the power men to work normally," said Sir Oliver cheerfully.

"And if they refuse?"

"Arrest them." It was Sir Charles' first contribution to the discussion. A small, dapper man with square shoulders and a trim moustache, he had been in the army thirty years and only ever seen action in Northern Ireland. In the absence of a Russian invasion this was his last chance before retirement.

"All twenty-two thousand of them?" said Perkins, raising an eyebrow.

"If necessary, sir," said Sir Charles, who did not appear to realise he was not being taken seriously. "We have the capacity. A string of camps up and down the country for just such an emergency. All in working order. Even some vacancies in the Salisbury Plain camps since the Trots were released."

Sir Oliver Creighton's face had assumed a pained expression, as though a secret had been let out of the bag. "I think Sir Charles is referring to our civil defence preparations which, if you'll forgive my saying so, are not relevant here," he said soothingly. Sir Charles was just about to protest that, on the contrary, he was referring to the plans for dealing with strikers drawn up by the previous government but never implemented, when he was silenced by an icy stare from Sir Oliver. The Prime Minister said nothing, but made a mental note to enquire further when the crisis was over.

"I don't understand," said Perkins to Fred Thompson over a late-night whisky in the Prime Minister's study. Spread out on the desk before them were the first editions of tomorrow's newspapers. "ACTION NOW" demanded the *Sun* in a front-page headline two inches high. The editorial below began, "How many more old-age pensioners have to die of cold before Prime Minister Perkins climbs down off his high horse and starts talking to the power men?"

Perkins read the sentence aloud and then tossed the paper back on to the desk. "I don't understand," he repeated miserably. "Last time the power workers came out the *Sun* was practically demanding they be boiled in oil and Reg Smith was described as public enemy number one. This time they treat him like a bloody hero." He turned to the centre pages of the *Daily Mail* which carried a sympathetic profile of Smith. It was headed "The Reluctant Militant" and showed a picture of the United Power Workers' general secretary with his family. "No one regrets this more than I," Smith was quoted as saying, "but the government just won't listen to reason." Perkins read it aloud.

"Hypocrite," said Thompson who was leafing through *The Times*. "The power men have a case" was the heading over the main leading article. For a full minute there was silence, broken only by the rustling of newspapers. It was nearly midnight and the silence pervaded the whole building. The private office was in darkness. The lady on the switchboard was halfway through a crossword. The policeman on duty in the entrance lobby was lightly dozing.

At length Perkins spoke again, "It can't go on like this, Fred. Sooner or later something's got to give." He was leaning back in his chair his head resting on the high back, the whisky glass cradled in his right hand. Thompson was perched on the edge of the desk. "The civil service are pushing for the use of troops. I'm coming under pressure in Cabinet. Even Jim Evans seems to be weakening. A week ago, I'd never have believed it, but now . . ." his voice trailed off. A police car raced up the Mall, its sirens wailing.

"For Christ's sake, Harry," said Thompson harshly, "if you send troops into the power stations, we'll find ourselves at war with the whole movement. The miners will black the coal. The supervisors will come out in sympathy, and we'll turn Reg Smith into a national hero."

Perkins did not reply. He knew that Thompson was right. He put the half empty glass on the desk and ran his hands over his aching eyes. He was dog tired. Since the dispute began he had averaged less than five hours' sleep a night. He no longer went home to Kennington, but slept in the flat in Downing Street. Another victory for Tweed and the private office. Since the day Perkins arrived in Downing Street Tweed had been taking bets on how long it would be before Perkins stopped catching buses and living at home and started behaving like a Prime Minister. It had taken just nine months.

Thompson took a last swig of whisky and said he must be off. He left behind a pile of letters to be signed. There was no need for the Prime Minister to sign any letters but Perkins had always insisted on the personal touch. As with riding buses and living in Kennington, he was finding it harder than ever to deal with letters personally. Tweed and the private office had been against the idea from the start. Prime Ministers have more important things to do, they argued. Perkins, however, was determined not to allow Tweed to chalk up another small victory. With a sigh he took the bundle of letters, each with an addressed envelope embossed with the Downing Street seal, and signed the top one in blue felt pen. It was to a Labour Party member in Glasgow who was advising him to stand firm against the power workers. The writer had said a number of uncomplimentary things about Reg Smith, even going so far as to suggest he was in the pay of the CIA. Thompson had drafted a tactful reply. Since the man had addressed Perkins as "Dear Harry" (so many Party members seemed to consider themselves on first name terms with the Prime Minister) Perkins signed himself "Harry" in clear blue letters. That would make someone's day in Glasgow.

In the distance Big Ben struck midnight. No other sound reached the Prime Minister in his study. Downstairs in the hall the policeman was still dozing, disturbed only by the occasional patter of an unattended telex machine somewhere on the ground floor. The telephonist had abandoned her crossword and was also dozing. Only one dim light lit the main staircase. The brighter light from inside the study showed clearly the crack between the door and the carpet.

After twenty minutes Perkins put down his pen; pushed away the bundle of letters with both arms outstretched and sunk back in the deep, comfortable chair. On the desk, by a tea mug full of old pens was a small framed portrait of an elderly woman, her face lit by a wide smile not unlike that for which Perkins was famous. She had the same full cheeks, the same wrinkles around the eyes. It had been ten years now since Perkins' mother had died. How chuffed she would have been to see her Harry in Downing Street. She wouldn't have stood any nonsense from those stuffed shirts on the Civil Contingencies Committee. She would have told them what they could do with their state of emergency.

He put the cap on his pen and returned it to an inside pocket. As he did so his eye caught the front of the *Daily Mirror*. It was dominated by a picture of Number Ten, taken at night with all lights blazing. The caption beneath explained that, unlike most houses, the Prime Minister's residence had a generator of its own and he was not inconvenienced by the electricity cuts. The headline above read, "ALL RIGHT FOR SOME PEOPLE."

As the work-to-rule entered its third week the snow stopped, the slush melted into puddles reflecting a clear blue sky. By now the electricity in the grid was down to half the normal supply. At the Streatham Switching Centre Wally Bates was on the edge of a nervous breakdown. Most factories were working only twenty hours a week. A huge balance of payments deficit was forecast for the end of the month. Television was reduced to a single channel, but that had not stopped the BBC from carrying a sympathetic profile of Reg Smith and a documentary setting out the power workers' case in terms which were broadly favourable. There were some isolated acts of public vengeance. Some power workers in Yorkshire had had the tyres of their cars slashed. A doctor in Manchester refused to treat power workers. By and large, however, the media was remarkably successful in laying responsibility for the dispute at the door of the government. Perkins' opinion poll rating dropped to an all-time low.

But Reg Smith knew he had to settle. As the days passed it became clear that many power workers did not have their hearts in the dispute. Many were saying openly that the claim was too high. The head office on the Euston Road received an increasing number of letters from members urging a settlement. Surprisingly, or so it seemed to many people, the newspapers did not highlight the opinions of the men in the power stations. An opinion poll commissioned by Sir George Fison's main daily newspaper had found that over eighty per cent of power station workers were prepared to settle. It was quietly suppressed on direct orders from the proprietor.

Smith knew he couldn't carry the normally docile members of the executive indefinitely. There had been rumblings at the last meeting. Even Tommy Walker, the ultra-loyalist from the North-East, had said he couldn't keep his members under control much longer. So, the day before the regular executive meeting Smith picked up the phone in his sixteenth-floor office and ordered his secretary to dial Congress House. "Reg here," he said gruffly when the TUC General Secretary came on the line. "We're ready to talk."

The talks took place by candlelight at the Department of Employment in St James's Square. The government had authorised the Electricity Council to go all out for a settlement. Smith took them to the limit, double the original offer. The newspapers hailed the result as a triumph for Smith and humiliation for the government. An opinion poll published on the morning of the settlement showed that an instant general election would result in a Tory victory. Reg Smith was not a Tory, but he could not suppress a secret smile.

13

Half a dozen senior ministers and their permanent secretaries attended the defence conference at Chequers. The Chiefs of Staff were also present together with sundry colonels, group captains and lieutenant commanders. All weekend military men in civilian clothes were to be seen bustling up and down the stairs between the Hawtrey Room and the Great Parlour, bearing huge rolled-up maps depicting the Soviet threat. Outside on the gravel forecourt gleaming black Mercedes were drawn up in a neat semi-circle. Government chauffeurs in green uniform and matching caps stood gossiping and smoking in clusters. Others reclined in the back seats of their cars with noses buried in the sports pages.

The forecourt was screened by a high brick wall and beyond the drive led away through an avenue of young beech trees to a pair of lodge houses which marked the main entrance. Here the press were assembled. Photographers festooned with cameras and long lenses stood, hands in pockets, wind-cheaters zipped to the chin, stamping their feet in frustration. There were to be no photo calls, no press conferences. All they could do was attempt to snap the participants as their cars slowed down to check with the policemen on the gate. Television crews with the latest lightweight cameras kept on the alert. Interest was not confined to the British press. Correspondents filled in the time by recording face-to-camera pieces describing the conference with phrases like "vital to the future of the Western alliance" and "a turning point in Anglo-American relations".

Security was tight. The policemen carefully scrutinised the passes attached to the windscreen of every car that went in. Away across the green parkland policemen with dogs could be seen patrolling the fields that divide the public footpath from the grounds of the Prime Minister's country residence.

Inside the atmosphere was tense. The Chiefs of Staff made

little secret of the fact that they regarded Perkins and his government as a greater threat than the entire Soviet army. The permanent secretaries sympathised discreetly. The ministers knew, or at least strongly suspected, that their civil servants were in cahoots with the Chiefs of Staff. Even the Wrens who served the tea remarked to each other on the atmosphere as they scuttled in and out of the Great Parlour.

The dozen places at the stout mahogany table were occupied by the ministers and the Chiefs of Staff. The permanent secretaries and the military advisers sat behind them in a wider circle around the table on chairs poached from the White Parlour. The Prime Minister sat with his back to the window. On a sideboard in the bay of the window rested a bowl of yellow chrysanthemums. God knows where you get chrysanthemums from at this time of year, thought Defence Secretary Evans, as he took from a red despatch box the paper he was about to present.

Perkins called the meeting to order without ceremony and invited Evans to speak first. Copies of his paper had been circulated in advance and he summarised it page by page, inviting questions as he went along. "So far as we have been able to establish," began Evans, "the United States has over one hundred bases and other military facilities on the soil of the United Kingdom. These you will find listed in Appendix One." There was a rustle of paper while everyone searched for Appendix One.

"What do you mean 'so far as we have been able to establish'?" interrupted Jock Steeples.

"To be perfectly frank," said Evans with a quick glance at the general on his left, "I have not had the co-operation I would have liked in the preparation of this paper." He went on to explain that it had taken three requests before his private office had been able to come up with what now appeared to be a complete inventory of American weaponry and related installations. Even now there was some dispute about the exact rôle of the communications facilities, some of which appeared to be targeted against the host country rather than against any real or imagined external threat. He would deal with this in more detail. Meanwhile he would only say that there were some members of the British defence establishment who apparently believed that the Secretary of State could not be trusted with all matters relating to the defence of the realm. At this, there was much foot-shuffling and sideways glancing among the Chiefs of Staff and their advisers, but no one thought it wise to argue.

Evans resumed his summary. "US forces in Britain have the use of twenty-one airbases, nine transport terminals, seventeen weapon dumps, seven nuclear weapon stores, thirty-eight communications facilities and three radar and sonar surveillance sites." He paused, "You will find details of each of these in Appendix Two." There was more rustling of paper and a rattle of tea cups as Wrens with the trolleys arrived.

"The United States," Evans went on, "has about seven thousand warheads and of these about two hundred are stored in Britain. Those for the Poseidon submarines are kept in underground chambers at Glen Douglas near Holy Loch. The other main storage depots are at Caerwent near Newport and Burtonwood near Warrington. There are also nuclear weapons stored on or near American air force bases at Upper Heyford, Mildenhall, Lakenheath, Bentwaters, Brize Norton, Wethersfield, Woodbridge, Greenham Common, Marham, Sculthorpe and Fairford." Evans recited the names slowly, in the manner of a British Rail announcer. A uniformed Wren leaned across his right shoulder and placed a cup of strong tea on the edge of his blotter.

"In the event of war," Evans was no longer reading from the brief in front of him, "especially equipped Boeing 757s would take off immediately from Mildenhall in Suffolk and would become the US European Command."

"Exactly how much control do we have over this little lot?" asked Mrs Cook, the Home Secretary. She was seated almost opposite Evans. Her bright red jacket made her conspicuous among the dark lounge suits and military uniforms.

Evans plopped two lumps of sugar into his tea and stirred gently. "None whatever," he said quickly.

"With respect, sir." It was Air Chief Marshal Sir Richard Gibbon, RAF Chief of Staff. "With respect, we have an *understanding*."

"Not worth the paper it's written on," said Evans without waiting for the air marshal to finish. He had had the same argument with his officials twice already this week. "I had my officials go back through the archives. No treaty was ever signed. All they could come up with was a note, dated October 1951, prepared by the British ambassador in Washington and initialled by an American under-secretary of state which says that the use of the bases in an emergency is a matter of joint decision 'in the light of the circumstances prevailing at the time.' The full text is in Appendix Three." They turned to Appendix Three.

"I can only say," snorted the air marshal, "that in the ten years I've been dealing with them, I've always found that our American allies work very closely with us." He leaned back in his chair as though that was the final word on the subject, but it was not.

"Fact of the matter is," said Evans quietly, "that over the years the US air force has installed its own communications network, and it can now operate quite independently of the MoD. Isn't that so Air Marshal?"

The air marshal did not reply. There was a brief silence during which Evans glanced triumphantly around the table as though expecting a round of applause.

"What I'd like to know," said Harry Perkins who had until now sat silently with his chin in his hands, "is against whom are we defending ourselves?"

"I'm sorry, Prime Minister, I don't quite follow." Air Marshal Gibbon had assumed, without any particular reason, that the question was directed at him.

"For the last forty years," said Perkins, "all our defence plans have been based on the assumption that the only threat to our security comes from the Soviet Union." He paused. Through the bay windows behind him two policemen could be seen pacing the north lawn, one of them held an alsatian on a lead. "Supposing," continued Perkins, "just supposing, that the real threat to our security were to come not from the Soviet Union, but from the other side of the Atlantic?

"We'd not be very well prepared, would we?"

Lunch was a buffet in the Long Gallery. Perkins spent most of the lunch hour describing the treasures on display there to anyone who cared to listen. There was Nelson's gold pocket watch, Napoleon's despatch case and a ring reputed to have belonged to Queen Elizabeth the First. Jock Steeples and Mrs Cook stood watching from a distance as Perkins stooped over a glass case trying to decipher a letter from Oliver Cromwell for the benefit of the navy Chief of Staff. "This place brings out the lord of the manor in Harry," said Steeples with a grin.

The Prime Minister's final remarks at the morning session were the main topic of conversation among the military men and the permanent secretaries. Nothing in their training had prepared them for the possibility that Britain might need protecting against the United States. One permanent secretary, having first glanced over his shoulder to make sure he was out of earshot of the politicians, said that so far as he was concerned the Atlantic alliance was all that stood between freedom and tyranny in Britain. And in a discreet corner, a colonel from the MoD Planning Department was heard to say that the way things were going he would not be surprised if Britain soon became a fully paid-up member of the Warsaw Pact.

The afternoon began with a slideshow downstairs in the Hawtrey Room at which a succession of military men sought to impress upon ministers the overwhelming superiority of Soviet conventional forces in relation to those of the West. As Jock Steeples murmured to Mrs Cook, it was a bit late in the day for this sort of argument. The government said clearly that it intended to get the Americans out and only the practicalities remained to be settled. That was why they were here: to work out the practicalities, not to go through the same old arguments all over again.

Steeples was still whispering when the first slide came up on the screen. It purported to show the balance of NATO and Warsaw Pact forces in central Europe. Mrs Cook had waited until the room was in darkness to put on her glasses. She peered through the haze of smoke from Jim Evans' pipe. "Where's France?" she asked.

"Madam," said the colonel who was giving the commentary, "France is not a member of the NATO Command." He spoke in the slightly patronising tone that experts sometimes use when dealing with the hopelessly ignorant.

Mrs Cook repaid in kind. "I am aware of that, thank you, Colonel." Her voice betrayed the tone of irritation that ministers sometimes use with experts who treat them like fools. "But if the Russians invaded Western Europe, I imagine we could count on the French to lend a hand, couldn't we?"

The colonel said he hoped so.

"In that case," said Mrs Cook flashing him one of her steeliest smiles, just visible in the light from the projector, "perhaps you could show us some figures that include the French?"

A major was despatched to find details of the French armed forces. Meanwhile the colonel pressed a button and a picture of a Soviet T-72 tank appeared on the screen. "One moment, Colonel," said a voice from the gloom, "would you mind taking us back again?" He pressed the reverse switch and the tank was replaced by the chart depicting the East/West balance. "Aren't the American figures a bit on the low side?" It was Ted Curran, Minister for Overseas Development. He was not in the Cabinet, but had asked to be included in the Chequers weekend since defence was his particular hobbyhorse.

The colonel shifted his weight from one foot to the other. His right hand clutched a stick, about the length of a billiard cue, which he used for pointing to the screen. "They include all American troops based in central Europe," he said stiffly.

"But not those based in the United States and earmarked for Europe in the event of emergencies?" asked Curran from the back of the room.

"No, sir."

"And the Russians?" Because he was looking into the light of the projector and the smokescreen thrown up by Jim Evans' pipe, the colonel was denied a view of Ted Curran's face.

"We count all Soviet troops west of the Urals."

"Not a very fair comparison, is it, Colonel?"

"That's how we've always done it in my time, sir." In the front row the Chiefs of Staff were on edge. Air Marshal Gibbon was plucking at the expanding metal strap on his watch. General Payne was brushing his lapel with exaggerated gestures of his right hand. The First Sea Lord affected to be dozing, but was in fact wide awake.

They moved on to tanks and it was the same again. Mrs Cook wanted to know if the figures included obsolete Russian tanks. Ted Curran wondered aloud whether precision guided missiles had not rendered the tank almost useless and, in any case, why had no mention been made of anti-tank weapons? Then they turned to aircraft. Did the figures include planes based in America, but earmarked for Europe? If not, why not? How many of the Soviet planes were interceptors? Why was no distinction made between interceptors and attack aircraft?

And so it went on. The beads of sweat that formed on the colonel's forehead showed clearly in the beam of the projector. By about the third slide the tone of crisp, military self-assurance that he had carried with him since Sandhurst had disappeared. General Payne, in the front row, fixed him with a glassy stare and did not let go for a full minute. The permanent secretaries were silently appalled. Surely the MoD could put up a better show than this? They must have known they were in for a rough ride. "Trouble with the chaps at MoD," whispered Sir Peter Kennedy to his opposite number at the Home Office as they filed out when the show was over, "is that, until now, they've always had ministers who accept whatever nonsense is put in front of them." He blinked rapidly as they came into daylight. "They don't seem to realise those days are over."

*

Perkins was the first to surface on Sunday morning. Or at least he thought he was until he crossed the landing overlooking the Great Hall and saw Mrs Cook ensconced in one of the deep armchairs with the papers. "Morning Joan." She looked up sharply as Perkins appeared at the balustrade.

"Ah, there you are, Harry. I want a word with you."

"Fire away." Perkins was leaning on the banisters which turned the first floor landing into a sort of gallery overlooking the hallway.

Mrs Cook, who was standing by now, shook her head. She placed the papers on the chair in which she had been sitting and indicated silently that he should come down. She was waiting at the foot of the stairs and without speaking, save a mumbled "Good morning" to the policeman on duty in the porch, they went outside. In the forecourt they turned left and through a gate in the brick wall that surrounded the south terrace. There had been a frost in the night and their feet made light imprints on the stone terrace. Mrs Cook did not speak until they were out of earshot of the house and going down the steps into the rose garden.

"Harry," she said, "there's something you ought to know."

"There's a lot of things I ought to know," smiled Perkins.

"I had the Prison Room last night," continued Mrs Cook. The Prison Room, an attic bedroom so called because it had once acted as a place of detention for a lady of the court who had fallen foul of Queen Elizabeth the First, stood apart from the other bedrooms at Chequers and could only be reached by a spiral staircase from either the Hawtrey Room on the ground floor or the Great Parlour immediately above. "After dinner I did some work on my despatch box and set off for bed around midnight. I was just about to cross the parlour on my way to the spiral staircase, when I heard voices."

Mrs Cook described how she had hovered in the doorway and managed to identify the voices as belonging to Lawrence Wainwright, the Chancellor, and Air Marshal Gibbon. The parlour was lit only by a single lampshade on the mantelpiece

154

and peeping round the door she could see that the two men were seated, port glasses in hand, close by the entrance to the staircase. Not wanting to disturb them she retraced her steps down the main staircase and into the Hawtrey Room. From there she had entered the spiral stairway up which she crept until she drew level with the first floor. "The door leading from the staircase into the parlour was ajar and I had not switched on the light on the staircase for fear of alerting Wainwright and Gibbon. I couldn't hear everything, but Wainwright was saying he had planned to resign but Craddock had advised him not to."

"Craddock?" said Perkins. "Would that be the D15 Craddock?"

"Who else?"

They had completed a circuit of the rose garden and were now back by the steps leading to the terrace. Mrs Cook indicated that her story was not yet finished and so they commenced a second circuit. "Wainwright said that Craddock had advised him to stay on at least until the Americans had been consulted."

"The sly bastard," said Perkins almost under his breath.

"Then Gibbon piped up and said that he'd be in Washington next week and would take the opportunity to sound out the Americans then."

"Sound them out about what?"

"They didn't say, but I imagine it's got something to do with the bases. Gibbon did say something about seeing the Secretary of State and maybe even the President."

As they returned to the house they ran into Wainwright on his way out. He greeted Perkins with a hearty "Morning Prime Minister", but Perkins could not help noticing that Wainwright avoided looking him straight in the eye.

When they assembled in the Great Parlour for the morning session there was one new face among them. A small man in his early sixties with thick black eyebrows and a shock of white hair. He was seated on the right of Perkins who introduced him as Sir Montague Kowalsky, chief scientific adviser to the Ministry of Defence. "Sir Monty's going to tell us how we get rid of the bomb," said Perkins.

The small man gave a nervous smile. "Gentlemen," he said and then, with a nod of the head in the direction of Mrs Cook, "and Madam." He fumbled with the documents in front of him. "You should all have a copy of my paper. I shall make a short summary."

He spoke with a central European accent. "A nuclear warhead is a very delicate instrument. To remain functional it requires constant maintenance and the regular replacement of sensitive components. Withdraw the facilities for maintenance and refurbishment and you lose the capacity to retain nuclear weapons." Sir Monty's forearms rested on the table. "Warheads rely for detonation upon such elements as plutonium, tritium and in the old days, polonium."

The mention of these words caused the eyes of the audience to glaze over. Seeing this, Sir Monty added, "I need not trouble you with the details."

He paused and looked around the table. "Suffice it to say that the effective life of a nuclear warhead is between four and ten years. After that time it has to be transported to the Royal Ordnance Factory at Burghfield for renewal. The simplest way to dispose of our nuclear arsenal would be, therefore, to dismantle each warhead as it arrives at Burghfield."

On the landing outside, the rattle of cups foreshadowed the coming of the Wrens with tea. Sir Monty joined the palms of his hands as though in prayer. "However," he said, "I imagine you would wish to complete the run down of our nuclear arsenal in somewhat less than ten years. There is some scope for speeding up the process at Burghfield. Reasonably, I estimate that you could dismantle all the warheads within three to five years."

This news he announced with just a trace of a smile. Sir Monty was a rare phenomenon among the defence establishment: a scientist who was opposed to nuclear weapons. He was a Jew born in Poland, the son of a goldsmith from Poznan. When the Nazis over-ran Poland he was living with an uncle in Golders Green. His parents were despatched to the concentration camp at Treblinka and he never saw them again. By the end of the war he was a student at Imperial College. His PhD was on the effects of radiation. Hiroshima and Nagasaki provided no shortage of case studies. From that time onwards he was convinced of the evil of nuclear weapons.

For years Sir Monty had concealed his aversion to the bomb, at least to his professional colleagues. He had taken care to speak in the measured, balanced tones expected of a scientist. He hoped that he still did so, even though he found it hard to conceal his excitement. He was within two years of retirement and had long despaired of seeing an end to the bomb in his lifetime. Now, suddenly here was Harry Perkins and his government pledged to rid Britain of the bomb. And here was Montague Kowalsky sitting at a table in Chequers, telling them how to go about it. Truly, these were exciting times.

The Wrens served tea and left. Jim Evans puffed at his pipe and Mrs Cook waved away the smoke with her hand. Ted Curran had a question. "How do we make sure," he asked, "that no future government is able to revive a nuclear weapons programme?"

The faces of the Chiefs of Staff simultaneously assumed a pained expression.

"You cannot be sure, but you can make it extremely difficult and very expensive," Sir Monty replied with what he hoped was the appropriate air of scientific detachment. "You must close and disperse the facilities at Aldermaston and the Royal Ordnance Factory near Cardiff. That is where the components for the warheads are made."

He paused to sip tea. "Also, as soon as all existing warheads have been dismantled you must close and disperse the facilities at Burghfield."

"And how many people will be put out of work?" It was Wainwright's first contribution to any of the discussions that weekend.

Funny how the Treasury never worried about putting people out of work if it involved cutting public spending in any other department, thought Joan Cook. Only when it comes to saving money on bombs that they start worrying about lost jobs. From the look on the face of Harry Perkins, she could see that he was thinking the same.

"There are about 5,000 people employed at Aldermaston," said Sir Montague calmly. "And maybe another 2,000 at Burghfield and Cardiff. You may also lose some jobs in the naval dockyards at Devonport and Rosyth. As regards the Polaris submarines or the Tornados and Jaguar planes which carry warheads, these need not necessarily be scrapped. They can easily be adapted for conventional use."

Wainwright pressed the point. "So you would estimate at least 10,000 lost jobs?"

"If I may make a personal observation?" Sir Montague turned to the Prime Minister. He was not in the habit of offering his opinion, but with the exception of Wainwright, the ministers seemed well disposed.

Perkins waved his hand as if to say, "All right by me."

Sir Monty proceeded to offer his opinion. "With proper planning there is no reason why these people should lose their jobs. Many of them are highly skilled. Certainly the scientists could be redeployed."

"Exactly," said Mrs Cook. Wainwright did not respond.

Jock Steeples spoke next. "You have said nothing about disposal of the American warheads based in Britain."

Sir Monty ran a hand through his white hair. "The Americans," he said, "are another matter. If you ask them to go, they will take their warheads with them, probably to Germany and Spain. They will take with them their submarines, planes and other delivery vehicles." He paused as though deliberating whether to venture another personal opinion. Why not? he thought. "After they have gone, you will want to dismantle all the storage facilities on the bases. Otherwise there would be nothing to prevent their return under another government."

Kowalsky looked innocently around the table. He hoped he had not overstepped his brief. Wainwright and the Chiefs of Staff, seated in a cluster at the opposite end of the room, looked aghast.

Unabashed, Sir Monty added one last personal observation. "I imagine," he said mischievously, "that the Americans will not be very keen to go."

14

The President was on a fishing holiday in Maryland when the cables from London confirmed that the British were going through with their plan to evict all American bases. And not just the bases. In his broadcast to the nation, recorded in the Great Parlour at Chequers that Sunday evening, Perkins had specified that the Americans would also be asked to withdraw from General Command Headquarters (GCHQ) at Cheltenham, to close Menwith Hill in Yorkshire and the chain of other communications facilities used for monitoring all telephone, telegram and telex traffic to Europe and the United States. The timetable, said Perkins, would be a matter for negotiations, but he envisaged that the American withdrawal would be complete within three to five years.

Within an hour of the broadcast the President was reading the full text in his log cabin by the Potomac river. Two fishing rods and a gaff were propped up against the wall by the door. Laid nearby were two gleaming salmon, the day's catch. The President was slouched in a folding camp chair the bulging canvas of which was hard put to accommodate his considerable frame. He sat there clad in an anorak, gumboots and old tartan trousers splashed with mud. Around him, motionless and with their arms folded, stood aides dressed incongruously in blue blazers and trousers with impeccable creases.

No one spoke while the President ran his eye down the three foot length of teletape. After several minutes of intense concentration he put the tape on the table, unwrapped a spearmint chewing gum; then he shouted so loudly that even the fish in the Potomac must have heard. "Damn, blast and shit," he said.

There followed a hurried conversation with Secretary of State Morgan over a scrambled radio telephone. Morgan was already in his office at the State Department. Their brief conversation over, the President walked out of the cabin and strode to a waiting jeep. Behind him doors slammed as aides and secret service agents climbed into their vehicles. Then the little convoy set off bumping along the rough forest track. After twenty minutes they came to a clearing in which stood a white helicopter, its fuselage emblazoned with a circular coat of arms around which was written in clear black letters, "The President of the United States." Two hours later, the President, still in gumboots and mud-spattered trousers, was back in the Oval Office.

They were seated in a semi-circle of easy chairs around the fireplace, logs freshly lit burning in the grate, and a portrait of George Washington above the mantlepiece. The President sat to the right of the fireplace, to his left Admiral Glugstein still in evening dress, having driven to the White House directly from the Hilton Hotel where he had been hosting a dinner for the head of the Chilean navy. Marcus J. Morgan, the Secretary of State was next. Morgan had brought with him a pile of cables from London, the latest saying that the Chiefs of Staff were threatening to resign. Opposite, on the sofa, was the President's national security adviser, Anton Zablonski, who was leaning forward with hands on his knees like a crouching rugby full-back expecting the ball to come his way at any moment. Beside Zablonski sat the CIA chief, George McLennon. On the way up in the elevator McLennon had been composing small talk to break the ice. He had planned to ask the President about his fishing trip, but changed his mind when he saw the look on the President's face. This was no time for small talk.

With the exception of McLennon, they were all big men with heavy jowls and large bellies. The heaviness of their jowls lent gravity to the occasion.

The President spoke first. "Let's be clear. There is no way we can afford to lose Britain. No way at all." Zablonski was nodding in agreement. The President went on, "We lost China in 1949 and got by. We lost Vietnam in 1975 and got by. But if we lose Britain, we're done for."

161

"Right on, Mr President," whispered Zablonski.

"If we were prepared to invest two-billion dollars a year and forty thousand American lives to try and save a dump like Vietnam, then the sky's the limit when it comes to saving Britain." The President spoke slowly, every phrase punctuated by the sound of his jaws processing chewing gum. "Whatever the cost we've got to stop those bases falling into enemy hands – and by enemy I mean the British government."

For a moment there was no sound save the crackling of the log fire. The President looked at each man in turn. "Gentlemen, this is war. I want to know how we get rid of Harry Perkins and his government." He nodded towards Morgan. "Marcus, you first."

The Secretary of State ran a plump hand across the stubble on his unshaven chin. "To start with, Mr President, we gotta play for time. Emphasise the technical difficulties. Slam in a nice bill for compensation. Demand the return of every piece of equipment that we've ever installed in the British defence system, down to the last paper clip. Meanwhile we get our European allies to pile on the pressure, get the bankers to heat up the economy a little and quietly prepare for the worst."

"Anton?"

Zablonski sat up straight, slicked back his hair and tightened the knot of his tie as though he were rising to address an audience of thousands. "I reckon," he said firmly, "it's about time we stopped babying the British. Tell them straight to get into line or else. We could start by organising a trade boycott and, if it comes to the worst, we could blockade the ports."

"That's plain crazy." McLennon could not restrain himself. "If we do that we'll end up taking on the whole world."

"So what would you do," snapped Zablonski, "put Perkins down for a Nobel Peace Prize?"

McLennon ignored this. In his view Zablonski was a dangerous lunatic who enjoyed far too much access to the President. Lunatics like Zablonski had already driven half the world to Communism and, if they continued to have their way, it would not be long before the other half followed.

"We have one thing going for us," said McLennon. "British public opinion. Perkins is not as popular now as he was six months ago. That dispute with the power workers was very damaging. On top of which many people in Britain are worried about the Soviets. We must play that one for all it's worth." He paused to look across at the President who was making notes. *Play Soviets*, the President had written on a pad of white paper embossed with his seal.

"And here," McLennon went on, "I must pay tribute to the British intelligence boys. We often laugh at them, but I must say they have got their media sewn up tighter than a gnat's ass-hole. Apart from a Communist rag, which no one takes seriously anyway, every national daily, every Sunday paper, just about every local newspaper from Surrey to the Scottish Highlands is on our side on this one. So is the BBC and most other television networks. All hammering Perkins and his crew every day. All playing the Soviet threat for everything it's worth. In most countries we have to pay for that kind of coverage. In Britain we get it for free." There was envy in his voice. If only the American establishment had a media half as friendly, half as unenquiring. "Sooner or later," he said, "public opinion in Britain is bound to swing our way." He paused and looked at Zablonski. "Unless we screw it all up by declaring war on them."

"George is right Mr President, we gotta play this cool." It was Marcus Morgan. McLennon looked up in surprise. It was not often he had the Secretary of State on his side.

"What we need," Morgan went on, "is a bit of so-phist-ica-tion." The word rolled slowly off his tongue. Sophistication was not something widely associated with corporate lawyers. "If Anton had his way, we'd be training British mercenaries in Camp Hale by now."

"As I see it," said Admiral Glugstein, who until now had sat back in silence, "our key objective must be to maintain the installations." He pinched his trousers at the knee to preserve the crease. "The warheads are no problem. If the worst comes

163

to the worst we can play the Brits along by flying them out to Germany or Spain. The submarines can also be temporarily relocated, if necessary. But the infrastructure, that's another matter."

The admiral's polished shoes gleamed in the light of a lampshade. His cuffs protruded a full two inches from the sleeve of his dinner jacket. "Yes sir," he went on, "we got thirty billion dollars tied up in infrastructure. Communications, storage facilities and the like. If we lose that little lot we're in trouble deep."

"That's where the British military come in." Morgan had taken a cigar from his top pocket and was fumbling for a lighter. "Providing we hand over to the British military, they should be able to babysit for us until the next election."

"And if Perkins wins the next election?" jeered Zablonski.

"That," said the President with a thin smile, "is item two on today's agenda."

The RAF DC10 bringing Air Chief Marshal Sir Richard Gibbon to Washington touched down at Andrews Air Force Base at around 9 am Washington time. Officially he was coming to talk to the American air force about an updated version of the F-18 which the RAF were hoping to buy. The visit had been scheduled months in advance. Unofficially, however, he had come to give the Americans a full briefing on the Chequers weekend and to sound them out on what was to be done. Although he was met at the airbase by a USAF staff car, he was driven not to the Pentagon, but to the State Department. To avoid the possibility of recognition he was dressed in civilian clothes. He entered the State Department by a service entrance at the rear of the building and was taken immediately to the office of the Secretary of State.

If anyone had suggested to the air marshal that what he was engaged upon was treason he would have replied crisply that, on the contrary, he was engaged in an act of patriotism. If pressed, the air marshal would have argued that the citizen's loyalty to the State was conditional upon the State recognising a responsibility to provide protection for the citizen. By withdrawing from the Atlantic alliance the British government was failing to honour its share of the bargain. Therefore, the air marshal was perfectly entitled to withdraw his loyalty from the State. He was not alone in this line of thinking. In one way or another such arguments were to be heard around the dinner tables and in the drawing rooms of gentlemen's clubs the length and breadth of St James's. They were to be heard in the officers' mess at the Army Staff College at Camberley. And in the boardrooms of some of Britain's grandest corporations. They were even, on occasion, to be heard between the four walls of a permanent secretary's office in Whitehall.

Very often such arguments were embellished by the suggestion that the loyalty of many government ministers was in doubt. If there was any treason going on, it was argued, it was more likely to be found in the Cabinet Room or behind the Georgian façade of Labour party headquarters at Walworth Road. To say nothing of some of the Marxist trade union leaders who made no secret about where their loyalties lay. This reasoning rarely made the newspapers, at least not in so crude a form. But it was what many very important people in Britain were thinking as the winter of 1989 faded into spring of 1990.

Of course no one in their wildest dreams would have envisaged a situation where any British Cabinet minister or even a Marxist trade union leader would actually undertake a trip to Moscow for the specific purpose of briefing the Soviet Foreign Minister on the secret deliberations of the British government. Everyone knew that Soviet sympathisers were a little more subtle than that.

Yet here was an air marshal, who only hours before had been party to the highest level and most secret deliberations of the British government, seated in the office of the American Secretary of State, spilling the beans with gusto. Call it treason or patriotism or what you will.

Marcus J. Morgan was in shirtsleeves, which did justice to his mighty biceps. Cold winds blew outside, but inside an air conditioner hummed gently. Or was it an extractor fan absorbing the endless screen of cigar smoke which wafted up from behind his paper-strewn desk? On a table by the window was a scale model of the B-1 bomber, the biggest, fastest and most expensive ever built. The air marshal gazed longingly at it and wondered aloud if the Royal Air Force would ever be able to afford a squadron of B-1s. "Don't worry," Morgan assured him, "Britain will get her share just as soon as we've extended the runways at Mildenhall."

"Let's get one thing straight right from the start," said Morgan after the air marshal had told him there was talk of resignations, "we don't want to see any resigning. The battle's only just beginning and we're going to need you boys to stick in there. So stay stuck in." The air marshal nodded. He could see the point, though he had never before heard the Chiefs of Staff of His Majesty's armed forces referred to as "you boys".

"Another thing," said Morgan after the air marshal had told him of the plan to dismantle the British warheads. "Instead of taking the warheads to Burghfield, just fly them to Germany and we'll take care of them for you until the all clear sounds. Then you can have them back again." He flicked the ash from his cigar into an ashtray made from the wing of a Soviet MIG shot down over Afghanistan. "You can put a few through Burghfield to keep Perkins happy. If necessary, soup up the figures a bit." The air marshal nodded again. Yes, he thought that could be done. The real problem would be when the time came for Burghfield and Aldermaston to be dismantled. When that happened there would be no hope of Britain ever again maintaining an independent deterrent.

"That's when you start to take it easy. Throw a spanner or two in the works. Tell the government it's more complicated than you thought. Get the workers to go-slow." Morgan chuckled. "Going-slow is what you British are good at, isn't it?"

The air marshal managed only a weak smile. At home he would have been the first to laugh at any joke about the idleness of the British working man, but he did not like to see a foreigner running down his countrymen. "That might not be as easy as you imagine," he said, "the running down operation is likely to be in the hands of the chief scientific adviser to the MoD, an old Pole named Kowalsky. We're not sure we can count on him to play ball. At Chequers on Sunday I rather got the impression that he might actually be in favour of doing away with nuclear weapons." The air marshal's voice betrayed incredulity, as though he could not conceive a scientist, let alone one working for the Ministry of Defence, who would be against the bomb.

"A pinko?" asked Morgan, one eyebrow raised.

"I wouldn't go *that* far," said Sir Richard quickly.

They talked for another half hour. Mainly about the chain of communications bases run by the American National Security Agency. This was really not Sir Richard's department. More an intelligence matter. But he knew enough to venture an opinion. He was slightly taken aback when Morgan remarked casually that it was being used to monitor all British government communications, including the Downing Street switchboard. "There's virtually nothing that bastard Perkins says that won't find its way to this desk within six hours," said Morgan patting a file of computer print-outs in his in-tray. At first Sir Richard assumed that American bugging the British government communications had been prompted by recent events, but Morgan soon put him straight. America, he said, had been bugging friendly governments for the last thirty years. Including all British governments, Conservative and Labour. "We started during the Suez crisis," beamed Morgan, "and never kicked the habit."

From the State Department Sir Richard was taken to see the President. They went in Morgan's car. To avoid leaks the meeting took place not in the Oval Office, but in a suite in the Executive Office Building which the President used for off-the-record meetings. The President asked mainly about the political situation in Britain. How long did Gibbon think Perkins would last? Was there anyone else in the Labour Party who could take over if Perkins was ousted? Gibbon had replied that being a military man he was not well up on politics, but it was his impression that Perkins would lead the

Labour Party into the next election and that he stood a good chance of winning.

With that Gibbon was driven to a house in Georgetown which the State Department used for VIP guests. Here he bathed, shaved and changed into his air marshal's uniform. From there he was taken to the Pentagon where he lunched with the USAF Chief of Staff. Even here the F-18s were discussed only perfunctorily. Most of the talk was about the bases in Britain. Finally he was driven back to the RAF DC10 which was refuelled and waiting for him at Andrews Air Force Base. By the small hours of Tuesday morning he was back in London.

The spring brought out the crocuses and daffodils in St James's Park. On the Thames the pleasure boats made their first trips of the season to Kew Gardens, and in Hyde Park military bands began playing again on Sunday afternoons.

Spring also saw the launch of a huge offensive against the government's plan to do away with nuclear weapons. It started a few days after the Chequers conference with a statement from the US State Department to the effect that while the United States would always respect the sovereignty and territorial integrity of the United Kingdom and any other NATO member, there were wider issues at stake. By effectively withdrawing from the alliance, the statement continued, the government of the United Kingdom places in jeopardy not merely the security of their own people, but that of Western Europe as a whole. The German, the Spanish, Belgian and Italian (though not the Dutch) governments each delivered separate protest notes. Meanwhile the Chiefs of Staff made what was supposed to be an unpublicised visit to Perkins to protest at the decision, but when they arrived at Downing Street batteries of cameras were waiting to record the event.

Press coverage grew steadily more outrageous. Ministers were presented as unwitting agents of the Soviet Union. One cartoon depicted Perkins standing on a map of Europe and opening a door for Russian tanks. Another showed a column of Russian tanks in front of the Houses of Parliament with America, Germany and other NATO allies, standing to one side, saying to Britain "Serves you right". The *Daily Mail* described the decision to ask the Americans to leave as the "biggest betrayal of Europe since the Molotov-Ribbentrop Pact". *The Times* said that Britain would never be able to hold her head high again and the *Guardian* commented that while a case might be made out for severing military ties with the

United States, now was not the time. Attempts to point out that Sweden and Switzerland had prospered as neutral countries were brushed aside, as was all mention of Canada which had unilaterally renounced nuclear weapons three decades before without any discernible ill-effects.

The public was still being given a wholly false picture of the balance of forces in Europe. Despite a personal memorandum from the Secretary of State's office and several reminders from Downing Street, the MoD press office continued to brief journalists using tables which omitted all mention of French forces and which excluded all British and American troops stationed outside central Europe.

Perkins staged a slight recovery in the opinion polls, which recorded a majority of British citizens in favour of the government's stand, but the findings were not widely reported. Only in May when in the face of a continuous propaganda barrage the majority against the bomb started to decline, were the opinion polls headline news again.

Gradually the going got rougher. The West German railways cancelled a ninety million pound order for locomotives and rolling stock to be built in Huddersfield. Spain pulled out of an order for two naval patrol vessels being built at Barrow. Saudi Arabia, which had been on the point of signing a contract with a British company for a huge construction project at a port on the Red Sea, withdrew at the last moment. These were the first in a spate of cancellations. The *Boston Globe* reported that American embassies around the world had instructions to persuade friendly governments to take their business elsewhere than Britain. Only the *Financial Times* took up the story.

Also about this time American-owned multinational corporations began transferring huge sums of money out of Britain. At first there appeared no reason for the transfer since British exchange rates compared favourably with those in Europe and the United States. Later a rumour circulated the money markets that the corporations were acting in response to pressure from the US Treasury which had privately guaranteed them against losses arising from these transactions. When the rumour persisted the American ambassador was summoned to the Foreign Office and asked to confirm or deny. His denial was less than watertight.

At the same time it was reliably reported from Washington that the Secretary of State had told a group of right-wing congressmen in an off-the-record briefing that America had no intention of vacating its bases in Britain. "When the time comes," he was quoted as saying, "we'll just sit tight and see what happens."

At this news the colour drained from Perkins' face. "I'm beginning to think we've bitten off more than we can chew," he said to Fred Thompson during one of their late night chats. Thompson was amazed. It was the first piece of pessimism he had ever heard from Perkins. "You know, Fred," Perkins had continued, "membership of NATO is about as voluntary as membership of the Warsaw Pact." He spoke as though he was kicking himself for not having realised that earlier. "We aren't going to be allowed to leave. If economic pressure doesn't work, they'll try blackmail. If that doesn't work, they'll try and subvert us. And if that fails, they'll send tanks. Just like the Russians did in Hungary."

Trade Unionists for Multilateral Nuclear Disarmament was launched at a crowded press conference at a suite in the Dorchester Hotel. The Dorchester was not an obvious venue but then, as Reg Smith never tired of saying, nothing is too good for the working classes. Smith was the chairman of TUM, as it became known. The secretary was a dapper young man called Clive Short who had lately graduated from Oxford. At Oxford he had formed a breakaway Labour club because the original one had, it was alleged, been taken over by extremists. It was in this capacity that he had come to the attention of Reg Smith.

Two other general secretaries, the leaders of the steel workers and the shop workers, shared the platform with Smith at the Dorchester. They were, however, careful to emphasise that they were present in a personal capacity. Also on the platform were shop stewards from union branches at

Aldermaston, Burghfield and the Devonport dockyard. Their interest was easily identified: their members' jobs were at stake.

In answer to questions, Smith did most of the talking. TUM, he said, was his brainchild. It was designed to act as a rallying point for the millions of moderate, sensible trade unionists who realised that Harry Perkins and his government were surrendering the country to the Russians. He wanted to stand up and show that it was not only Tories who cared about their country and about freedom.

Was TUM in favour of nuclear disarmament? Yes, of course, but not at any price. It was not right to ask the Americans to pull their bases out of Britain, unless the Russians pulled out of Eastern Europe.

Where was TUM's money coming from? From affiliation fees and a large bank overdraft. So far only the United Power Workers' Union had affiliated at national level, but a number of union branches had already signed up and at least one of the major civil service unions, which had a lot of members in the defence industry, was expected to affiliate shortly.

Was TUM a CIA front organisation? This question came from a reporter on the *Independent Socialist* who had managed to slip in to the invitations-only press conference. But Smith was an old hand at his game. He easily parried the question with just the right blend of indignation and humour to be convincing. "And while we're on the subject of front organisations," he added to general laughter, "is there any truth in the rumour that the KGB is funding the *Independent Socialist*?"

Press coverage the next day was lavish. Every paper carried a picture of Smith and ten to twenty column inches of sympathetic reporting. Papers which had only half heartedly supported the power workers' go-slow a few weeks earlier now had a campaign they could get their teeth into. The *Daily Mirror* was particularly effusive. Here at last, said an editorial, was a man prepared to stand up to Perkins on his own ground. A trade unionist who put the security of Britain before party politics.

TUM placed a series of advertisements in national newspapers appealing for members and money. Donations poured into its third-floor office in a terrace of early Victorian houses near the Euston Road headquarters of the United Power Workers' Union. So great was the flood of mail that Smith had to second a couple of union secretaries to help. By the end of the first week, Smith was able to announce donations totalling forty thousand pounds. He wisely declined to speculate as to the kind of people who would contribute funds to Trade Unionists for Multilateral Nuclear Disarmament. For one thing, many of the donations were anonymous. For another, as many of the accompanying letters made clear, much of TUM's support was coming from people who believed neither in trade unionism nor disarmament.

Sir Peregrine Craddock knew even before most CND members that the Campaign for Nuclear Disarmament were planning a major demonstration. Quite apart from the routine telephone taps, he had a man on the CND general council. It was one of DI5's most successful penetrations, yielding a complete set of minutes, not only of executive meetings but also of the secret discussions that took place between leading members of CND and Harry Perkins when he was leader of the opposition.

Sir Peregrine had long regarded CND as the most subversive organisation on DI5's books. Its subversive nature lay in the breadth of its appeal. Besides the usual gaggle of Communists, Trotskyists and layabouts, CND's membership took in Christians, Social Democrats, Liberals, Buddhists, vegetarians and even a few Young Conservatives. In the early days DI5 had made a number of hamfisted attempts to discredit CND as a Soviet front. Sir George Fison's newspapers even helped out with stories of CND delegations on expenses-paid trips to Moscow or by quoting from articles in *Pravda* in praise of CND. But none of this had the slightest effect on public opinion and CND's membership continued to grow. Worse still, it was effective. For years DI5 had invested thousands of man hours and weeks of computer time meticulously infiltrating, bugging and logging the details of every little Trotskyist sect that had ever raised a placard outside Brixton tube station on a Saturday morning. Yet none of these had ever caused the slightest hiccup in the orderly conduct of the nation's affairs. CND, meanwhile, had turned the nation's defence policy upside down in the space of a decade. And there appeared to be nothing DI5 or any other organ of the State could do to stop it. Yes, thought Sir Peregrine turning a half circle towards the window in his swivel chair, CND was a very dangerous organisation indeed.

From below in Curzon Street, a screech of car brakes momentarily penetrated the double glazing and lace curtains of Sir Peregrine's inner sanctum. He spun his chair sharply back from the window towards the desk and pressed a button by the telephone which caused a red light to flash in the outer office. The door at the far end of the room opened and Fiennes entered. As usual he was wearing a white shirt with blue stripes, a dark blue suit and the thinnest of thin smiles.

"Fiennes," said Sir Peregrine without looking up, "I think we ought to lay something on for this CND demo next month. Get on to Special Ops and see what they suggest."

"Good idea, sir." Fiennes would have said it was a good idea whether or not he thought so.

"What I have in mind," Sir Peregrine went on, "is a bit of a punch-up. Something that will detract from any favourable press coverage."

"I'll get on to it right away, sir."

Fiennes had turned back towards the door when Sir Peregrine spoke again. "Just a punch-up, you understand, Fiennes. I don't want anybody killed or maimed." As an after-thought he added, "Above all, I don't want any of those psychopaths from Hereford involved."

"No sir," said Fiennes quietly, though he could not bring himself to think of the members of the Special Air Services as psychopaths.

The crowd began to assemble at Speakers' Corner long before midday. All weekend people had poured into London for what CND had promised would be the biggest demonstration in British political history. It had been billed in CND literature as "The Final Push". The aim, according to the leaflets, was to show that "in spite of the unanimous hostility of the media and the establishment the British people stood behind their government's decision to do away with the Bomb."

The organisers had confidently predicted a quarter of a million people and even by the normally cautious estimates of the Metropolitan Police it seemed they could be right. Special trains and coaches were streaming into London from Scotland and the North of England, from Wales and the West Country. To the dismay of Jim Chambers, who was observing from the American embassy, there were even contingents from the West German Social Democratic Party and from Holland, Italy, Greece, Norway, Belgium and Spain. Nearly every country in NATO was represented. The spectre of a neutral Europe which had haunted Pentagon defence planners for so long was looking more and more probable.

As is customary at such gatherings, the Special Branch was well represented. Though not carrying banners they were readily identifiable. Heavy young men in green anoraks, faded jeans and plimsols. Some posed as press photographers, but gave themselves away by chatting too readily with the uniformed officers. Others were given away by the tell-tale bulge of a police radio under their jackets. They were to be glimpsed operating long-range cameras from rooftops all along the route of the procession, but particularly from vantage points overlooking Trafalgar Square, which would be the climax of the demonstration.

Fred Thompson was pointing all this out to Elizabeth Fain as they walked hand in hand along Park Lane towards Speakers' Corner. "Those cameras are so powerful," he was saying, "that they can identify an individual at a hundred and fifty yards." Thompson waved cheerfully at the men on the roof of the Hilton.

"By now," he teased, "they'll have you on file and before long all your friends in high places will know you have been seen in the company of a dangerous extremist. It'll be the talk of Annabel's."

"I wouldn't be seen dead in that place these days," said Elizabeth nudging him playfully. It was true, Elizabeth's outlook on life had changed since she first met Thompson. She had started to read between the lines of what she read in newspapers and, at Thompson's prompting, was now halfway through a book on the origins of the Cold War. Unlike many of her friends, Elizabeth had always been prepared to accept that the Americans were not necessarily the champions of freedom that she had been brought up to believe. However, it came as a revelation to discover the existence of a point of view, apparently supported by documentary evidence, which saw America as the centre of a worldwide network of tyranny, terrorism and suppression. It had turned her world upside down. She was not exactly converted. She was confused.

"I can see it's going to take a long time to repair the damage caused by that expensive education of yours," Thompson had said when she questioned him one evening about the coup in Chile. He had added with a grin, "Count yourself lucky that you've been saved while there was still time."

He had put his arm around her and kissed her lightly on the cheek. "Just imagine if you'd married one of those awful Hooray Henrys from the Cavalry Club."

"Do shut up, Fred," she had said half in anger, but she knew he was right. In her mind there suddenly loomed a vision of the awful Roger Norton and his tales of "bopping wogs" in Oman.

"Think about it," Fred had continued, "by now you might have been living in the Shires breeding a new generation of Hooray Henrys to run our country for us."

With that they had both burst out laughing. She had kissed him. "Yes," she admitted, "I had a very narrow escape."

By now they were more or less living together. Elizabeth had taken a job in an oriental bookshop near the British Museum, and during the week she would stay at Thompson's flat in

Camden Town. At weekends Thompson went to her house near Sloane Square.

This was the first demonstration they had ever attended together. "I can't imagine what my father would say, if he could see me now."

"He'd probably disinherit you."

"Probably." She squeezed his hand.

They were nearing Speakers' Corner now. A stream of people, some clutching banners headed in the same direction. In the park itself the crowd was so dense that it stretched as far as the cafeteria on the corner of the Serpentine. A policeman said he had not seen anything like it since the firework display the night before Prince Charles got married.

Stewards were trying to marshal the throng into some sort of order. "North-East region to the front, South Wales in the middle, trade unionists in the third column," a man with a loudspeaker was shouting. By a miracle, Thompson spotted the Holborn Labour party banner and he and Elizabeth fell in behind that.

All around there were people selling magazines and newspapers. Obscure journals with names that Elizabeth had never heard of before: *Tribune*, *Militant*, *Sanity*, *New Socialist*. To pass the time while they waited Thompson bought a copy of a paper called *Socialist Worker*. The front page led with a story about a police plot to sabotage the demonstration with an outbreak of violence. It said secret instructions had been given to units of the Special Patrol Group, but offered no clue as to the source of this information. "That's the trouble with all these Trot journals," said Thompson, "high on hysteria, low on facts."

Far away the head of the demonstration, led by a brass band of Yorkshire miners, was now moving off into Park Lane. Through a gap in the railing they could see wave after wave of banners passing, but still the numbers in the park seemed to grow no smaller.

In the centre of the crowd the speeches had begun. The speakers were crowded on to the back of a lorry with a hydraulic platform normally used to repair street lights, and one by one they were elevated above the crowd. Thompson and Elizabeth were too far away to recognise the speakers by sight, but their voices came over clearly on the carefully placed amplifiers: Labour politicians, a Church of England bishop, and even a well meaning brigadier who was received politely, but without enthusiasm. The biggest cheer of all was reserved for a Methodist peer in his late eighties. And all the while a police helicopter, with huge zoom lens cameras on either side, whirred above the great throng.

Thompson and Elizabeth waited more than two hours before their section of the crowd started to file out of the park. Even then more than half the crowd still remained to follow. "At this rate," said Thompson, looking at his watch, "we are going to miss Harry's contribution." The Prime Minister was scheduled to speak at 3.30 pm, the first time anyone could remember a serving Prime Minister addressing a demonstration in Trafalgar Square. The private office had come out strongly against, sending memos all week advising him not to speak. First they gave security as the reason. Then they tried to persuade him to entertain the Irish Prime Minister to lunch at Chequers instead. Finally, they said it demeaned the dignity of his office. "Nonsense," Perkins had replied, "the only thing that demeans this office is the long list of broken promises by successive Prime Ministers."

The demonstrators moved briskly to Hyde Park Corner shepherded between a thin line of policemen. The demonstration was a good-natured affair, with some singing, some chanting of inane slogans such as "Yanks out," and "Americans go home." It was only as they moved into Piccadilly that the police lines thickened. Behind the railings in Green Park, clearly visible from the road, stood uniformed police in helmets with visors, riot shields and truncheons at the ready.

"Expecting trouble, are we?" said Thompson quietly. Elizabeth held his hand tighter. Above, the police helicopter whirred. The air of goodwill began to evaporate. "Aren't our police wonderful?" shouted someone behind.

They passed the Ritz. St James's was cordoned off. Behind the cordon Thompson caught sight of half a dozen identical mustard coloured vans with rear windows blacked out parked in a convoy. "The Special Patrol Group," he whispered to Elizabeth.

Twenty yards further on, outside Fortnum and Mason, a group of heavy young men in plimsolls and green anoraks stood smoking nervously. Just before Thompson and Elizabeth reached them, the police cordon parted and four of the men slipped through to mingle with the demonstrators about five yards ahead of Thompson. The other demonstrators gave them a wide berth. Thompson was not the only one who noticed what was happening.

The strangers marched in step with the demonstrators. Thompson saw that two of them were carrying plastic bags that appeared to contain something heavy. They passed Hatchards and the Church of St James's, crossed Piccadilly Circus and moved into the Haymarket. By the time they reached the American Express office beyond the Haymarket Theatre, Thompson had almost forgotten them. It was then that he heard the sound of breaking glass.

He looked round in time to see one of the plate glass windows on the American Express office splinter inwards. Instantly a burglar alarm began to ring. As he watched a half brick arched up from the crowd just ahead of him and smashed through another window. He looked around for the four strangers, and identified them trying to push their way out of the crowd on to the pavement on the opposite side of the road from the American Express office. One man was still clutching a half brick.

"Fred, look out." It was Elizabeth, holding his hand tighter than ever. The crowd around them began to scatter. Everyone was shouting. From distant amplifiers came the sound of the speeches in Trafalgar Square. To judge by the applause it sounded as though Perkins was speaking. The original burglar alarm had now been joined by others. Above the din Thompson could hear clearly the sound of horses' hooves. "Look out," Elizabeth screamed again. The crowd around them parted to reveal police, scores of them on horseback, pouring out of Charles II Street wielding batons to right and left.

The first of the horsemen had already overtaken them. Wailing police sirens now vied with the burglar alarm. So did the screaming. The noise drowned the whir of the police helicopter directly above. No one even looked up.

They were running as fast as they could now. Elizabeth had still managed to keep hold of Thompson's hand. The horsemen were in hot pursuit clubbing to the right and left. Banners were trampled underfoot. They passed one boy with blood pouring down his face from a wound in his forehead. Ahead of them a girl was screaming.

The panic spread in both directions. It passed up the Haymarket in waves and back towards Trafalgar Square which was already jammed with people. For some reason the section of the crowd in the north part of the Haymarket, instead of retreating, continued to press forward forcing those at the front into the path of the horsemen. This may have been because, as Thompson later learned, both ends of the demonstration had come under attack. At almost exactly the moment the bricks went through the window of the American Express building, the police with riot shields had emerged from behind the railings in Green Park and started to lay into the demonstrators. Those in the middle had at first been unaware of what was happening.

Thompson and Elizabeth continued running until they reached the bottom of the steps at Carlton House Terrace where, they reasoned, the horsemen could no longer follow. It was here that they again caught sight of the four strangers jogging along the edge of St James's Park that borders the Horse Guards Parade. Following them was easy. By the time they drew level with the end of Downing Street they were walking. Two of the men paused to light cigarettes. They were laughing and joking as they climbed over the low rail at the edge of the park, crossed the Horse Guards Road and made for the steps leading into Downing Street.

Two uniformed policemen were on duty at the end of Downing Street. The men spoke briefly to them and then disappeared up the steps. When Thompson and Elizabeth arrived one of the policemen held out his arm to bar the way.

"Not today, thank you, sir." He pointed in the general direction of Piccadilly. "A bit of bother up the road, you see."

"I work here," said Thompson flashing his plastic laminated Number Ten pass under the policeman's nose.

The policeman stood aside without another word. The four strangers were almost at the top of Downing Street by the time Thompson and Elizabeth entered and they had to run to catch up. Whitehall was practically deserted, having been sealed off to keep the demonstrators away from the government buildings. The men had crossed Whitehall and were passing up the side of the Ministry of Defence. Thompson and Elizabeth ran to catch up. As they closed in, the men turned right and disappeared through an entrance just before the Embankment.

"Where's that?"

"Three guesses."

A convoy of mustard coloured vans overtook them and turned in behind the men. A uniformed policeman closed the gates. Thompson and Elizabeth arrived just in time to glimpse the four strangers greeting the occupants of the mustard coloured vans.

They seemed to be congratulating each other.

"Cannon Row Police Station," said Thompson.

"Oh," said Elizabeth quietly, "aren't our police wonderful?"

The next day's newspapers were full of it. Perkins had the early editions delivered to his flat in Kennington that evening. He continued to spend weekends there in preference to the flat at Downing Street.

"Anti-Bomb mob on rampage," screamed the *Sun* front page headline over a picture of the American Express building with its two broken windows. The inside pages displayed pictures of an injured policeman and a crowd charging helter-skelter down the Haymarket. The caption said they were running wild, but in fact they were fleeing the police horsemen. "Mob attacks American Express – 400 arrested," said the *Telegraph* headline. All the other papers carried similar reports and pictures. There was scarcely any mention of the size of the demonstration or its purpose. Perkins' speech was referred to only in passing.

The only comment that was reported with any prominence was a statement from Reg Smith in his capacity as chairman of Trade Unionists for Multilateral Nuclear Disarmament. The riot, he said, proved what he had always argued. Namely, that CND was run by a number of irresponsible hotheads who were motivated more by hatred of the United States than by a desire for nuclear disarmament. He appealed to all decent, sensible people who may have allowed themselves to be misled into supporting CND to reconsider their position.

"Bastard," said Perkins as he flung the papers in a heap on the floor. For weeks he had been looking forward to today as a chance to get the case for removing the bases across to the public in a way that not even Sir George Fison's papers could ignore. He was sure the disruption was organised, but proving it was going to be another matter.

Thompson had telephoned soon after Perkins arrived home and described what he and Elizabeth had seen. Perkins had rung the Metropolitan Commissioner immediately and demanded an explanation. "But I don't suppose I'll get one," he had said to himself as he replaced the receiver. "After all, I'm only the bleeding Prime Minister."

Sure enough, an hour later the Metropolitan Commissioner rang back to say that he had personally checked with Cannon Row police station and no men answering the description given by Thompson had been seen on the premises.

Meanwhile Thompson, on the advice of Perkins, had contacted the BBC and ITN offering them his eyewitness account of what had happened. The BBC Television news desk referred him at once to a senior executive, Jonathan Alford. Mr Alford was courteous, but sceptical. He said he would ring back, but did not. ITN, on the other hand, immediately whisked Thompson to its Wells Street studio. But the recorded interview was not shown. "You know how it is," said an embarrassed news editor when Thompson rang to enquire what had happened, "you were crowded out, not enough time."

But both BBC and ITN did find time to show the demonstration leaving Hyde Park. They used near identical clips in both of which a Communist Party banner stood out clearly.

Perkins switched the television off and poured himself a whisky. He had not felt so depressed at any time since he became Prime Minister. The other side were winning the propaganda war and he was almost powerless to hit back. For a moment he caught himself wishing he ran a dictatorship where he could simply order the newspapers to print what he said.

When he climbed into bed that night he felt lonelier than for a long time. As he drifted to sleep he found himself thinking of Molly Spence. It was getting on for thirteen years since she had passed out of his life. She was the last woman he had slept with. She would be getting on for forty now. He wondered whom she had married. How many children she had. Whether she had voted for him in the election. He did not suppose he would ever find out.

How wrong he was.

16

Molly Spence had married her boss, the managing director of British Insulated Industries. They had two children, a girl aged twelve and a boy aged ten, and lived in a converted mill in the Peak District of Derbyshire. Her husband commuted each day to British Insulated's twelve-storey head office in the centre of Manchester.

The mill, which could not be seen from the road and was approached by a winding drive of grey stone chippings, was on the floor of a valley and overlooked on three sides by sloping bare hills which were green, grey or purple depending on the time of year or the disposition of the sun. The highest of the plateaux, Kinder Scout, was a favourite place in the summer for parties of campers and ramblers.

Despite its isolation the mill was never a silent place, what with the sheep on the hillside and the running water from the nearby stream. Only when the wind howled too loudly or the rain beat too hard upon the windows could the water not be heard. And every hour or so there was the rattle of a one-coach diesel railcar that ran along the floor of the valley. It was one of those lines that British Rail was always threatening to close, but never did.

Molly's husband, Michael Jarvis, was fifteen years older. Even by Molly's standards that was pushing it a bit. She had thought hard before accepting his persistent offers of marriage. He had two children by his first wife and she did not get on with them. He drove a Jensen, though that was neither here nor there. He was powerful and, if Molly was honest with herself, she did have a soft spot for powerful men. In the end she said "Yes" because it seemed less trouble than saying "No". Off and on she had been going with Michael Jarvis for four years. Everyone in British Insulated knew. She did not want to devote the best years of her life to being someone's mistress and then end up being dumped in favour of a woman younger and prettier.

She had not told Michael about the affair with Harry Perkins. It had only been possible because he had based himself in London to negotiate the reactor deal. Although she had told Perkins that she shared a flat in Kensington with another girl, she in fact lived with Jarvis in an apartment owned by British Insulated. On Thursday nights Jarvis usually returned to Manchester to deal with business at head office. He would stay the weekend in Manchester and always spent Sunday with his children. It was these weekly visits to Manchester that made Molly available for Harry Perkins at weekends.

She had never loved Harry Perkins though she was as fond of him as she had been of anyone. She had liked him for being different. She liked his sense of humour. She liked him because he was famous. She liked him because he was interesting. But she always knew there was no future in the affair. Every Sunday when she caught the tube to the Oval she wondered whether to tell him it was the end. As the tube sped under the river, and through Kennington, she would sit composing her opening lines. But when she arrived, she could not bring herself to do it. There was Harry as warm and witty and optimistic as ever. There was the Handel organ concerto on the stereo. The bottle of Côte du Rhône on the table. She knew that deep down Harry Perkins was a lonely man. She knew that behind his façade of self-assurance, behind his steely willpower and his crammed appointments diary, there was an area of emptiness which she filled. She could tell by the way he clung to her. By the way he closed his eyes so tightly when they made love. By the way he lay with his head on her breasts.

So when the time came she had not the heart to tell him. She had carried on seeing him right up to the end. Right up to the Saturday before the wedding. The nearer the day came, the harder it got to tell him. In the end she had written him a long letter explaining about Michael and going into all sorts of unnecessary detail about her feelings. Then she had torn up the letter and substituted a simple statement of fact: *On Saturday I'm getting married so we'll have to call it a day. Please understand. Good luck. Molly.* She told herself that this was the sort of memorandum Cabinet ministers liked. Short and to the point.

Even so, she had not forgotten Harry Perkins. How could she? There he was in the newspapers every day. There he was every time she turned on the television. Not the Harry Perkins she knew. This was a much harder man, tough talking and belligerent. All the same, she felt a pang of guilt every time she saw him. She thought how much older he looked and wondered if the daily barrage of vilification was getting him down. She noticed too that the optimistic twinkle had disappeared from his eyes.

Molly kept her souvenirs of Perkins in a blue vanity case amid a pile of old boxes in the attic. They included that first note on official paper. *Lunch Sunday? Ring me at midnight.* And then the telephone number. Not even signed.

There was *The Ragged Trousered Philanthropists* with the message inscribed on the inside cover: *To a slightly Tory lady in the hope that she will see the light. Love, Harry* and then the date. There were several other notes, mainly re-arranging the time of their weekly rendezvous, one on ministry notepaper, a couple on House of Commons paper and the rest on blank scraps. There was also a cheque for £5.20 drawn on the account of Harold A. Perkins at the Co-operative Bank, Leman Street, London, E.1, in payment for shopping. Because he was famous she had decided the cheque was worth more to her uncashed. And that was it. Not a lot to show for a love affair that lasted more than a year. She kept her souvenirs hidden because she did not want Michael to know. He would have seen the dates and worked out for himself that she had two-timed him almost to the day of their marriage.

Perkins would have been pleased to know that she voted Labour in the election. Actually it was no big deal. Michael and most of the top management of British Insulated had probably voted Labour, if the truth were known. After all they owed their jobs to Perkins. Had he not fought so hard for

186

their reactor, British Insulated would have gone to the wall. Instead it had landed contracts to build four nuclear reactors in Britain with an option on two more. That in turn had led to orders from Saudi Arabia and Brazil. Thanks to Harry Perkins British Insulated had gone from strength to strength. And, who knows, they might one day have led the world, but for the disaster at Windermere.

The Windermere reactor was not simply a triumph of technology. It was also a triumph of politics. The splitting of the atom was as nothing compared with the five-year battle that raged between the Central Electricity Generating Board and the Save Windermere Society. There were public inquiries, High Court injunctions, parliamentary select committees and, when all else failed, sabotage.

The scientists argued that their nuclear power station was clean, safe and aesthetic. The Save Windermere Society said it was dirty, poisonous and ugly. The society argued that the Windermere reactor would drive away tourists, destroy wild life and one day perhaps incinerate Lancashire. The society had mobilised the National Trust, the Countryside Commission, Cumbria County Council and the Lake District National Park Authority, to say nothing of the Kendal Conservative Association and the Newby Bridge Amenity Society. Between them these organisations could count on more colonels, brigadiers and generals than the Duke of Wellington took to Waterloo. Yet in the end they met defeat. Whitehall decreed that the Windermere reactor should be built. Parliament and the judges endorsed it. And up it went.

But slowly. The building of it took four years longer than scheduled. Sugar was poured into the fuel tanks of the bulldozers that came to clear the site. There was an interunion dispute over the lagging of pipes which led to a six-month shutdown. When the pipes were finally fitted many were found to have faulty welds. Then the boilers leaked. And then there was the little matter of the uranium that came off the rails somewhere between Liverpool docks and Preston.

There were times when British Insulated teetered on the edge of bankruptcy. There were times when the board seriously considered pulling out of reactors. There were times when Michael Jarvis wished he had been a schoolteacher, a postman or anything but the managing director of British Insulated. Yet in the end the Windermere reactor was built.

It occupied a shelf of land blasted out of the hills that run along the west shore of the lake. By no stretch of the imagination was it a thing of beauty except perhaps to nuclear engineers and architects. But neither was it dirty or poisonous. Not to begin with anyway.

The reactor dwelled in a huge windowless temple of sheer white concrete inlaid with aluminium. Inside the temple was crisscrossed by steel pipes and walkways all as spick and span as a hospital operating theatre. Down the centre a towering structure of yellow steel, not unlike a lighthouse, ran back and forth on rails feeding the god on enriched uranium. In all of this the intervention of human beings seemed irrelevant.

The god itself was encased in a concrete holy of holies seventy feet high and twelve feet thick and lined with steel, capable, or so it was said, of enduring heat at temperatures of up to seven hundred degrees centigrade and pressure of six hundred pounds per square inch.

The uranium pellets on which the god was fed were passed to it through the roof of the concrete chamber. The great heat given off by the uranium was blasted by carbon dioxide into water boilers which produced steam, which drove turbines which in turn produced electricity. That at least was the theory. And so it was in practice, until that fateful day in May when the Windermere reactor went out of control and almost took out Liverpool.

Jerry Turnbull was in charge of the control room when the temperature gauges started to rise. "Bloody gauge is playing up again," he muttered, hammering the glass panel with his fist. The needle on the gauge did not move.

Phil Prescott, control assistant, came and stood behind Turnbull. He was yawning. It was the first hour of the night shift. "No sign of the red light." He gestured towards the panel of lights which came on automatically in the event of an equipment failure. "Must be the gauge."

Turnbull hammered on the gauge again. Still it didn't move. He was not unduly worried. There had been two false alarms in the ten days since Windermere had been operating at full capacity and both had been traced to faulty wiring in the instrument panel. "Marvellous, isn't it?" said Prescott. "We can split the atom, but we can't wire a bloody circuit."

Turnbull picked up a phone and dialled the instrument maintenance engineers. There was no answer. "Another fucking tea break," he said loudly and slammed the phone down. Opening the log book he wrote the following entry: "2130, reactor coolant temperature gauge reading too high. Rang instrument maintenance. No reply." At least my arse is covered, he thought as he closed the log.

Jerry Turnbull had risen about as far as he was going to get in the hierarchy of the power industry. Even now he was working above his grade. The regular nightshift controller had taken sick two days ago and Turnbull was filling in. He was forty-nine years old and bitter. He worked nightshifts because his wife had left him and because nights were quieter. "Mr Turnbull likes a quiet life," his annual report had said. And it was true.

Unfortunately for Mr Turnbull, however, tonight was not going to be quiet.

He was dozing lightly when somehow his eye came to rest on the meter that measured radiation in the reactor hall. It was reading two hundred and fifty millirems per hour. He came to with a jolt. Carbon dioxide was leaking.

Turnbull looked at his watch; it was 0215. The reactor temperature gauge was still creeping up although there was no sign of a red light. He looked around for Prescott, but Prescott had gone for an early breakfast.

Trembling slightly Turnbull switched on the video scanner that monitored the pipes carrying the carbon dioxide into the reactor. The camera ran along the length of the pipes, hovering over the welds. There was no sight of a leak. He looked again at the radiation meter. It had gone up another twenty millirems.

Next, he turned on the scanner that monitored the pipes taking the steam out of the reactor to the generator. He scanned them once, twice. Turnbull was panicking now. He had worked seventeen years in nuclear power stations without once being near the scene of an accident. Now for the first time he found himself in sole charge.

He rang the canteen. Where the hell was Prescott? Gone down to the lakeside for a smoke. He rang instrument maintenance. The bastards still were not answering.

Even at this point, so the manuals assure us, there is no cause for alarm. All the reactor components essential to its safe functioning are duplicated. If the pumps which bring the coolant gas into the reactor fail, there are duplicates waiting to take over. If one of the pipes bringing the coolant into the reactors or taking the steam away should leak, there are others which will take the strain.

If all else fails, so the text book says, the reactor will automatically shut itself down. But none of this happened at Windermere that night.

By the time a nearly hysterical Turnbull got the general manager out of bed the meter reading for radiation in the reactor hall had risen to four hundred millirems an hour, ten times the permitted level.

Engineers in protective clothing were inside the hall searching for the source of the leak. The temperature gauge had reached seven hundred degrees but there was no sight of an automatic shutdown. When the general manager appeared on the scene around 0545 he found Prescott and Turnbull arguing furiously. Prescott wanted the reactor shut down. Turnbull was shouting that he was not going to be the man who shut down the Windermere reactor.

By the time the dayshift came on duty the radiation level in the reactor hall was over six hundred millirems. Medical checks on the engineers who had been inside the hall showed they were seriously contaminated. The general manager immediately ordered a shutdown of the reactor but some of the control rods appeared to have warped, making a complete shutdown impossible. Inside the reactor the uranium was melting. In the reactor hall automatic sprays had been activated, but they were insufficient to cope with the huge quantities of radioactive carbon dioxide now leaking from the reactor.

Tests in the atmosphere outside the reactor building showed no significant radiation leakage, but it was clearly only a question of time. The police were asked to stand by to evacuate everyone within a five mile radius. At 0800 Downing Street came on the line. The Prime Minister wished to be kept informed.

He was not the only one. A twenty-mile-an-hour wind was blowing due south. At that rate a cloud of radioactive carbon dioxide would take just fifteen minutes to engulf the village of Newby Bridge at the end of Windermere. Then, assuming no change in the direction of the wind, the radioactive cloud would continue south over Morecambe Bay and would reach Blackpool within little over an hour. Within three hours it could be over Liverpool.

"Facilities for the orderly evacuation of Liverpool do not exist," said the Chief Constable of Merseyside when informed of the news.

By 0935 the Windermere engineers managed to get the emergency cooling system working which stopped the uranium melting, but the radiation level in the reactor hall was higher than ever. The meter reading was showing nearly one thousand millirems in the area of the reactor and even men wearing protective clothing could only work there for a few minutes at a time.

By midday, with the help of experts from London flown in by army helicopter, the engineers managed to insert the warped control rods and close down the reactor. Tests outside the building showed that radiation was reaching dangerous levels. Disaster had been averted. Just.

*

The preliminary investigation showed that the cause of the leakage was a series of hairline cracks in the base of the concrete pressure vessel which contained the reactor. The cracks had developed into fissures when the reactor over-heated due to the failure of the emergency cooling system. Later enquiries revealed that the cracks occurred because the concrete used in the construction of the pressure vessel did not match the specifications laid down by the designers and approved by Nuclear Installations Inspectorate. Neither had the vessel been adequately tested despite documentation that said otherwise. In other words, British Insulated Industries had a few questions to answer. A public enquiry was immediately announced, but it was not only British Insulated who would face questions.

On the Sunday morning after the accident at Windermere, David Booth made himself a pot of tea and sat out in the garden with the papers. It was the first time that year that the weather had been good enough to sit outside. His wife had taken the children to lunch at her mother's, so he would not be disturbed.

The papers were full of the Windermere disaster. The *Sunday Times* Insight team had traced the whole history of the project and their report filled a special four-page pull-out. Most of the papers had been quick to pounce upon Harry Perkins' role in the affair. There were long articles describing how he had forced the deal through in the teeth of bitter opposition from his own civil servants, the Atomic Energy Authority and the Central Electricity Generating Board. Several editorials called on Perkins to make a statement.

David Booth took more than a casual interest. He was a principal in the foreign exchange department at the Treasury, but thirteen years ago – exactly at the time the deal with British Insulated had been negotiated – he had been on a six-month secondment to the nuclear division of the Public Sector Department. Indeed he had actually taken part in some of the negotiations.

At the time, Booth had formed a sneaking regard for Perkins. He had been deeply impressed by the way Perkins had stood his ground over the reactors against virtually the entire establishment. He had also been appalled at the way his civil service superiors had behaved: refusing to circulate briefing documents; withholding from the minister information that did not tally with the case they were putting forward. There had been times when he had seriously wondered whether or not some of his colleagues were actually in the pay of the American reactor company.

But none of this concerned Booth that sunny Sunday morning. He was worrying that he knew what the *Sunday Times* Insight team did not, something that would cause a sensation if it became generally known. David Booth knew that, at the time Harry Perkins had been pushing British Insulated's case through Cabinet he had been having an affair with the secretary to the managing director of British Insulated. Booth had seen the Secretary of State discreetly hand the girl that envelope during the negotiations at the department one morning. He had watched them drinking coffee together by the window overlooking the Thames. And in the weeks that followed he had seen the knowing winks and nods, the occasional pat of the elbow that the Secretary of State and the girl had exchanged.

The question was, what should he do about it? In all probability the affair was entirely innocent. Foolish perhaps for a man in Perkins' position, but nevertheless innocent. He had no wish to do Perkins down. God knows, the man had enough trouble on his hands without all this being raked up. In any case he had worked with Perkins. The man was as straight as a die – even his worst enemies would concede that.

On the other hand, a doubt nagged him. Supposing the girl had influenced the decision over the reactor? Supposing she had led him, however unwittingly, to come down in favour of British Insulated? Almost certainly there was nothing in it, but it was his duty to report what he had seen.

Booth wrestled with the problem all weekend. He did not

finally make up his mind until he arrived at his desk on Monday morning. Then he asked for an immediate appointment with his permanent secretary, Sir Peter Kennedy.

17

When the memorandum from Sir Peter Kennedy arrived on Sir Peregrine Craddock's desk the DI5 chief's eyes lit up. Sir Peregrine was not much given to displays of emotion, but he got up, paced his office and slapped his thigh with the flat of his hand. If this is true, he said to himself, we've got the bastard at last.

Composing himself Sir Peregrine returned to his desk and buzzed Fiennes.

"There's a man called David Booth who works in the Foreign Exchange Department of the Treasury. I want to see him immediately."

"Yes, sir."

"Then I want to get on to our man at the Public Sector Department. Ask him to get me the names and addresses of everyone from British Insulated Industries who took part in the reactor negotiations at the Department thirteen years ago." He looked up at Fiennes who was standing almost to attention. "Everyone. Do you understand? Typists, clerks, stenographers, the lot."

"At once, sir."

"And when you've done that," Sir Peregrine was still looking at Fiennes, "get on to the Special Branch inspector in charge of the Prime Minister's security. Tell him I would like to see him as soon as possible, but that he is not to let anyone know he is coming here. Neither his superiors nor the Prime Minister. Especially not the Prime Minister."

What's all that about? wondered Fiennes, as he closed the door behind him and returned to the outer office. He knew better than to ask questions, however. He would find out soon enough.

David Booth arrived at Curzon Street House within the hour and was shown straight to Sir Peregrine's office. His hands were shaking slightly as Fiennes showed him in. Even now he was not sure he had done right. Perhaps there was something in it after all. All the same, he never expected to be summoned by the head of DI5.

Sir Peregrine was in an affable mood. When Booth entered, he leaned across his desk and shook hands. "So good of you to come, Mr Booth. I shan't keep you long." He waved Booth to an armchair.

The interview lasted about ten minutes. Booth repeated what he had already told his permanent secretary that morning. Sir Peregrine went over the details carefully. Had he actually *seen* Perkins hand the envelope to the girl? Yes, he had. Did he have any idea what was in it? No, he did not. Could it have been connected with the reactor negotiations? Yes, possibly. Perhaps the Secretary of State had simply handed over some document for safe keeping that she would afterwards pass on to her boss? Possible, but unlikely. And in any case there was all that nodding and winking.

"Quite so," said Sir Peregrine crisply, "but even Secretaries of State are not above occasionally making eyes at a pretty girl. That didn't mean he was sleeping with her."

Not necessarily, agreed Booth. He was beginning to feel that it was all in his imagination. There was nothing in Sir Peregrine's reaction to indicate whether he believed the story or not.

"One final question," Sir Peregrine was saying. "Have you told anyone about this apart from Sir Peter Kennedy?"

"No sir."

"No one at all? Not even at the time."

"No."

"Good." Sir Peregrine smiled benignly. "Then I'd be obliged if you would continue to keep the whole thing under your hat."

The DI5 chief rose and Booth rose with him. They walked towards the door. "I am sure you appreciate," said Sir Peregrine confidentially, "that if any of this got out, there would be the most awful stink."

*

Inspector Page nearly fell over backwards when he received the summons to Curzon Street. Of course in his job he often dealt with DI5, but only with the liaison man in Downing Street or other government departments. Usually these dealings only involved routine checks on people scheduled to meet the Prime Minister. Occasionally he drew the odd threatening letter to DI5's attention. But a meeting with the chief himself, that was another matter.

Page arrived at Curzon Street House in the early evening. Fiennes had stressed that he was not to tell anyone and so he waited until he went off duty before setting out. Fiennes met him in the lobby and took him by lift to the second floor. He offered no clue as to what it was all about. The truth was that Fiennes did not know. When he had handed over the list of names and addresses of the British Insulated Industries people that had arrived that afternoon, Sir Peregrine had received it without comment.

When Fiennes entered with Inspector Page he noticed that the list was lying on Sir Peregrine's desk and that one of the names had been circled in red. He was not close enough to see which one.

Sir Peregrine waited until Fiennes had left the room before he spoke. "Inspector," he said, "does the name Molly Spence mean anything to you?"

The inspector's forehead creased to a frown. After a moment's thought he said, "No, sir."

"Mrs Jarvis, perhaps?"

"No sir."

Sir Peregrine was sitting sideways on to the window, his elbows resting on the arms of his chair and his fingers joined at the tips. To look at the inspector he had to turn his head sharply to the right. "Am I correct in thinking that you have been looking after the Prime Minister since the day he took office?"

"Yes sir."

"And as far as you know, no one of that name has visited him during that time."

"That's right sir."

Sir Peregrine stared straight ahead, his chin touching the tip of his joined fingers. "Is it conceivable that a lady of that name could visit him without your knowing?"

The inspector smiled. The idea of Harry Perkins receiving secret visits from a young lady was one that appealed to his sense of humour. "Possible, but not likely, sir."

"When he visits his constituency in Sheffield perhaps?"

"If he goes to Sheffield either I or the sergeant go with him. Normally he returns to London the same night."

"Or to his flat in Kennington."

"Nowadays he only stays at Kennington one or two nights a week," said the inspector. "In which case there would be a uniformed man on duty in the lobby downstairs, day and night. I would expect to be told of any visitors."

Sir Peregrine turned back towards the inspector. Reaching his arm forward, he pressed the switch on a desk lamp. It illuminated the space between them, giving the inspector his first clear view of the DI5 chief's face.

"Do you have access to the Prime Minister's flat, Inspector?"

"Yes sir, I have a key."

"Good." Sir Peregrine smiled. "I want you to do something for me."

The inspector stiffened a little. "Sir, I normally get my instructions from the Branch."

"I'll clear this with your superiors," said Sir Peregrine brusquely. He went on to explain that he wanted the inspector to search the Prime Minister's flat for any trace of the woman called either Molly Spence or Mrs Jarvis. He was to look for photographs, letters, dedications on the inside of books and to search desks, cupboards, drawers and filing cabinets. He was to leave everything exactly as he found it. He was to take no one with him and, above all, to breathe not a word to anyone.

Sir Peregrine scribbled a number on a scrap of paper which he passed to the inspector. "This is my direct line. You are to report to me personally and to bring with you whatever you find."

*

Inspector Page waited until Friday when the Prime Minister left for his weekly visit to Sheffield under the watchful eye of Sergeant Block. Then he drove to Kennington. He felt distinctly uneasy. It was not every day he was ordered to commit burglary, let alone in the home of the Prime Minister. He might have felt happier had he been told the reason for the interest in this woman Spence or Jarvis or whatever her name was. In any case, why couldn't DI5 do its own dirty work? And so what if Perkins was having it off on the quiet? Good luck to him.

Page had been looking after Perkins for over a year now. Politically they were miles apart. Page was a bit of a law and order man himself, but he did not mind admitting that Perkins was a decent enough bloke. Over the last few months Page had often found himself alone with the Prime Minister. Sharing compartments on trains, sitting together in the back of an official car on the way to a speaking engagement, even sharing a seat on the top deck of those damn buses that Perkins still insisted on riding now and again. Perkins had listened patiently to Inspector Page's views on what should be done with strikers, rioters and Northern Ireland and sometimes they had engaged in good-natured argument. Perkins was forever asking about the inspector's family. On one occasion he had even invited Page to bring his wife and two small sons to Downing Street and had shown them round in person. The inspector would not exactly have described himself as a close friend, but he was as close as a bodyguard is ever likely to get to a Prime Minister.

And now he was being asked to sneak into Perkins' flat and sift through his personal effects. Page would do it because he was under orders, but he did not like doing it. Not one little bit.

To avoid prying neighbours he parked his car in the Clapham Road and walked back round the corner about fifty yards to Perkins' flat. He glanced quickly up at the window of neighbouring flats and, when he was sure no one was looking, let himself into the front entrance hall with a Yale key. He glided up the three flights of stairs, taking the steps two at a time, turned the two Chubb locks on Perkins' front door and let himself in, closing the door quietly behind him.

It was, thought Page, a very modest home for a Prime Minister, being rather smaller than the inspector's own semi in Willesden. There were two bedrooms and a medium-sized living room. The smaller of the two bedrooms was a store-room. There were boxes of papers and magazines, piles of bound volumes of Hansard, and two metal filing cabinets. This is going to take all bloody night, thought Page, as he surveyed the flat.

He started by looking at the photographs. The one on the desk in the living room of an elderly lady with grey hair was, he guessed, Perkins' mother. On the mantelpiece there was a picture of Perkins with some orientals. On the wall in the bedroom a large photograph, taken in the bar of a Sheffield Labour club, showed Perkins surrounded by party members. In the wardrobe Page found an old shoebox full of black and white prints, some of them dating back to Perkins' childhood. There was one girl in her early twenties, but it seemed to have been taken years ago and the name Anne was scribbled on the back.

Next he went through the letters on the desk. They were in wire baskets labelled 'Constituency', 'Personal' and 'Party'. Page flipped through the basket marked 'Personal'. It consisted mainly of unpaid bills, some bank statements and two or three letters from people who appeared to be relatives. There were drawers in the desk and he went through them one by one. Postage stamps, typewriter ribbons, paper clips, a pile of old election addresses and several books of old Co-Op coupons. Jesus, thought Page, it must be ten years since the Co-Op stopped giving stamps.

He had been there about an hour when he started on the small bedroom. He tugged at the top drawer of one of the filing cabinets. It was open. Inside it was crammed with green folders, all neatly labelled. He ran his eye quickly along the labels which were in little plastic mounts clipped on to the metal ridge of the files. Every so often he came to a folder that was not labelled and drew it out for inspection. They mostly contained newspaper cuttings, many of them about Perkins, some dated years back. There were copies of letters sent on behalf of constituents to various government departments and to the housing department of Sheffield City Council.

Page did not strike lucky until he reached the third drawer. The folders now seemed to consist of old newspaper cuttings arranged under subject headings . . . CIA . . . Indian Ocean . . . Income Tax . . . they did not seem to bear much relation to each other . . . Microchips . . . Molly . . . Multinationals . . . Molly, Molly. That was it. The name of the girl he was looking for. He whisked the folder out and walked with it into the living room. Opening it, he laid the contents out on the desk. There was very little: a postcard from Austria dated March 1977 and half a dozen notes on scraps of blank paper. These were variously signed Molly, Moll and M, but bore no address. Some were dated, some were not. They mainly concerned shopping arrangements. Surely the head of DI5 had more important matters with which to concern himself? Page shrugged. His was not to reason why.

He scooped the notes and the postcard back into the green folder, closed the filing cabinet and glanced around the flat to make sure everything was as he had found it. Then, with the folder under his arm, he let himself out of the front door.

At the end of the street he found a phone box and rang the number Sir Peregrine had given him. It was after seven o'clock on a Friday evening, but the DI5 chief was at his desk. Page drove directly to Curzon Street.

If Sir Peregrine was disappointed at the meagre contents of the Molly folder, he did not show it. Using the photocopier in the outer office he made two copies of each item and then returned the folder to Page. "Put this back where you found it," he ordered. "And remember, not a word to anyone."

Molly Jarvis had just finished loading the dishwasher when she noticed a tall man striding down the gravel drive towards the house. He would have stood out anywhere in Derbyshire, indeed anywhere north of Mayfair. He was dressed in a perfectly cut navy blue suit with a waistcoat. On his lapel she caught the glint of a watch chain. On his head he wore a hat, a homburg she thought it was called. An umbrella was hooked over his left arm and in his right hand he carried a black leather briefcase of the sort that is standard Civil Service issue.

Drying her hands on a teacloth she went to the front door. She had opened it even before the man reached the house. The man doffed his hat. "Mrs Jarvis?" he said from a distance of about five yards.

"Yes."

"My name is Craddock." He had reached the doorstep now and was standing, hat in hand. Molly guessed he was aged about sixty. A handsome man by any standards. His greying hair still covered the top of his head. His square chin and straight back suggested he might once have been an officer in the Guards. "I'm with the security people in London," he added in a voice which reflected generations of refined breeding.

"Oh," said Molly.

"One or two questions to ask. Hope I'm not disturbing you." He took another step forward.

"Not at all," said Molly standing aside to let him enter. If the man had said he was the Prince of Wales, she would not have argued.

They passed into the living room. The man had to stoop slightly to avoid hitting his head on the oak beams in the ceiling. There was a Handel organ concerto playing softly on the stereo.

"Like Handel, do you?" asked the man.

"Yes," said Molly.

He arranged himself on the sofa and laid down the hat and the briefcase at his side. The umbrella he propped against the arm of the sofa. Molly went to make a cup of tea and while she was out of the room the man got up and inspected the bookshelf. When she returned he was standing by the window leafing through a biography of Harry Perkins. It was not a very good book. Molly had bought it on the spur of the moment at a shop in Sheffield two years ago.

"You once knew Harry Perkins, I believe." Molly nearly dropped the teatray.

"Yes," she said, "in my old job at British Insulated we had to go and negotiate with him once or twice. About reactors."

"No," said the man turning to face her, "that wasn't what I meant."

Molly was seated by now. The tray was on the floor at her feet. The Handel concerto was still playing softly. "How did you know?" she whispered.

"Never mind about that." His voice seemed harder now. He walked to the bookshelf, replaced the volume and returned to the sofa. Molly poured the tea. "Mrs Jarvis," he said eventually, "I want you to tell me everything you know about Harry Perkins, starting from the day you first met him."

She told him of the meetings at the Public Sector Department. About the note Perkins had slipped to her. About that first lunch at his flat in Kennington. About all the other Sundays. About how she used to ring first from the Oval tube station so that he would leave the door open for her.

The man had taken a notepad from his briefcase and a felt-tipped pen from an inside pocket. Occasionally he scribbled on the pad. Sometimes he asked a question.

"And all this time you were living with Michael Jarvis?"

"Yes," said Molly quietly, her eyes downcast.

"And all this time Mr Jarvis was negotiating the sale of his company's reactors with Perkins."

Molly's eyes widened. Suddenly it dawned on her where all this was leading. No, she protested, her affair with Perkins had nothing to do with the reactors. Michael knew nothing about it. Even to this day she had not told him. She had never discussed the reactors with Perkins. No, never. Not once, not ever. It was a love affair, nothing more.

The more she protested, the more the man probed. Had she ever given Perkins a present? A watch, a pair of cufflinks perhaps? Not even at Christmas?

No, she said, it wasn't like that. She was crying now and the man's voice became more gentle. The chimes of the grand-father clock in the hall reminded her that it was almost time to collect the children from school. The man said he would soon be finished.

"Mrs Jarvis," he said, "did Perkins ever give you a present?"

"No," she said quickly. And then she remembered *The Ragged Trousered Philanthropists*. He asked if he could see the book and she led him up the wrought iron spiral staircase to the attic room where she kept her souvenirs of Perkins in the blue vanity case.

She blew the dust from the case. It had been at least two years since she last opened it. The key was in a jamjar on the window sill. She unlocked the case and took out the book. Its paperback cover had faded. The man opened the book and read the dedication on the inside of the cover: *To a slightly Tory lady in the hope that she will see the light. Love, Harry*, and then the date. Molly looked embarrassed.

"And these letters," said the man indicating the half dozen or so envelopes bound together with an elastic band. "From Perkins, were they?"

Molly nodded.

The first was the note Perkins had passed her that day in the Public Sector Department: *Lunch Sunday? Ring me at midnight*. It was undated, but the notepaper was inscribed at the top: 'From the Secretary of State.' The man shook his head in amazement. How indiscreet politicians could be.

Taking each of the other notes from the envelopes, he inspected them and put them back. Molly stood in silence, watching.

Then he came to the cheque for £5.20 drawn on Perkins' personal account. "For shopping," said Molly quickly.

The man raised an eyebrow.

"What the hell do you think it was for?" said Molly sharply.

The man said nothing. He collected the envelopes and the cheque together and bound them again with the elastic band.

They went downstairs in silence. The man was carrying the letters and the book.

"Mrs Jarvis," he said when they were back in the living room, "I am afraid I must borrow these."

What was he going to do with them, she demanded? Michael would be furious if he found out about her affair with Perkins. And as for Perkins . . . Her voice trailed off as the awful panorama of possibilities opened up before her eyes.

The man's voice was reassuring again. "My dear, you have nothing to worry about. All this will remain a secret between you and me." He was putting the book and the letters in his briefcase. "In due course they will be returned to you." He paused and glanced around the room. "It's just that, if any of this got into the wrong hands, the Prime Minister would be gravely embarrassed." He spoke as though embarrassing the Prime Minister was the last thing he wanted to do. "Particularly," he added, "in the light of the accident at Windermere."

The man then collected his hat, umbrella and briefcase and walked to the front door. Molly offered him a lift to the station. He thanked her, but said he would rather walk since he did not get to the country very much these days.

With that he strode away up the gravel drive. Molly stood on the doorstep and watched him go.

Sir Peregrine was back at his home in Queen Anne's Gate by about eight that evening. His maid had prepared a light meal which he ate alone in his study overlooking the park. Before settling down for the evening with a glass of port and a book of John Donne's poems, he made just one telephone call on the scrambled line. It was to Sir George Fison at his home in Cheyne Walk.

"George, dear boy." He toyed with the port glass. "The PM's been looking a bit off colour this evening, don't you think?"

Fison said he thought so too.

"Strain's beginning to tell at last," said Sir Peregrine.

Fison gave a little snort of laughter and said he would not be in the least surprised.

"I was wondering," said Sir Peregrine, "if you could get your chaps to run a little speculation on the PM's health."

Fison said he would see what could be done.

18

Indeed Perkins had not been feeling well for months. The colour had drained from his cheeks. The optimism had gone from his eyes. He smiled less often now and when he did his smile looked artificial. Thompson had been advising him for months to take it easy, but the advice went unheeded. Everyone in Downing Street was talking about how worn he looked. The garden girls, the policemen on the door, the housekeeper, even Tweed and the civil servants in the private office.

There was a time when he had ignored what the newspapers said about him, but nowadays he seemed obsessed by them. Every night when the first editions arrived he would spend an hour poring over them, sometimes by himself, sometimes with Thompson. "Lying bastards," he would shout as he read the editorials, particularly those in the *Express* or the *Mail*.

"Take it easy, Harry," Thompson would say.

But Perkins did not take it easy. As the attacks in the media mounted, he became bitter and short tempered. It showed in his performance on the floor of the House. The Tories could see when he was riled and jibed him mercilessly.

For some weeks now, ever since the Chequers conference, there had been reports of a plot against him in the Parliamentary Party. There was talk in the tea rooms of a substantial revolt over the proposed cuts in the defence budget. Up to one hundred MPs were, it was said, prepared to abstain or vote with the Tories. There was even talk of the Parliamentary Party choosing a leader of its own. A small group of MPs around Wainwright were said to be behind the rebellion. Relations between the Prime Minister and the Chancellor had sunk to an all-time low.

The accident at Windermere had shaken Perkins. Though he maintained a studied silence in public, in private he held himself responsible. "If only I had listened," he said to

Thompson. There was nothing anyone could do to convince him it was not his fault. At one stage he was talking about resigning and it was all that Thompson, Jock Steeples and Mrs Cook could do to talk him out of it. From the wall of his room in the House of Commons he took down the framed letter from Sir Richard Fry: *You were right. We were wrong*, it said. Perkins wondered what Fry was saying now.

On top of everything else, there was the growing crisis in relations with the United States. The US ambassador had been to Downing Street with a list of impossible demands for compensation and assurances before his government would even consider withdrawing the bases. Indeed American leaders were now saying openly that they had no intention of going, but would sit it out until the next election. And the way things were going Perkins was unlikely to survive the next election. The opinion polls were showing a substantial Tory lead and the last two by-elections had seen Labour seats fall to the Tories.

By the time the newspapers began carrying a spate of reports about his health, it no longer seemed like a media conspiracy, just a reflection of what people around the Prime Minister had been saying for weeks.

Whatever the state of Perkins' health, it was not improved by a memorandum from Sir Philip Norton, the Co-ordinator of Intelligence in the Cabinet Office, requesting an appointment for himself and Sir Peregrine Craddock to discuss a security matter of the utmost urgency.

They came one Wednesday evening in July, entering through the secret door that divided Downing Street from the Cabinet Office. Tweed unlocked the door to admit them and locked it again after they had passed.

As usual they formed a solemn little procession as they made their way along the ground floor corridor and up the main staircase to Perkins' study. They walked in silence, one behind the other. Their footsteps fell in unison. They wore long, doleful faces which seemed to say that they had a regrettable but necessary public duty to perform. Pinky and

Perky, Perkins had taken to calling them behind their backs.

"Come in gentlemen," said the Prime Minister as the two intelligence chiefs hesitated at the doorway of his study. And then Perkins could not resist adding, "Which of my ministers have you come to stick the knife into this time?"

Craddock and Norton looked at each other blankly and sat down in the comfortable chairs. Perkins joined them.

Craddock and Norton looked again at each other as though they had not decided who should speak first. Craddock clutched tightly at the thin green folder on his lap. Norton broke the ice.

"Prime Minister," he said quietly, "it concerns the reactor at Windermere."

"Oh," said Perkins sitting bolt upright. He had not been intending to take the intelligence chiefs very seriously, but now they had his full attention.

"I believe," continued Norton, "that you were the minister responsible for commissioning the reactor."

"I was the Secretary of State, but it was a Cabinet decision," corrected Perkins.

"Quite so." Norton avoided catching Perkins' eyes.

"Prime Minister," Craddock was speaking now, "did you know a girl called Molly Spence?"

Perkins gulped. Where the hell had they dug her up from? "So what if I did?" he said quickly.

Craddock ignored his question. "And were you having an *affair* . . ." his tongue lingered over the word, "with her at the same time as you were negotiating with British Insulated over the purchase of their reactor?"

"Now look here," said Perkins struggling to suppress anger, "if you think there was any connection between . . ."

He did not finish. Craddock cut in with another question. "And were you aware that during the whole time of her relationship with you, she was living with Michael Jarvis, the managing director of British Insulated, the man with whom you were negotiating?"

"Impossible," Perkins almost shouted. And then he stopped because he realised it was perfectly possible.

"And were you further aware," Craddock was heading for the winning post now, "that she subsequently married Jarvis and that the wedding took place only three days after she finished with you and only three weeks after British Insulated won the contracts for the reactor?"

Craddock could not have delivered a more devastating blow if he had hit the Prime Minister square on the head with a cricket bat. Perkins fell back into the chair, his hands rested limply on the arms. The silence was broken only by the distant hum of traffic in the Mall and by the laughter of children in the park. Perkins could even hear the ticking of his watch.

When he spoke again, he did so quietly, "Has she been trying to sell her story to the newspapers?"

"No," said Craddock, "but there's always the possibility."

"It was just an affair," said Perkins weakly, "just a small love affair."

"*We* know that Prime Minister," said Craddock, "but it doesn't look very good, does it?" As he spoke he handed Perkins the green folder that until now had rested on his lap.

Perkins opened it. The contents were photocopies of notes he had written her. Craddock had omitted to include the copies of notes that she had written to him. There was no point in letting Perkins know his flat had been raided.

There were no more than ten sheets of photocopy. Perkins examined each in turn. There was the inscription from *The Ragged Trousered Philanthropists*. He remembered how he teased her about her ignorance of working class history. There was the note that had started it all. On Department notepaper. Perkins shook his head. He must have been mad. There was the cheque. He could not even remember writing it.

"She said it was to pay for some shopping she did for you," explained Craddock seeing his bewilderment.

The rest of the notes would have meant nothing to anybody but himself and Molly. Just meeting times and who was going to do the shopping. As he leafed through them it all came back to him. The Sunday lunches. The Côte du Rhône. The Handel organ concertos. The afternoons in bed. For a whole

210

year she had been the bright spot of his life. He shook his head sadly. How could she do this to him?

For a moment he tried to put a brave face on it. He closed the folder and returned it to Craddock. "Nothing very incriminating there," he said, trying to sound cool.

"Except the dates, Prime Minister."

He shook his head. Of course, it was the dates that landed him in it. For a moment he glimpsed the headlines when the newspapers found out: P.M. IN REACTOR LOVE TANGLE or PERKINS IN WINDERMERE SCANDAL – TORIES DEMAND ENQUIRY. He shook his head again. It was going to come down very hard.

Sir Philip Norton had apparently sensed what the Prime Minister was thinking. "There is another way," he said.

"Oh?" said Perkins numbly.

"Ill health, Prime Minister. You have been looking poorly recently. Everyone's been saying so."

"Go into hospital and then resign, you mean?" It was the first time anyone had used the word *resign*. "Who the hell is going to believe I resigned through ill health?"

"Don't see why not," said Norton, "Eden got away with it after Suez."

"Of course there will be a fuss," said Craddock, "but it will soon die down. People have very short memories." And then he added almost hopefully, "We could make the necessary arrangements very quickly."

Perkins took a deep breath. "I'll let you know in half an hour," he said.

After they had gone Perkins remained seated for five minutes exactly as they had left him. Then he got up and walked to the window. His head came just above the bullet-proof shields. He looked out over the empty garden of Number Eleven, over the wall to the park beyond. He saw children playing. He saw lovers walking hand in hand. Why had she done this to him? He shook his head again.

Then he walked slowly to his desk and tried to raise Fred Thompson on the internal phone. There was no answer. He

211

rang Thompson's home number. Again no answer. Then he rang Jock Steeples' room in the House. Then Mrs Cook's direct line at the Home Office. Then her House of Commons number. No answer. No answer. No answer. What else did he expect at dinner time on a fine summer's evening?

He sat down at the desk and ran his hands over his eyes. All his instincts told him that he should never make a decision like this without seeking advice. But he was tired, very tired. Besides which, who was there to advise him? For the time being Molly Spence was a secret he shared only with DI5. If he delayed another twelve hours, he might find himself sharing Molly with the whole world.

He was still seated at the desk, rubbing his eyes when Norton and Craddock returned. They knocked gently and entered. He looked at them, blinking.

"Shall we go?" said Norton as though the answer was a foregone conclusion.

"I'll go upstairs and pack," he said.

"No need," said Norton, "we'll take care of that."

From the desk Perkins picked up the framed picture of his mother and slid it into the pocket of his jacket. It was only a small picture and so fitted easily. He walked to the double doors where Craddock and Norton awaited him. He turned and looked around the room in the last fading light of the summer's evening. Then the three men stepped on to the landing. A footman outside silently drew the doors closed behind them.

They went down the main staircase in silence. Norton in front, Craddock behind. They walked across the hall into the lobby. The policeman on duty stood up when they passed but Perkins did not acknowledge his greeting. There was no sign of Inspector Page or Sergeant Block or of any of the other Special Branch officers responsible for his security.

Outside there were only a couple of passing tourists. They waved when they recognised him, but he did not respond. They were the only witnesses to the fall of Harry Perkins.

A black Rover was waiting, one of the last off the production line before British Leyland had collapsed. A policeman held the door while he climbed into the back seat followed by Sir Philip. Sir Peregrine walked round the back of the car and climbed in through the rear door on the other side. That was how they sat, one on either side of him, as if they were afraid he might try and jump out at the traffic lights.

The Rover moved out of Downing Street and turned left into Whitehall. It was not the Prime Minister's official car and Perkins did not recognise the driver. They drove around three sides of Trafalgar Square, cutting through the lane reserved for buses and taxis. They turned left after the National Gallery and sped away towards Hampstead.

One hour later the following statement was issued from Downing Street:

At 2130 hours the Prime Minister was admitted to the Royal Free Hospital for medical tests. On the advice of his doctors, he will be receiving no visitors.

The first the Prime Minister's doctors knew of his illness was when they read about it in the newspapers next day.

19

Perkins remained immured on the ninth floor of the Royal Free Hospital for seven days. An entire ward had been evacuated and sealed off, the corridors patrolled by unsmiling young men who talked to each other through walkie-talkie radios and whose jackets featured a prominent bulge under the left shoulder.

Shortly after the Prime Minister was admitted the hospital switchboard became jammed and for some hours callers heard only the engaged tone. When it was possible to get through again the operators had been instructed that no calls were being put through to the ninth floor. After failing to get through by telephone Jock Steeples drove to the hospital. He arrived a little after midnight and found Fred Thompson in the main hall. Thompson had apparently tried to get out of the lift at the ninth floor and been bundled back again by the unsmiling young men who were patrolling the corridors. The production of a Downing Street pass had made no impression.

Steeples and Thompson made one more attempt. This time getting out of the lift at the eighth floor and making their way up the fire escape to the floor above. On arrival they found the doors locked and curtains drawn.

The battery of pressmen who had descended on the hospital had no better luck. Some had put on white coats and posed as hospital orderlies. Others tried bribing genuine orderlies to go up and take a look. But everyone who tried to get out on the ninth floor had the same reception.

Steeples was fuming. He demanded to speak to the hospital's chief administrator. The man was eventually woken up at home and brought to a telephone. All he could say was that the matter was out of his hands. The ninth floor had been taken over by DI5. Next, Steeples rang the Cabinet Office and demanded Sir Philip Norton's home number.

The duty officer declined to believe that the caller was Steeples and refused to part with the number. Steeples then drove to the Cabinet Office and virtually beat the number out of the wretched man. All to no avail. Sir Philip's telephone did not answer.

At ten o'clock next morning Downing Street issued a further statement. It read as follows:

> The Prime Minister has been advised by his doctors that he is suffering from exhaustion and requires a long period of complete rest. He has, therefore, tendered his resignation to His Majesty the King, effective from noon today.

Copies of a signed statement to this effect were circulated to the press. The signature was quite clearly Perkins'.

When Steeples eventually ran Sir Philip Norton to ground and demanded to see Perkins, all he got was "Terribly sorry old boy. PM was adamant. No visitors."

As deputy leader of the Labour Party it naturally followed that Jock Steeples would now take over as acting Prime Minister until the autumn when the Party would elect a new leader at its annual conference. It only remained for an emergency meeting of the Labour MPs to be convened to confirm Steeples in his rôle.

It soon became apparent, however, that events might not follow the anticipated course. A meeting of Labour MPs was called for the following Monday, but the statement convening the meeting spoke of 'electing' a new leader. This did not go down well with Labour Party members since it was nearly ten years since a party conference had relieved MPs of sole responsibility for choosing the Party leader.

All weekend delegations of Labour MPs were seen going out of the Chancellor's residence at Number Eleven Downing Street. The Sunday papers were full of speculation that Lawrence Wainwright would shortly announce that he was a candidate for the leadership. When the General Secretary of the Labour Party rang to ask Wainwright to confirm or deny the speculation, she found Wainwright evasive.

Sure enough, when the MPs assembled on Monday evening Wainwright was a candidate. In the election which followed he beat Steeples by a comfortable majority. About fifty left-wingers abstained on the ground that the election was unconstitutional. The following morning an emergency meeting of the Labour Party National Executive unanimously endorsed Jock Steeples as acting leader.

The result was an unprecedented constitutional crisis. The King found himself with a choice of two Prime Ministers, both claiming to represent the Party with a majority of seats in the House of Commons.

The King was at Windsor when the crisis occurred. Three hours before the Parliamentary Labour Party was due to meet, a black Rover containing Sir Peregrine Craddock was admitted to the castle. He was received in a drawing room overlooking the long straight sweep of the Great Park.

There is no record of what was said. It is known only that Sir Peregrine was closeted with the King for about twenty minutes, after which he was driven back to London. Later the same day several prominent members of the judiciary were received and still later four senior members of the Privy Council.

The next day it was announced from Windsor Castle that His Majesty had asked Lawrence Wainwright to form a government.

The news was received with dismay by Labour Party members throughout the country. There were a number of arrests for the daubing of anti-Royalist slogans. In Glasgow serious rioting occurred on successive nights. In London all police leave was cancelled and security was intensified in public buildings.

The Labour National Executive applied to the High Court for an injunction, arguing that Wainwright was not the properly elected leader of the party. This was refused on the ground that it was established practice for the sovereign to choose as Prime Minister the person who commanded the confidence of a majority of members of the House of Commons. The fact that he did not command the confidence of the Labour Party was neither here nor there. The case was thrown out by the Appeal Court and the House of Lords for the same reason.

Wainwright's Cabinet did not contain a single member of the outgoing government. Steeples was offered a minor post, but declined.

At its first meeting the new Cabinet announced that the request to America to withdraw its bases and other military facilities would be revoked. Britain would remain a full member of NATO and would only renounce nuclear weapons when the Russians did the same.

It was also announced that Chequers, the country residence of the Prime Minister, would be placed at the disposal of Harry Perkins for the purpose of convalescence. Ministers were unanimous in wishing him a speedy recovery.

That night at the Athenaeum rejoicing was unconfined. The head porter said afterwards he could not remember anything like it since VE day. Members who had not been seen in town for years showed up. Sir Arthur Furnival was there, looking fit and tanned after a sojourn in the South of France. The Bishop of Bath and Wells was there too, looking years younger. So was Sir Lucas Lawrence, a retired permanent secretary. Lord Kildare had come down from his castle in Scotland for the first time since that awful night when Perkins had been elected.

There was much backslapping and handshaking. Champagne corks popped late into the night (so much so that Berry Bros. and Rudd had to be especially opened to bring in fresh supplies).

Away from the hubbub, in a quiet corner of the dining room, Sir George Fison was giving a small dinner party. The editor of *The Times* was present. So was Sir Philip Norton from the Cabinet Office and Sir Peter Kennedy from the

Treasury. There was also a younger man called Alford, who was said to be a rising star in the BBC. And there was the mysterious Sir Peregrine Craddock.

Not all their conversation was audible to the waiters or the other guests, but the gist was overheard. "This time last year," Fison was saying, "who would have dreamed we'd be sitting here tonight celebrating the survival of all we hold dear." A waiter poured champagne as Fison went on to enumerate, "The Atlantic alliance, the Common Market, the House of Lords . . ." He had been going to propose a toast, but was interrupted by a telephone call. It was the night editor of his principal daily newspaper with a query on the front page editorial that Fison had dictated that afternoon. It was to be headed "A victory for sanity."

When Fison rejoined his guests, Alford was telling a story about how a fellow called Jack Lansman, the anchorman on the BBC Radio Four breakfast programme, had done a little jig in the corridor outside the studio when he heard that Perkins had resigned. "Been nothing quite like it since the night Allende was overthrown in Chile," Alford was saying.

Sir George proposed a toast to Craddock. "The British public," he said, "would never know how much reason they had to be grateful to Sir Peregrine."

Craddock smiled modestly and raised his glass of orange juice. "Everyone should feel proud," he said. There had been no tanks on the streets. No one had gone to the firing squad. Apart from the odd demonstrator on the receiving end of a police baton, no one had even been injured.

In fact, he said with a wan smile, "It was a very British coup."

Postscript

Harry Perkins was not seen again in public for nearly a year. For most of that time he remained in seclusion at Chequers. Security was very tight. Once or twice a photographer with a long lens managed, by sneaking round to the back of the house, to get a shot of a lonely figure pottering around the rose garden. Fred Thompson, Jock Steeples and Mrs Cook were allowed the occasional visit. If the sun was shining they would sit with Perkins on the south lawn, drinking tea and reminiscing about what might have been. Neither Steeples nor Mrs Cook ever held office again.

When Perkins did return to the House of Commons he seemed a broken man. He wandered the lobbies and the tea rooms and sat on the occasional committee, but he contributed little. He remained popular with his constituents in Sheffield, however, and the City Council put a little plaque on the council house where he and his mother had lived.

When the New Year's honours were announced, Reg Smith of the United Power Workers became Lord Smith of Virginia Water. Sir George Fison also received a peerage. "For services in the cause of truth and freedom," the citation said. Jonathan Alford was knighted and is widely tipped as a future BBC Director General. There was one surprise buried deep in the honours list: a CBE for David Booth, a young civil servant in the Foreign Exchange Department of the Treasury. No one – least of all Booth himself – seemed to know why he had been honoured.

Sir Peregrine Craddock retired to Somerset where he now grows prize-winning roses and plays the occasional round of golf. Once in a while he comes up to town and has a quiet lunch at the Athenaeum and a browse around the bookshops in Bloomsbury.

After the Windermere disaster Molly Spence's husband, Michael, lost his job with British Insulated. He now works in

Saudi Arabia. Molly and the children live with her parents in Sheffield. When she realised what had happened, she wrote Perkins a long letter explaining that it was all a terrible accident, that she had never meant to harm him, and begging him to forgive her. There is no reason to suppose Perkins ever received the letter. Anyway, he did not reply.

As for Fred Thompson, he married Elizabeth Fain and they moved away to Scotland where he now has a job on the *West Highland Free Press*. Thompson is said to spend his evenings writing a book which will tell what really happened to the government of Harry Perkins. There must, however, be some doubt as to whether it will ever be published.